Erotic Travel Tales 2

Erotic Travel Tales 2

❧

Edited by Mitzi Szereto

CLEIS
PRESS

Published in the United States by Cleis Press Inc., P.O. Box 14684, San Francisco, California 94114.
Printed in the United States.
Cover design: Scott Idleman
Text design: Frank Wiedemann
Logo art: Juana Alicia
First Edition.
10 9 8 7 6 5 4 3 2 1

"Vin Ordinaire" © 2003 by Gabrielle Coyote, was originally published on www.mindcaviar.com (Fall 2002, Volume 3). "The Shape of Cities" © 2003 by Maxim Jakubowski, was originally published in a different version under the title "Friends and/or Lovers" in 13, by Marc Atkins (The Do-Not Press, 2002). "Rapture at Cartagena" © 2003 by Michèle Larue, was originally published in French in Passion de Femmes" (Editions Blanche, 1996) and in the Swiss magazine Untel (2001). "Seven Cups of Water" © 2003 by Mary Anne Mohanraj, was originally published in Aqua Erotica, edited by Mary Anne Mohanraj (Three Rivers Press, 2000). "Butterfly" © 2003 by Lisabet Sarai, was originally published in a different version on www.erotica-readers.com, the Erotica Readers and Writers Association website (2002). "Lost in the Translation" © 2003 by Alison Tyler, was originally published in Bad Girl, by Alison Tyler (Venus Book Club, 2002 and Pretty Things Press, 2003).

CONTENTS

INTRODUCTION

TO THOSE WHO ARE NEW ARRIVALS TO MY *Erotic Travel Tales*
anthology series, welcome. And to those who have been with us
before, welcome back. I am pleased to once again be offering up
a delicious helping of travel tales with an erotic flavor. Indeed, an
exciting variety of voices can be found on these pages — from the
lyrical, to the sassy and snappy, to the in-your-face. *Erotic Travel
Tales 2* gives you the best of all worlds.

Travel in itself — leaving behind the known for the unknown —
is a highly erotic concept. Things happen when you travel that
might never happen when you're at home. You become a different
person; after all, you might be in a place where nobody knows
you. You can be free to explore your location as well as yourself.
You can set aside your inhibitions. You can even remake yourself
into something entirely new. The possibilities for adventure are
unlimited, just as they are in these stories.

The tales in this volume range from the fun and flippant to the
serious. There's plenty of escapist fare to be found, if that's what
you're looking for, but there's a lot more than that. Here you will
find the unique experiences of life away from home: the unknown,
the unpredictable, the crazy, the sublime, the poignant.... These are
not one-dimensional sex stories, but finely crafted gems that are
certain to draw you into their special worlds — to take you outside
of yourself, which is what good fiction is all about!

A collection of international stories would not be authentic
without an international cast of writers, and my tireless search

has reaped an excellent harvest. As in the last volume, some of the writers in this collection have lost their virginity, albeit *willingly*, by seeing publication in print for the first time. Of course, there are enough familiar names to satisfy even the most diehard erotica lover, yet an interesting mix of people makes for interesting stories — and you'll find them in abundance here. I am pleased to welcome back several writers from the first *Erotic Travel Tales* as well as a number of new contributors. A special welcome to our Royal Fellow of Literature, Lesley Glaister — probably the first ever to grace the pages of an erotica book. But then, *Erotic Travel Tales* has always aspired to be more than just "an erotica book." An emphasis on original, high-quality writing, on stories that stand out in their uniqueness, and on that delightful sense of having the rug pulled out from under you — *this* is what *Erotic Travel Tales 2* has to offer.

City girl meets local farmer in a clash of cultures in rural Wales... A woman experiences *la séduction* in off-season St. Tropez... An English tourist combs the Hollywood Hills in search of Keanu Reeves... A man's middle-aged angst comes to the fore on the beaches of North Carolina... Wine tasting and men turn out to be one and the same for a roving reviewer... A dam worker falls for an exotic dancer in Bangkok and gets more than he bargained for... A gay man waxes poetic on the Hemingway trail in Havana... Two women go undercover in the Reeperbahn to catch out their partners... A swimmer rescued by a boatload of fishermen off Cartagena becomes their willing catch... A woman visiting Barcelona fantasizes about a street performer until fantasy and reality converge... The search for Nirvana in Tibet leads a pair of backpackers to a sordid room and a Buddhist monk... An innocent young gay man looking for a bathhouse encounters a shady character in Prague... A second honeymoon amid the pastel shades of the Bermudan landscape provides a couple with what might be their final chance at love... Ceylonese sisters-in-law find themselves hopelessly drawn to each other in a culture that will never accept them... A woman is tormented in the night by the sound of lovemaking while staying at a matchmaker's *hostale* in coastal Portugal... A transitional journey to Milan reaches completion in the Simplon Tunnel... Two women have their passion ignited by the art of Florence... A lonely man finds himself left with only his memories of hotel rooms... A young

Mexican-American woman discovers her true nature while visiting her dying grandmother in Guadalajara... The desire for a local taste treat leads to the rediscovery of a childhood love in the Derbyshire village of Bakewell... A repressed Scottish woman gets unexpectedly loosened up while visiting Kandy...

Okay, I've probably teased you enough. So get ready, as I invite you to sit back, grab onto your armrests, and experience the journey of a lifetime!

Mitzi Szereto
January 2003
Yorkshire, England

Traditional Ayurvedic

ॐ

GRISELDA GORDON

MR. ABDULLAH AND HIS DANISH WIFE ARE ON THE doorstep to greet the Macrae family as they arrive. Their guesthouse is not quite as described in the Macraes' well-thumbed guidebook. *Tucked neatly into the hillside above Kandy, the Nirvana Inn boasts magnificent views of the lake and the Temple of the Tooth.* From the rooftop maybe, Mrs. Macrae thinks. Only then might one catch a glimpse of the gray silken water, which she remembers so well.

Mrs. Macrae is nevertheless glad of her choice. She wants her family to experience a humble, local establishment, somewhere altogether earthier than a large resort hotel. She yearns to capture something of the essence of her life then.

Their room on the second floor is spacious and clean, and while there is no sign of the lake, the balcony affords an excellent view of the guesthouse garden. Everywhere fecund greenery steams and heaves with moisture: hibiscus bushes frothing with pink bloom; a Na tree in the corner, providing shade to a visiting dog; thorny yellow bougainvillea entwining itself through the balcony railings. The shrill ring of birdsong. The smell of damp earth rising. It is the start of the rainy season.

At dinner they sit around a table covered with a red-checked cloth, hungry and tired after their long journey. The night air is damp and still. The heat has taken its toll on their three children, Alastair, Eilidh and Fiona, who loll over their chairs like rag dolls. Mr. Macrae cracks open a bottle of beer while Mrs. Macrae stares into space, a battered journal lying open next to her. Mosquitoes dive-bomb around their ears.

Mrs. Abdullah appears from the kitchen with dinner. Large steel platters of steaming curries are placed on a long lace-covered table: bright green mung bean dhal; hotly spiced, pickled aubergines; ash plantain curry; coconut sambols; a yellow curry of dried fish, and Mallung, a dish of shredded and stir-fried greens. Mrs. Macrae is surprised to hear Mrs. Abdullah speaking Singhalese with Nifal the cook, a wiry Tamil from the hill country. Mrs. Macrae was once able to talk as fluently as that. A few scattered phrases and odd fragments are all she can remember now.

Their fellow guests are mostly British, forty-something couples who have finally relinquished their backpacks. They all clutch the same guidebook as her own, the blue one with the two fishermen on the front. Perhaps they have chosen the Nirvana Inn for the same reason she has: its glowing reference and the emphasis on "clean." Ethnic, but undeniably safe. She goes up to the buffet and piles her plate high. She feels suddenly far removed from the girl in Punjabi pants, silver anklets and frizzed-up hair who arrived here twenty years ago, a gap student with a whole new world at her feet. Where was that free spirit now?

As they eat, Mrs. Macrae glances over at two sisters on the table opposite. They stoop over their plates, and pick neatly at their food in tandem. Tied around their waists are two matching green batik *longhis*, bought from the Kandy covered market. Mrs. Macrae had lived in *longhis* for an entire year. She worked the fields in them, bathed in the village river with one wrapped around her chest. She slept under another on the hard dung floor of her mud hut. At the time, she had been so desperate to live the life of the native, and would scoff at the tourists in their air-conditioned cars, while she sat hot and squashed on a sack of pawpaws at the back of the local bus. And if it had been possible to change the color of her skin, she surely would have done.

Toward the end of the meal Mr. Abdullah appears in the doorway. He claps his hands and starts to bellow orders to his houseboys. They scuttle off like beetles. He swaggers over to the Macraes with the air of a man who holds sway over many things.

"Everything OK?" he shouts.

"Wonderful." Mrs. Macrae makes a ball of rice and curry with her fingers, then lifts it to her mouth and flicks it deftly in with her thumb.

"Ah, I see you eat like a native." He slaps a mosquito from his neck. Mrs. Macrae smiles.

"We've arranged with your driver, Pathi, to go to Sigiriya tomorrow as you suggested," she says.

"Ah, our wonderful ancient fortress. Lion Rock. King Kassyapa. What an old scoundrel he was. You know, he had five hundred wives up in that rock palace of his." He chuckles, his belly, fat as a village merchant's, wobbling like a *wattalappam* pudding. "And you must see the frescoes of the maidens. They are not to be missed." He puts a hand on her shoulder and leans toward her. His eyes are black, hard as marbles. "When you return, I shall arrange a little traditional Ayurvedic massage for you." He points at some photographs on the wall of a massage clinic. "He's very good, you know, is Patrick. I go once a week." He squeezes the top of her shoulder. "You should go and release some of this Scottish tension." He wanders over to the other guests and his laughter resounds around the room like a king in his court.

Mrs. Macrae returns to her journal. She reads another entry while Mr. Macrae cracks open another bottle of Lion beer, ice cold from the dining room fridge.

"Just like you remember?" he asks.

"I was just thinking how strange it is, how memory plays such tricks on us." She takes a sip from her husband's beer. "When I came home—oh, I don't know—I felt I'd left some of my heart out here. I loved this place. But reading these again," she fingers the yellowing pages of the journal, "I'd forgotten how unhappy I was at first." Her journal has reminded her of the tropical ulcers, the endless searing heat, the loneliness, the loss of everything familiar, her wish to feel the cold Edinburgh *haar* on her face again. Her

3

memory has painted everything differently, embellishing the good, erasing the bad. She watches the condensation dribble down the brown beer bottle, like sweat off an oily limb.

. . .

The climb is more arduous than she remembers. To her, this fifth-century fortress has always looked like an immense red-brown rump rising up from an ocean of jungle as if from nowhere. Sigiriya. The rock throbs with the sun's midday heat. Everywhere dust clouds hang above the rust-colored earth. They have long drunk their stores of water. Above them, as they climb, two kites swirl in the thermals. A guide has appeared from nowhere to help Eilidh up the long ascent. Eilidh wants none of it.

"*Yande!*" Mrs. Macrae shouts, somewhat abruptly, but the guide grasps Eilidh's hand even more firmly and drags her protesting upward. She knows she will have to hand him a hefty tip. The sundress she is wearing, a white halter-neck splashed with red poppies, is tight fitting and totally impractical for climbing. And the red dust is everywhere, under her armpits, around the edge of her knickers, itching inside her bra. Her face feels gritty. Sweat blooms in gray patches through the cotton fabric. She sees the sensible attire of all the other visitors: cool polo shirts, airy shorts, stout boots, and feels a fool.

They continue their ascent. Solid iron steps manufactured and installed by the British are still riveted to the side of the rock. Wasps buzz out from the nests that collect in the overhangs. She grasps the stout metal handrail and doesn't look down. At the top, Pathi beckons them to a large flat stone, King Kassyapa's throne. They sit on it and look out over the plain below, an unfurling carpet of foaming jungle all the way to the ocean.

"The Tamil Tigers hide in there—waiting to pounce." Pathi springs like a civet toward them. They all jump. Mrs. Macrae frowns at Pathi. She wishes he hadn't mentioned the war. It is not the Sri Lanka she remembers.

"Hey, they not interested in the likes of you," he says, and his sad eyes look down at his feet.

"I must show you the frescoes," she says to Mr. Macrae, changing the subject. There is a clamor of resistance from all three children. Mr. Macrae shrugs. Pathi agrees to take them back down to the jeep where he has cold drinks waiting.

"You two go," Pathi says. "You go make love with the Maidens." He winks at them both.

Mr. and Mrs. Macrae tread carefully back down the steep staircase, and weave their way through to a walkway gouged out of the rock, shielded by a tall highly polished wall. She takes his hand, leading the way. It is hot and slippery.

"It's called the Mirror Wall. Look!" She points at swirls of ancient graffiti etched into the rock. "Over fifteen hundred years old. They're all verses inspired by the frescoes. Erotic poems of love."

Mr. Macrae lets go of her hand and squeezes her bottom.

"And lust?" he growls.

"Not here!" She moves quickly away, avoiding his gaze.

The bejeweled damsels chalked into the rock are even more beautiful than she recalls. The colors still vibrant. The perfect breasts swelling out of the red granite. The full and sensual lips. The deep, mango-curved navels. Translucent veils as thin as butterfly wings fluttering against their nipples as if in a soft breeze.

They stand there for some minutes, lost in contemplation. Did these creatures really exist, she wonders, or are they a fantasy made perfect by their artist?

She continues to ponder this question on the drive back to Kandy in the cool of their air-conditioned jeep. They pass another army checkpoint. Since Pathi has spoken of it, she notices every one; the wooden shacks shrouded in palm fronds and piled high with oil drums and sandbags, over which white eyes flash out from dark faces, guns glinting.

• • •

The sign above the door is modest. *Patrick U. Guneratne, Ayurvedic Masseur.* The black letters have been hand painted on a rough piece of bare wood. Mrs. Macrae leaves her shoes at the door and enters. Her poppy sundress is now soaked through with dust and sweat. There has been no time to freshen up. The door opens onto a small reception area with cheap plastic seats and a low wooden table. On it stands a vase of red anthuriums. She marvels at their waxy red heart-shaped flowers and the long creamy spikes that protrude from their centers. They don't look real. Beneath her feet the asphalt floor is cool and smooth. To the back of the reception area yellow moth-eaten curtains are drawn. There is a shuffling of feet.

"Patrick?" calls Mrs. Macrae, and a man emerges from behind the curtain drying his hands. She had expected a wiry individual clad in a sarong, not this huge bulk of a man in pink shorts, flip-flops and stripy shirt.

"Sorry for delay." Patrick smiles, his clean white teeth gleaming like strip-lights next to his dark skin.

"Mr. Abdullah rang on my behalf. Grace Macrae." She extends her hand to his. His grip is strong and her hand feels crushed. He beckons her to sit down on one of the red plastic chairs. She knows her thighs will stick to them in this heat, and will peel off like Elastoplasts, so she perches carefully on the edge.

"Here—read some of these while I get ready." He hands her an old blue jotter, just like the ones she used to have in primary school, with ruled feint, red margin and rough scratchy paper. She reads:

> *Man! There are massages and massages, and jeezo, does Patrick do the latter.*

> *Patrick's fingers are the strongest I've encountered. A deep tissue massage of the first order.*

> *I'd recommend Patrick's massages to anyone. His kind demeanor, and sensitive touch makes this an out-of-body experience.*

Every entry glowed.

"You read them?" he asks, smiling, as he returns with a clay pot in his hands.

"*Hari hundai.*" Very good.

"So, you speak Singhalese?"

"*Okome mateke ne.*" Forgotten all of it. He laughs.

"Come." He ushers her into a changing cubicle in the corner. "Just take your clothes off and wrap up in this towel."

A rusty nail is the only thing Mrs. Macrae can find on which to hang her discarded clothes. A full-length mirror leans against the wall in front of her. It is cracked through at head height and is clouded with dirt. Her body is streaked with Sigiriya dust and her shoulders and neck are an angry red. If somebody gave her husband a piece of chalk and a granite wall, is that how he would draw her? Just as she is. Or would he modify the Camembert stomach, the low-slung breasts, erase the mole on her shoulder, give her a waist again, smooth out the lines on her face? Would he depict truth or fantasy? She picks up a towel and hurriedly wraps it around her. It is damp and grubby, and stained with oil. She pulls back the curtain. Patrick has placed a wooden chair for her just outside. She sits down in front of the cracked mirror. He stands behind her and begins to massage her head and shoulders with some of the oil from his clay pot. Her burned face shines like a grilled prawn.

"If you prefer, you can lie, but I prefer this. Better contact." He thrusts his hips forward, burying his fingers in her dust-caked scalp. He is good. She loses herself to the sensations, watching him in the mirror. He tells her he has just returned from Good Friday Mass. Mrs. Macrae has clean forgotten. Not a chocolate egg in sight to remind her. Of course, with a name like Patrick, he has to be a Christian. He talks of his eight brothers and sisters with whom he still lives in a small village a few miles from Kandy. She tells him of Scotland, of her family, of the ceaseless rain they have left behind. They fill the room with harmless chatter and laughter. He continues to knead her shoulders, head and neck, his fingers firm and sure.

"Grease! You're so tense — come back tomorrow and I do it free of charge. OK?"

Grease. Mrs. Macrae laughs inwardly at the pronunciation of her name. She feels exactly like that. A filthy grease ball. Patrick towers above her, still working on the muscles at the top of her neck. The crack in the mirror makes him appear beheaded. She watches his flexing biceps. He tells her of his seven years training.

"You have to be strong. Very strong." Patrick shows her his fists, clenches and unclenches them. Pink. Brown. Pink. Brown. So pale his palms, she thinks. So white his teeth. And almost as an afterthought, how kind his eyes. She feels her body begin to float. She asks him what *Ayurvedic* means.

"*Ayu*, this mean 'life.' *Veda*, this mean 'knowledge.' Life knowledge. It's very ancient, Grease. A medicine that's been around for thousands of years."

Life knowledge. She likes that. The oils are absorbing into her hot skin. Sesame oil, a waft of sandalwood perhaps, and the smell of rusting metal. Patrick does not know the English words.

"Special, rare oils with herbs. All sorts," he shrugs, guiding her up from the chair over to a slatted wooden bench. Fragrant oils in clay bowls line one end. Mrs. Macrae clambers onto the high bench, trying not to lose her towel, which she has to unfasten and throw over her back. She is aware of Patrick watching her. It would have been easier to throw the towel off and slide on elegantly, but it's too late now. It has become bunched under her stomach and Patrick has to wrench it out from under her and rearrange it over her back so that only her legs are visible. He closes the moth-eaten curtains and begins with her feet.

"Hikkaduwa, you go Hikkaduwa?"

"No," Mrs. Macrae says, "not that hippy dump. I've heard it's ruined now."

"Sad place, Grease. Very sad. Lots of drugs and bad people. Men paying for small boys. This place Hikkaduwa is where I first practice."

Mrs. Macrae tries to imagine this gentle giant on the white sand among the ponytails and clouds of hashish smoke. It seems incongruous. He pummels her stiff calves. She flinches.

"I hurt? Sorry, Grease. I will be gentler with you. My hands too strong sometimes." He begins to work on her back. Mrs. Macrae feels herself falling into a soporific haze of contentment. Outside she hears the grumble of rush-hour traffic on the Sangaraja Mawatha, the persistent horns of the *tuk-tuks* as they weave in and out, the shrill signature tune of the Walls Ice Cream vendor. She is utterly relaxed.

Then quite without warning he removes her towel and flips her over onto her back. His head looms close. His breaths are hot on her cheek.

"Grease. Is it OK to do here?" His voice is almost a whisper. He points at her stomach.

"Yes, of course," she says, grateful that he should ask.

"And here?" He points at her breasts. Mrs. Macrae hesitates. She is unsure of how to respond, but Mr. Abdullah's words *traditional* and *Ayurvedic* ring loud in her ears. She thinks it would be priggish to refuse.

"And down here, too?" He points vaguely in the direction of her lower abdomen.

"Sure."

He begins to smooth her belly with both hands.

"Terrible, these stretch marks," she says, and she tries a nonchalant laugh, but it comes out all strangled.

But Patrick says nothing, spiraling inward over her navel with his fingertips, like two cobras coiling down to sleep. His palms lie hot and unmoving for several moments, then, as if the snakes are slowly stretching awake, they slide upward over her oiled belly and gently cup her breasts. She does not breathe. There is no sound in the room save his soft breaths that feather in the hot air above her.

"People say Patrick have magic fingers." His voice is slow and thick. Nothing moves. She looks up. His dark eyes stare down at her. And then it comes, and she knows it's coming and it is too late to stop it, this blush of skin-pricking intensity that rises to the surface of her skin from the tips of her feet to her scalp. She closes her eyes. Her pulse is thumping. She lies immobile, waiting.

And, briefly, as she lies there under the heat of his palms, a memory looms. She's at the top of the slide, the really big, shiny steel slide in Inverleith Park, the one that reaches halfway to the sky, the one she's always wanted to go on, and now that she's five years old she can, and she's sitting up there at the top for the first time, up high like a bird in a tree, but she can't go down. It is a cold winter afternoon. She is shivering. The pom-pom on her knitted woolen hat is buffeted by the stiff easterly wind. Her red Start-Rite shoes kick the steel, making a booming sound. Her legs are bruised with cold. She grasps the green metal rail with its blistering paint. Her knuckles are white. Her nose is running. Her mother stands with outstretched arms at the bottom, calling encouraging words, but Grace can't hear her, and there's a queue of other kids bunching up behind her, all taunting "Come on ye fearty—scaredy custard!" And her stomach is in her mouth and she can't look down at that vast river of steel, polished by thousands of others. She just grips the rails with her tiny pink hands and cannot let go.

And Mrs. Macrae cannot move as Patrick slowly encircles her breasts, then her nipples. And she chooses to interpret the first brush of his hands between her legs as an accident. It is only when he parts her legs a little further and a finger slithers in that she knows what is about to happen. She is aware only of the tremor of his breath, and the wet sound of his fat finger moving inside her.

9

Flesh on flesh, flesh in flesh. And all the while the fingers of his other hand encircle her nipples, first one, then the other, slowly, slowly and then with increasing speed. And Mrs. Macrae is five years old again. On top of the slide and terrified.

Jesus, think of something. Should she jump up, slap his face? Tell him where to shove his goddamned fingers? She plays out a series of scenes in her mind, scenes of outrage and indignation. But she knows she cannot do it to him. And she knows the reason why: she is too scared to *offend* the man.

And she begins to think that if she can't offend him, then perhaps she should play the part that Patrick wishes. Yield to his touch. She could tilt her hips, arch her back, and move to his rhythm. But what does Patrick intend? If she does surrender to his delicate foreplay, might Patrick then clamber on top of her, thrust in deep, and continue where his finger left off?

And, for a moment, she is back on her silver slide, gripping tight with her heart in her mouth, but it is not her mother who stands there at the bottom waiting for her. It is Patrick, smiling, his arms outstretched, his hands clasping and unclasping, pink brown, pink brown like giant Venus flycatchers. She gasps and opens her eyes. Patrick is staring at her with a curling smile and a gaze of such intensity that she has to turn her head away.

"*Lassenae*," he whispers, "so beautiful," and he strokes a wisp of stray hair from her forehead. Mrs. Macrae's stomach flips. His words touch her deeply. How long has it been since her husband has called her that? When they were first together he would often cry the word into the dark on the creaking bed as he creamed into her, over her. Her eyes smart with tears.

"It's OK, Grease. It's OK," and he lowers his head toward her breast and takes it gently to his mouth. He runs his tongue and lips around her nipple with such exquisite tenderness that Mrs. Macrae cries out "Oh!" in shock and wonderment as he licks and sucks and fingers first one, then the other until they stand firm and pert like two stiff peaks of shining meringue.

"Oh, oh!" she cries out again, and clutches the sides of the bench, then in horror realizes she has inadvertently said the words "Yes, yes!" in Singhalese for Patrick at once inserts another finger into her hot and silky and swelling insides, and probes so deeply and with such care that her tears spill over in shame that her body should betray her so. But she cannot help it. He is making her climb, nudging her up and up the long flight of steps to the top. Pimples of steel prick into the soles of her feet. She can hear her quiet moans, smell the spices on his skin, the tang of his hair oil as he flicks her nipples, now hard as raisins, with the tip of his tongue and shafts his two hot fingers in and out like pistons. It is too much. She props herself up on her elbows, arches her back and lifts her chest high to his devouring mouth, feeling the pull and ache of his suck deep in her groin. Then his fingers stop their pounding, and slither out to her red and moistened sex and start to tease her hard little nodule now electrified with desire for his touch, and he prods and tweaks and presses until she can stand it no more and jerks her hips upward and throws her head back making her long mane of hair fall into the clay pots behind her and swirl in the aromatic oils. And it is as though he senses her urgency for he plugs his fingers in deep again, increases his pace, bringing her up and up and nearer to the brink. She wordlessly follows his rhythms, twisting her hips around in a wide and glorious ellipse, hugging tight his two flickering and thrusting fingers. She feels her juices trickle down the crack between her buttocks, ashamed yet excited that she has produced so much. Then he changes his hands seamlessly and with the hand that has just been inside he snail-trails his glistening fingers down her neck and between her breasts to her navel. A scent of seashells mingles with the sandalwood.

"*Lassenae*," he whispers again, and before she realizes what is happening, he grasps the flesh of her buttock with his fingers and travels around its firmness into the curve and with his forefinger pushes gently into the mouth of that tight dark hole that she has always thought a forbidden place. She gasps. There is a feeling of unbearable, exquisite fullness, a delirious pressure. "Yes, Grease, yes!" Patrick cries as she shudders against him, and she knows she's there, up at the very top, standing high above the clouds, teetering on the topmost step as the cold wind roars around her, every hair on her body standing on end. And below her miles upon miles of gentle slope undulating and swirling down like a silver ribbon through the clouds. With arms outstretched Grace takes a giant leap and lands with a shriek on her mirror of steel, slipping down over the joyous bumps and curves that send her rising falling, rising falling through the vaporous mists and cool breezes. And as she coasts the endless corrugations, she rediscovers for an instant the essence of herself she has forgotten, of who and what she is, and she kisses the moment as she descends, crying out a guttural moan that transcends time and continents, toward Patrick and his magnificent hands. But when she breaks through the cloud barrier it is not Patrick she sees at the bottom. It is her husband with her three children, waiting expectantly and patiently for her return. The terrible realization dawns as her body convulses and she prays she will keep on falling, falling, because then it will all be a dream, from which she will never have to wake.

"Enough, Patrick. Enough." Her words are fractured, barely audible, her mouth dry, her tongue thick. She feels a nausea rising in the back of her throat. What has she done? He stops immediately, removing his fingers as though a fish has bitten them. She opens her eyes, her body still trembling with the aftershocks. He paces the room for a few moments like a trapped tiger, then is beside her again, his face close to hers. It is wet with perspiration and his eyes are afraid. He speaks between clenched teeth.

"Grease, Grease. I asked you and you say *yes*. OK? You say *yes*."

"I didn't think you meant where you did." It sounds feeble, unconvincing. He grabs a cloth from behind her head and dries his hands. He does not speak for some moments. When he does, there is the slightest hint of menace to his tone.

"You want me to say to your husband what we did together? What do you think he would say, I wonder?"

We did. His words hit her like a thrust stone. But she must look appalled, as he sits down quickly beside her and takes her hand.

"Of course, Grease, I won't tell. What goes on behind this curtain is a secret, OK?" His hand trembles. "Listen, I just poor village boy doing job for my boss."

Mrs. Macrae thinks of a man on a hillside not far from here with marble eyes and a belly that wobbles. And there is one last question that she knows she must ask, that hangs in the hot air like a lifeboat from a sinking vessel.

"Was that, you know, what you did, was that *traditional* Ayurvedic massage?" It will still be all right, she thinks, if she can put this thing into the realm of something ancient and oriental.

But Patrick looks at her in horror, as though she has desecrated a holy shrine. "Not that last thing. Oh no! Not *that*."

• • •

Later, back home, Mrs. Macrae will tell her story many times over many dinners. Her words will silence the clink of crystal and clatter of silver on bone china, and she will revel in the telling, in the drama of the moment: the shifting discomfort of the men, the squawks of disbelief from the women. And the tight laughter when it comes will burst forth from their throats like escaping champagne and cause their ribs to ache. This will be her comedy act, her public version.

Privately, though, as Mr. Macrae lies beside her on the cusp of sleep, she will call out softly into the dark, "*Langete ende mathe*." Come closer. And she will begin to scratch another kind of curling script into the Mirror Wall of her memory: verses inspired by the perfect fresco of a black man with kind eyes and magic touch, an image that she will chalk and chalk with bare hands into the rough red granite, until her knuckles bleed.

good-bye, cuba

ॐ

GERARD WOZEK

BECAUSE I WANTED LOVE, THE UNBIDDABLE KIND. Because I wanted the ungovernable heart, *amor prohibido*. Because I scratched his name on my neck with a scorched needle and because I handed over forty dollars to Esperanza at the psychic fair, who told me to bring her one of his shoelaces and a pillowcase that he'd drooled on, and a peso that he'd carried in his pocket. And because I handed those things over to her, I expected him to stay with me. Because I purchased three tall red votives at the *botánica* just as I was told to do and lit them and spun around my studio trying to pronounce the Spanish words of a spell until I was woozy and crying and finally calling out his name, "Herman, Herman!"

I sang his name like a Backstreet Boys' chorus and the angel harmony was like powdered cinnamon on my tongue. I wailed out in my loft studio and the walls echoed back his name, "Herman," and no one was there, no one came to answer. It was just me and those Spanish syllables pouring like hot wax over my skin, dripping down the crevice of my back. But I was compelled to speak his name out loud, because to swallow it and keep the feverish tones inside of me was like eating red embers and smoldering ash. So I said it. I declared his name over a tongue that needed his tongue, and it was a relief to pronounce, "Herman, Herman." I said it the way they say it in the city of Havana where he was raised. I said it the way he taught me with the *m* sounding like an *n* and with a faint trill over the *r* and the soft flute accent at the end like a desirous whisper. "Herman." I said it with *fuerza*. I said it with sparks and flame spitting out of the corners of my mouth. I said it with buried hope. I said it with a bitter singe on my lips.

It wasn't that he was handsome. Because if I said to him he was *hermoso* or *guapo*, he would turn mute and look away and tell me that in another life he wanted to be pretty, one of those airbrushed boys with slicked-back hair featured in the soap opera tabloids or on the covers of the *Enquerio de Mundo*. Not this geeky Afro-Cuban aspiring writer. Not this hopeful novelist with thick-rimmed glasses and a slight overbite. Not this dark, brooding man I had sunk into love with.

I had a fetish for his ears; they were small and perfectly round and close to his shaved afro. I would peck and bite his tiny lobes and he would pull me onto his torso, begin to pump into me and breathe harder until sweat would drip down his forehead and rest in the cradle just above the edges of those sweet conch shells. His right ear was deaf so I could move my lips over it and let the softest breath come out, "*Te adoro*, Herman." Then he would raise his shoulder to erase the tickle, never hearing my words, my desperate poem to claim him.

When he slept, I would touch his forehead, write my name over his brow. First the *G*, then the *E*; I had to trace my own simple consonants and vowels over the place where he worried and dreamed. When he woke in the morning, I would imagine that he had seen me running next to him on the Cuban beaches, or holding onto his waist as we scootered through my dream of old Havana; he and I riding along on a Vespa with the radio playing Gustavo Sanchez or an Afro-Cubano jazz troupe. And all the tender *abuelas* leaning out over the old wrought iron along the *Prada*, would be singing our names over the geranium pots and the tops of ceibas blowing in the wind.

In my dream of Havana fire, we were perfect. Our bodies were lithe and supple and we wiped the gritty soot off each other's faces. We touched openly amid the dilapidated buildings and old *calles;* we were *el negro y el blanco,* two *caballeros* in the sunstroked air, flaming without umbrellas, brave *compañeros* without our wide-brimmed hats to fend off the relentless heat.

Whenever we kissed, he would call me his *cielo.* He called me *chulo* and *chulpo* and I would wait for his emails and look for him to make my name a Spanish name. He'd call me "Gerardo" or "Geraldo" or sometimes, "Diego *pequeño.*" I wanted him to change me. To mold me into a scintilla of heaven, a hazy orange sunset, or a rainforest. And I would ask my friends at the cantina, "*¿Cómo se dice,* 'lover', in Spanish? *¿Cómo se dice,* 'amaryllis of my dreams', or how do you say, 'rabid wolfhound at my torso'?"

And everyone would laugh and say that a "gringo like me" could never hold onto one fleck of lightning in his African blood. "You can see it in that boy's crooked walk," the bartender would say to me. "The way he turns his heel and looks away when you close your eyes during the dance. The way he smiles at all the pretty twinks. What, you think you're the only white boy who knows how to *merangue?*"

When Herman took me, it was his black *pinga* unshod in my wet hole. It was his salty whitecapped ocean pouring inside of my hot rose cove. And with each thrust, each mustard kiss, he would say, "*Closer Gerardo, closer!*" And I would wrap around him, suck his trembling lower lip and tell him he was my *papi bueno* and it didn't matter that he was married once and still looked at women that way. It didn't matter that he was leaving for New York, that everything had to happen in the moment and we could count on no more *mañanas.* "It doesn't matter," I said to him. "Herman, *solamente esta noche.*" I said that. "*Solamente tú.*"

And though I lit the red votive and placed crushed black rose petals onto the wick (the glass votive shattered when the flame finally went out), and though I spoke the *bruja's* spell into his deaf ear, and though I memorized his profile, saved his beard hairs from when he shaved in my loft studio, wrote our names together on plum leaves and made a poultice of chestnut pods and grape seeds to entice him toward me, nothing ever came of it.

Only his cigarette butts in the ashtray. Only his torn up sheets of paper with character sketches or story outlines under my sofa. Only his monstrous toothbrush, cold on my bathroom sink for six weeks before I could throw it away. Only his musky scent on my sheets that I could not wash out. Only his fingerprints in my soap dish, on my lube bottle, on my cheek. His teeth marks permanent on my thighs.

I held onto hope because I didn't want to say good-bye. Because I didn't want to let go of Cuba and the wicked furnace of his mouth, his coal arms that wrapped around me. Because he said I was his "madness broker," his "perfect smile," his *chulpo*. He called me all sorts of things I could never decipher. Slang words from his boyhood in Havana. Words he would whisper in a passionate tango, or sometimes weave into his stories. Words he never translated for me.

We made a pilgrimage to his homeland during the summer we broke up. We boarded a plane in Toronto and arrived in Havana seven hours later. His cousin picked us up at the airport and took us to the Miramar district where elite residences and chic restaurants lined the wide avenues. We spent our first night in a colonial-style mansion that was converted into a hotel with purple velvet wallpaper and a duty-free shop in the plush lobby.

While Herman spoke Spanish to the reservation clerk, I purchased a miniature effigy of Oshun, the Santeria goddess of seduction. The woman in the shop said the statue was more than a souvenir, it was the embodiment of true power. She told me I could speak my desires into the ear of the goddess and the best of all outcomes would happen. So I whispered my beloved's name into this clay replica, this mold of the mother of romance, and plunged the deity safely into my satchel filled with condoms and silk boxers.

That night, we drank sediment-laden rum out of plastic cups and I toasted this mysterious goddess of love. We lit indigo votives around our tiny suite and gently dripped candle wax on the rim of the bathtub and each other's belly. We singed the frilly lace on the shower curtain. We spilled our seed over the opulent orange satin bed sheets. Salsa music trickled in through the open windows, and the moonlight caressed our exposed shoulders as we collapsed into sleep, entangled in each other's arms.

In the morning we moved into a tiny neo-Gothic style room

near the ancient seawall of the Malecon and spent four days meandering about the boardwalk and the adjacent district with its nineteenth-century homes, their Moorish windows garlanded with plaster roses, caryatids, and ornate ironwork railings. Old men lingered in the weathered plazas, nearly motionless in the heat and the haze of their *cohiba* cigars. Stray dogs climbed into rusted fountains, turned-over Ali Baba urns or benches of bright patterned tile.

In the mornings, we would linger at a café popular with the locals. We'd stare at each other, sipping mugs of *Cubita* Espresso and picking at our plates of tortillas filled with potatoes, onions and *chorizo*. Herman would pull out his journal and write and I would stare at his rugged caramel hands, the three gold wedding bands on his thick fingers, the way his wrist would turn as he made those bold strokes with his pen.

The light was different in the Malecon. The sun scrubbed the faded colors of decaying art deco facades and hurricane-scarred buildings: coral pink infused with purple, green with cobalt, mustard yellow mixed with a mermaid's turquoise. It was August and the rubber soles of our sandals almost melted onto the worn stones of the plaza. Our T-shirts stuck to our skins and our wrists would graze each other's as we tripped over rusted tin and broken bottles of rum. We lost ourselves in a wash of pastels and in the rabid heat we felt growing for one another.

In the early evenings when it was cooler, we'd step onto our room's outdoor front balcony and stare at the Soviet Ladas and prerevolutionary Studebakers on the boulevard below. I bent over the rusted railing covered in bougainvillea vines and he thrust himself into me. He claimed me, right there in the open, overlooking the exhaust fumes of traffic and the far-off Vedado skyline, the lovers leaning into each other on the top of the Malecon seawall.

"One, two," I whispered to myself, counting the slow pulsing movement of his hips.

"You like this?" Herman was breathless.

"Fifteen, sixteen." I closed my eyes to imagine the effigy of Oshun hovering over the scene.

"You want me?" Herman moaned. "You desire me?"

"Twenty-four." I began to imagine the benevolent goddess

glowing in the center of orchids that grew on the sides of white stucco houses. Her arms outstretched among the tiger lilies that sprawled on the trunks of the jacaranda trees.

"You want me to call you *cabrón*?"

"Thirty-three, thirty-four. Don't stop," I prayed aloud.

"You want me to call you *pendejo*?"

"When you explode."

"*¿Chulpo?*" His voice cracked. "*¿Mi puta?*"

"Forty-two." The sweat from his face poured onto my back and rested in the crevice between my ass and spine.

"*¡Paraíso!*" he exclaimed. His voice seemed to quiver off the crumbling seawalls that separated Malecon Drive from the Caribbean. Then the pale lamplights on the street below suddenly went on.

On the afternoon before we left Havana, we went to the *Museo* Hemingway and wandered among the relics of the famous dead writer. The roped-off desk where Papa Hemingway had written *For Whom the Bell Tolls* was still intact. On the desktop rested an exquisite cartridge pen in a holder made from conch shells and next to that was a dried-up inkwell.

"Imagine how he must have held that pen," Herman mused.

"Like this?" I said, covertly touching his crotch with my thumb and forefinger.

In the backyard of the *Museo* was a succulent garden. We strolled alone among the mangoes and *flamboyantes*, the palm leaves and the wet *aguacates*. In the center of the backyard was a large ceiba tree that dwarfed everything around it. Someone had carved *Viva Fidel* into the bark. I gently nudged Herman up against the enormous elephant-colored tree trunk. "Am I your true *novio*?" And in the shade of the dense branches we kissed deeply.

I kissed the gray-blue sea on his tongue that afternoon. I kissed the salty semen of my cock that had shot there last night. I kissed the residue of his divorced wife and the aftertaste of his nine boyfriends who had each tattooed their arms with a pierced heart and the name "Herman." I kissed the strange birthmark floating like an island above his naval. I kissed the clouded moon that smeared across our ephemeral Havana nights. I kissed the *adiós* slowly forming on the curve of his full lips.

And when we came back to the States and he began talking

about being a writer in New York, I knew he wouldn't linger for too long. I could taste the sea breath of the Caribbean that had settled on his eyelids, (or was that salt I tasted, his private tears?). I could see the haunt of Havana in his posture that told him to go, to write out his childhood, to make a memoir of his swallowed-up days.

And what could I give him to remember me? One thing only. I wrapped it in a waxed plantain skin and placed it in his coat pocket. I gave him back our Havana. That afternoon by the ceiba tree in the backyard at the *Museo*. That sun that washed everything into soft greens and amber and parrots and sweet kisses. The moon that lingered on the bed sheets. I gave him back all that. I gave him the pen I stole from Hemingway's desk.

"Go. Write your stories," I told him. "But come back to me."

He said, "It's what you wanted *chulpo*. You wanted to walk in a dream of fire for a little while." And then he smiled that invincible smile. "But just for a little while. *¿Verdad?*"

And he kissed me then. He kissed me without saying a word. And that's when I said it to myself. "Good-bye, Herman." I let it pass over my own tongue, my own lips. "Good-bye." And that's when it really counted for me. And that's when I began to shrink.

Because Herman didn't like to give in to sentimentality, or because he could not bring himself to say the words, he made his fictional characters engage in romantic farewells for him. On the day he left for New York, he called from the airport to tell me to look in my mailbox. There was a page from a story he had written where two *novios* part ways on the promenade in the Malecon. There was something written about pointing at the cliff-top El Morro fortress and the fading summer light on the Havana skyline. Something about making love on a patio the night before. Something about running off with an ice cream vendor from Trinidad and a yellow finch that curiously hovered over their heads like a halo or a bad omen, as one says to the other, "So long *amigo. Amigo.*"

It wasn't how I wanted to say good-bye. I wanted it for real, not written on a page. I wanted it with sweet lingering caresses on an afternoon patio and lots of sangria-drenched fruit on our tongues and our heads full of Rumba music and a whole bunch of *maybes*. And *besos*, I wanted *más besos*, and the tugs on each other's shirts, and tears running over our lips and two raging hard-ons, and passionate embraces and my breathless, "Don't go Herman! *¡Te adoro!*"

Good-bye, Cuba. Good-bye to all the wound of you, the piercing want of you. Your soft chest hair. (Yes I built temples to the sun there.) Your crimson nipples, two darts of spark. (Yes I did my penitence there.) Your narrow torso and your hot flaming wand. (Yes I kneeled there.) The smoky musk I inhaled in your armpit. (Yes I was anointed there, yes I found relief in your sweat, in your sea-brine scent.)

But I still can't vanquish this smoldering within. These ashes, these memories I keep spooning over my tongue. What do I say to the effigy of a goddess who stares back from my bed stand with a blank expression? What do I do with a spell that won't work? These used up votives? The crumpled boarding pass into Havana I keep under my pillow? This blue flame feeling?

LOST in the translation

ᘓ

ALISON TYLER

"WHAT DID SHE SAY?" I whispered to Johnny, staring at the angry flush of heat in Birgit's cheeks.

Johnny shook his head. Together we were lost in a foreign world. Whenever our friends wanted to talk privately, they simply reverted to their native tongue of German, plunging the two of us into instant helplessness. How could we get involved in a conversation that we didn't understand? So we watched them bleakly, and waited in silence, knowing that eventually they would translate.

This evening, Birgit was the one who finally explained the situation. She wanted to take us out to her favorite restaurant. Wolf wanted to show us the red-light district. The decision was up to us, and there was no way of guessing what had been lost in the translation. As could be expected, Johnny instantly voted for Wolf's plan, squeezing my hand hopefully. I agreed, curious myself, and the four of us drove to the Reeperbahn.

Once there, we wandered along the sidewalks, glancing in shop windows and observing the erotic sights until the harsh throb of a foreign phrase caught my attention. Unlike the flurry of normal conversations floating around us, these words were different, a come-on aimed directly at me.

"What did he say?" I asked Birgit, who had been designated as my perverted tour guide for the evening.

"The women in there," she began, indicating the darkened doorway that led to a hidden strip club, "they're all of legal age. But they're shaved, so they look younger." Then she pulled me along at a trot because we'd fallen behind the boys.

I glanced back at the heavyset barker, who winked at me before continuing his fast-talking German spiel, hawking his human wares to any passersby, even well-dressed girls like us. *What use would we have for shaved strippers?* I wondered, but the sinful gleam in his eyes made me feel instantly dirty, as if he knew all of my secrets. As if he might call them out to the next customer.

Swiftly, we fell into place behind our boyfriends, who were oblivious to the fact that we'd dropped back from them. Both men were fully captivated by the line of attractive prostitutes standing nonchalantly across the street from the police station. Our little foursome was clearly connected, but this didn't stop the hustling women from approaching anyone with a cock. Each girl had a different move—a sensual head nod, a seductive lower lip lick, an air kiss. Some were far bolder than that, stepping forward to actually speak to Johnny and Wolf, making pointed conversation in their lilting, foreign tongue.

"What did *she* say?" I hissed to Birgit after a kitten-like blonde in sleek leopard-print slacks and a zipper-encrusted leather top spoke to my beau.

"She asked if he was interested," Birgit told me, translating the words without hesitation. "She said that she's the best—too good to pass up. Better than his wife."

This last bit made Birgit's eyes narrow, as if she couldn't believe the nerve. I watched Johnny carefully for his response. He was looking the prostitute up and down, as if he were actually considering the offer. I tried to imagine what Johnny could possibly whisper to me so that I'd let him go and experience "the best."

"We're only here for a few days," he'd say. "And we *did* agree that we wanted to savor all of the international delights before returning home."

Then I'd give him a kiss and tell him, "Sure, baby. Enjoy yourself. Here's a handful of euros. Have a blow job on me."

As if reading my thoughts, Johnny turned around and gave me a sheepish smile, letting me know that he was simply a tourist on a sex-charged ride. *No problem, honey*, his expression said. *No worries*. On we went, heading toward the main drag of the Reeperbahn, where Birgit told us we could watch dirty movies, visit the erotic art museum, hear a late-night concert, buy a gun, fulfill any one of our decadent appetites. But before we reached the corner, Wolf stopped.

"No, Wilfried," Birgit said immediately. She was calling him by his full name, which showed me how serious she was. "Don't do it."

"He'll never get another chance," Wolf told her.

Birgit shook her head fiercely. Once again, our German hosts engaged in a short, heated discussion in their own language. Johnny and I stood with raised eyebrows and listened to the friends we'd known since grad school. What wouldn't Johnny get a chance to do? And why wouldn't Birgit want him to have that opportunity? Birgit shrugged angrily, as if to say *do what you want*, and Wolf said in his perfect, unaccented English, "Leave it up to them, right?" and Birgit nodded, blue eyes blazing.

"There's a street," Wolf began, "where the women are."

I knew that he was leaving out something important, because as far as I could tell, the "women" were everywhere. Turning my head, I spotted several prostitutes moving in our direction. One statuesque brunette was wearing gold hot-pants and lace-up boots, not even shivering while the rest of us were bundled against the chill. Apparently, she had an internal heater. Johnny and I waited silently for further explanation.

"Down there," Wolf said, indicating a glossy, scarlet-painted gate that towered over our heads. "Behind those doors, there is a street where only men can go."

"Why?" I asked, my shoulders tightening automatically. I didn't like the sound of this at all.

"They don't want the competition," Birgit explained. "Or simply curiosity-seekers. They want customers. Males mean sales."

"Would you like to go?" Wolf asked Johnny. His tone made it clear that *he* was the one who really wanted to take that stroll. "Just to look," he continued. "They sit in the windows and you choose."

"It's nothing," Birgit said, shaking her head. "Sluts under glass. That's all." But Johnny wanted a peek, I could tell, and so did Wolf. "I hate that we can't go, too," Birgit muttered, revealing genuine frustration. "If they're so good, they should be able to handle another woman walking by."

But they wouldn't want to compete with a girl like Birgit—that was my instant thought. So lovely, with her long blonde hair fanning loose over her black cashmere sweater. Bright blue scarf tight around her throat. Pale blue gloves matching her suede slacks. She was far prettier than any of the stunners we'd seen so far, and she gave Wolf what he wanted for free. Although, from the furious expression on her face, I thought he might not be getting any tonight.

Johnny looked at me, a question beating in his deep green eyes, and I nodded. Regardless of how left out I felt, who was I to keep him from a once-in-a-lifetime journey?

"How long will it take?" I asked.

"An hour," Wolf promised. "Maybe less."

He wouldn't meet my gaze as he spoke. Was there something else in the plan, something that Wolf wasn't telling me?

"We'll see you back at home," Birgit said suddenly, surprising me by how easily she was giving up. "I'm going to take our little one here out drinking. She's never had a Hefeweizen, if you can believe it. Don't worry. We'll cab." Wolf grinned like a kid, obviously thrilled that his girlfriend had acquiesced. Had he never been allowed down the street before? I didn't have time to ponder that, because the boys were moving in speeded-up motion before we could change our minds. I watched Wolf open the red gate, saw the two men disappear behind the wall. Then Birgit was tugging my hand, pulling me toward a waiting taxi.

"Where's the bar?" I asked as we settled ourselves in the plush leather interior.

"We're not going to a bar. We're going down that street," Birgit said forcefully, her ice-blue eyes gleaming. "It'll just take a little doing."

• • •

Back at their Hamburg apartment, Birgit rifled through Wolf's wardrobe. "We need guy clothes," she said, "and hats. We're lucky it's winter. Less exposed skin means less exposed features." I stood, bottle of beer in hand, as I watched her gather what she wanted. Honestly, I wasn't that interested in seeing women behind windows, but I was excited at the prospect of an adventure. Besides, I liked the way Birgit moved, telling me what to do and how to act. It meant that I didn't have to make any decisions.

"You'll need to tape those," she told me, indicating my full chest with a casual motion as she tossed over a roll of bandages. I'm slim, but I have curves. "Get yourself as flat as you can."

Now that it was really happening, my heart started to race. *Go fast*, I thought. *Don't think.* Modestly, I faced away from her as I pulled off my shirt and sweater and started to roll the bandage around my breasts. But Birgit moved next to me, helping, her fingers cold on my warm skin as she tucked in the end of the bandage.

"Wipe off your makeup," she told me. "No lipstick. No liner." I retreated to the bathroom to follow her orders, then returned, clean-scrubbed and fresh-smelling, although feeling something like a mummy in the bandage.

"Perfect," she said. "Now a button-up shirt, I think. Good that you're so tall. Makes things easier." She cocked her head, looking me over. "Keep the jeans, but put on a pair of my Docs. Your boots are too femme." I followed her commands, fingers trembling as I did the laces up on her heavy black shoes. "Leather jacket," she said to herself, nodding. "And some hat. Baseball hat? Yes, Johnny's got one, right?" As if on automatic pilot I found myself in the guest room, grabbing Johnny's vintage ball cap from the dresser and putting it on backwards.

"Your short hair is a godsend," Birgit said, fussing impatiently with her own intensely silky blonde mane. She wrapped it tightly, tucked the length down her turtleneck collar, and then grabbed a striped woolen hat. She'd dressed similarly to me, but without needing to wrap her small breasts. Standing side-by-side in front of the mirror, we looked like two young boys.

"If anything," she said, "they'll hassle us for being underage. We need something else." She rummaged a bit more, and then ran into the kitchen, coming back with a pack of Wolf's Marlboro Reds.

Our friends smoke American brands, while we think we're cool to buy the European ones.

"Smoking will keep our hands busy and give us something to cover our faces."

Again, we stood in front of the mirror, staring. Then Birgit snapped her fingers and said, "I know. I know —" and she reached into Wolf's dresser and pulled out two socks. "Roll 'em up and stick 'em down," she instructed, and soon there we stood: two insecure youths with smoking habits and serious hard-ons. "Let's go."

The cab ride was a tense five minutes as I tried to decide whether or not I could go through with this bizarre charade. "What happens," I whispered, "if they realize we're girls?"

"They'll throw ice water on us," she said matter-of-factly, "and bits of garbage."

That sounded like a whole lot of no fun.

"Maybe we should just go to the bar," I suggested softly, struggling to find a comfortable way to breathe with my chest so firmly wrapped. "We could have another heffer-whatever —"

"No." Birgit had her mind set. "This is it," she told the cab driver, and he murmured something back to her as he handed over the change. Birgit responded with a dark smoky chuckle that sounded nothing like her normal laugh.

"What did he say?" This was my mantra for the evening.

"He said, 'Have a good night, gentlemen.'" Birgit grinned, pushing me out the door. Then there we were, back in front of the red gates.

"What if Johnny and Wolf find out?" I asked, my last-ditch effort to talk sense into my friend.

"What can they possibly say?" she responded. "They've already done it. And who knows what else —"

She was right, and I took a deep breath and followed her through the gate and into another world. Instantly, I saw that we were in a sort of human sex mall. Lining both sides of the narrow street were tiny storefronts with floor-to-ceiling windows. Behind most windows sat a woman, waiting. I was surprised to see that the windows were actually lit with stark red light bulbs — hence the term "red-light district." Each window held a comfortable-looking chair, like an old-fashioned recliner. The chairs were decorated in a variety of different styles: some had flags draped lushly over the seats; others featured more luxurious fabrics, comforters made of velvet and satin.

As we strolled by, I noticed that several windows were dark. These were the ones that had customers, Birgit explained. "It's early," she said, looking around at the light pedestrian traffic. "Men with their needs come out later in the evening." But although this meant that there were many women for us to look at, this also meant that we were scrutinized as potential customers by each one. Some waved. Some stood in open doorways and beckoned. I could see their eyes, the red embers of their cigarettes, their bodies encased in shiny, revealing clothing.

"Hey, tall dark and handsome, come back—" one called, and I wondered how she knew I spoke English, and then remembered my baseball cap with the SF Giants logo on it. A clever guess. Birgit gave me a wink as she walked away from me, over toward the woman. The two spoke quietly in a heated conversation, and I sensed dollar figures were being discussed. What was she thinking? Nervous, I lit a cigarette, glad to have an activity to focus on while I waited.

"Two for one," Birgit told me when she came back, cheeks flushed with excitement. "What do you say? Can't beat a price like that."

At her words, I felt myself growing wet. Wetter than I already was. What would it be like to share a bed with Birgit and the knockout redhead in the doorway? Skin on skin on skin. But what would the prostitute do when she learned the truth?

"You could just touch her," Birgit whispered. "Don't even have to take off your clothes. Just touch her. Trail your fingers over her naked body. Half-price for that. Half-price when no sex is involved. You do that, and I'll watch. She'll think we're kinky, but it won't be the worst thing she's ever done. Believe me."

I shook my head quickly, and Birgit laughed immediately, throwing her arms around me in a quick, impulsive hug. Now I didn't know if the whole concept had been a joke. Or if she'd simply been interested in my response. Would I do it on a dare? Would I do it because I could?

As we made our way down the rest of the street, I looked out for Wolf and Johnny, but there was no sight of our mates.

"The boys are long gone," Birgit said. "They scurried down fast."

Turning to stare at her, I understood in a mental flash that she was smarter than Wolf, that when he played his little boy games with her, she was always the one in charge. "All macho in front of us," she continued, "but when women are offering sex for real, they get scared."

Maybe, I thought, *but maybe not*. I peered into the hazy gray of one storefront as we strolled by. *Maybe they're each behind one of those darkened windows. Playing for pay. Maybe they're the ones with needs that must be filled.*

I started to say this, to explain it to my friend, but I couldn't find the words. Not the right ones. Because there are some things that defy translation. Expressions. Wounds from old secrets. And there are other things that simply don't require translation—like the fact that I knew Johnny would sleep with one of the prostitutes if he had the chance, that I knew he'd done so before. Nuances like the heat between me and Birgit, the questioning glances, sly smiles, accidental brushes up against one another. You don't need a phrase book to understand certain concepts even if they are foreign as of yet. Even if you've never done them before.

At the end of the block, we turned around, walking faster down the other side until we reached the starting place. Now that we'd actually succeeded, there was no need to linger. Birgit smiled at me, and herded me through the gate.

"We did it," she said, gripping onto my hand tightly.

My cigarette had burned down to the filter, becoming one long piece of silvery ash. Birgit plucked the butt from my fingers and crushed it out on the concrete sidewalk. Then she took a step closer to me. Her breath was icy, puffs of wispy frozen air. Behind her, the barker called out to us.

"What did he say?" I asked, desperately.

"He said that his girls inside are young and pretty and shaved." She paused before adding her own opinion in a different tone of voice, "But they're not as pretty as you." As she said the words, she kissed me. Her cold lips pressed to mine, and I felt her arms pull me forward till I was wrapped in her tight embrace, her sock cock jammed into my side.

"Is that a tube sock in your pocket?" I whispered, "or are you just happy to see me?"

She laughed hard, her real laugh, and then took my hand

again, pulling me back to the taxi stand where a line of cabs waited. "They won't be back yet," she predicted. "If Wilfried thinks I took you drinking, then he knows he has a couple of hours to kick around town with Johnny. They're probably in one of the kino houses."

"Kino?"

"Movie. *Dirty* movies on this street. Two men, jacking off in the darkness."

I didn't have to ask what we were going to do. Her fingers played with mine on the ride home, squeezing. The cab driver kept his eyes intently on the rearview mirror, watching.

"He thinks we're fags," Birgit said, pulling her woolen cap off to reveal her long honey-blonde mane. The driver seemed to visibly relax. And then Birgit wrapped one arm around my neck and pulled me in for our second kiss. Sweet, at first, and then hot as her lips parted and her tongue met mine.

"Here—" she said, just when I was losing myself in the wonder of it all. "Right here." She paid the driver and hurried me back up the four flights of steps to the apartment. There were no words then. Just Birgit unwrapping me as if I were a Christmas present. My hat off. Sweater on the floor. Long strand of bandages unwound and discarded. Shoes pulled free. Jeans in a faded denim puddle. Birgit took me to the bed, spread me out on the soft duvet, and started to speak German.

"What—?" I begged. "What did *you* say?" Now, I needed to know. I didn't want to miss any words.

"Relax," she told me, her body soft and warm on mine, curved and dipping in all the right places. She straddled my waist and looked down at me, then traced her fingertips along the line of my forehead, the bridge of my nose, before bringing them finally down to my mouth. Her fingertips rested on my lower lip and I drew them in, sucking on two, gently, softly.

I felt the place where our bodies were joined, felt the heat as it seemed to move from her to me. Felt the wetness when it started and I bucked up against her body, letting her know. But she knew. Easily, she moved down, kissing along the rise of my collarbone, down the hollow of my flat belly, making her way to the wet opening between my legs.

I thought of Johnny and wondered whether he was behind a smoked-glass door, making love to a stranger. I thought of the barker, offering nubile women for viewing pleasure, or more. And then I thought of nothing, as Birgit spread my nether lips wide open with her slippery fingers and brought her hot mouth against me. She touched my clit gingerly with the tip of her tongue, then ringed it with her parted lips. I felt the wealth of expertise in the way she touched me – she knew what she was doing. Her fingers came into play, holding my lips apart, dancing along the slick wet split. Then she moved her head down and her long hair tickled my inner thighs as she drew a line with her tongue from my pussy to my ass. I groaned and raised my hips, anxious to take whatever she would give.

Mouth glossy, she moved back and forth, licking and sliding, playing tricks and hide-and-seek games with her tongue deep inside of me. I turned my head and stared at the gold-painted wall, seeing our shadows there, growing and stretching with our movements. There were four of us in the room. Me and Birgit, and the two lovers on the wall. When I could take no more, I put my hands on her shoulders and made her look up at me. "Please –" I begged.

"What?" she asked, an echo, a murmur, "What did you say?"

"I want to taste you," I told her, and quickly she swiveled her lithe body around so that her sex was poised and ready above my waiting mouth. Then we were connected again. My tongue inside her pussy, her whole face against my cunt, pressing hard. I didn't think. There was no need to. I only acted. Lips on her nether lips. Tongue flat to tickle her clit and then long and thin to thrust inside of her. I mimicked each move she made until we were in perfect rhythm. One creature, one being, riding together on that bed.

Nothing has ever felt that good. The way we connected to each other. Skin sliding on skin. Fingers moving, caressing. Searching together to find the end – the answer.

With my eyes shut, I saw the women in the windows, the sluts under glass. With no sound but our hungry breaths, I heard the barker offer up his strippers, smooth and shaved, and then I was coming, and I heard only my heart in my ears as I drove hard against her mouth, sucked hard against her clit, taking her with me, taking her over.

• • •

Hours later, the boys found us curled in the bed together, me wearing one of Johnny's shirts, Birgit in one of Wolf's.

"Sleeping off a drunk," chuckled Johnny knowingly.

"Far prettier than the women in the cinema—" Wolf said, and I understood from his tone of voice that Birgit had been right all along. The boys had fled that sex-charged street in favor of the less-challenging turn-on of a dirty movie.

Johnny and Wolf stumbled down the hall toward the tiny kitchen, where I could hear them trying, and failing, to be quiet as they looked for more alcohol. There was a loud bang and then Wolf groaned something in rapid-fire German.

"What did he say?" I asked Birgit, nuzzling my lips against her soft cheek.

"Nothing," she assured me, "nothing important." Her fingers once again found the secret shaved skin of my pussy. Then quietly she spoke to me in German, and I closed my eyes and listened to the delicate murmurings of phrases that I knew promised pleasure, for once not worrying myself about the translation.

Rapture at Cartagena

MICHÈLE LARUE

(Translated from the French by Noël Burch)

IN THE '70S, PIRATE-NOVELIST HENRI DE MONFREID'S tales of gunrunning in the Middle East inspired many a would-be globetrotter. I devoured those books; everything that happened to me seemed redolent of *Secrets of the Red Sea*. In those days, I roamed the rowdiest port cities of South America with a streetwise American who loved his big game fishing and could recognize CIA agents by the shoes they wore. He was puritanical to the point of never doing anything: leaning on the bar in some sailor's haunt, he would describe the day's catch, watching me dance the salsa.

In Cartagena, our only copy of *Secrets of the Red Sea* was a dog-eared English translation. I was sure that he was poring over the book to find out what made me tick, perhaps to woo me. We shared a bungalow, and he took it to bed with him every night, in the bedroom next to mine. Then one morning, on the beach, I saw a fishing boat in the distance, bobbing on the rough sea, long and thin like Monfreid's Swahili cargo boats. I began swimming toward the murky horizon.

The boat was only a few strokes away when my strength failed me. I cried out. The sky became suddenly threatening, the sea was sucking me down. Tossed by the crashing waves, I was about to drown. Echoes, voices in an unknown tongue rang out across the gray shimmer of merging sea and sky — approaching, calling.

The Red Sea boat was filled with half-naked men, silhouetted against the metal sky. The hashish smugglers (in reality, Colombian fishermen) lifted me on board. The smack of forearms, a profusion of smooth flesh against my back and belly, the animality of dark skin, the intoxicating virility. My breasts brushed against their rough blue loincloths (some wore turbans of the same material). The boat was bobbing on the waves and I collapsed on the scummy planks. Unable to rise, I lay like a fish out of its element, gaping for water. With great peels of laughter, my "smugglers" poured *aguardiente* into my mouth. Their hot organs touched me. Eyes shut, I breathed in their chocolaty aroma as they forced the bottle between my teeth. In a state of ecstatic alacrity, I began to sizzle. Take me! There's no "me" here.... A feeble sailors' prey, all willpower gone. So be it: and I arched toward them, thirsting for flesh, eager, bewitched. My whole body atingle, ready to swallow cocks by the score, orifice yawning for phallic vigor, pubis stiff as any cock. Get your breath back, swim ashore, said "me." Shut up, said I, let me revel in ecstasy, shudder and shake and die to my "me!" The reek of lust in that boat made thinking out of the question. My mind was in my sex, hungering for brutal caresses and heaving chests.

Breasts and belly strained against their firm, sticky palms. Three men carried me to a pile of nets and squatted over me. Hot suction cups tugged at my flesh, irradiated breasts, excited tummy; a tide of foam ran down to my toes, spittle, snot.

To look? Did I dare to look? I opened my eyes and gazed upon the new secrets of the Red Sea: other men were gesticulating over my body, one wore the top of my suit around his neck. I was slapped on the back, glancing, stroking blows. The mouths came up for air, gaping, laughing. Onomatopoeia. Mobile tongues, pink palates. My body desecrated like a torn rose. I skidded.

A boatman's arm prowled between my thighs. I arched my back like a bow, my bottom hollow and gaping. He drove in, thrust, expanded, climbed all ten octaves. My voice was inside me, I panicked in the treble, took heavier pleasures in the bass. A sense of weight returned, I could feel the meshes digging into my back, my skin had regained sensation. Rhythms, sublime rushes back and forth between us, deep dancing, dizzy spells. I was no sooner grasped than gone. One human suction cup forced his member under my armpit. Sticky chunk of flesh. My body stiffened, pressing it to my ribs. The aroused seaman's milk curdled on my reddened skin. As the spunk spurted, an orgasm shot down my legs. Trills. Tides of shifting orgasms. On the surface. Deep in the ass. Back to sculling. Corrugations: my diaphragm in my mouth. The sky was bristling with flagpoles. I grabbed one from below and it emptied itself at one go. I seized another to pull myself up, put it in my mouth, swallowed it to the curly hairs. It spouted but remained stiff enough to carry my weight. Suddenly, I saw the Colombian coastline: Land! Land! Two strides and I was into the water, splashing down on those crests of liquid sensuality. I dived and felt the refreshing delight of the deep, of my own movements in the water.

When the waves coughed me up on the sand, I didn't know where I was. I hadn't been dreaming: the boat was sailing out to sea, I could still feel the contractions in my sex, and the nets had marked my shoulders. A crowd of people brushed past me laughing, rushing every which way. I went looking for my towel. Dozens of dark-skinned boys crowded around a shower bath, their sexy laughter reaching me through a halo of sound and once again my tingling skin was drawn like a magnet. I plunged. They caught me, shoved me to the center of the mêlée. Their arms slid over my belly, my hips, their fingers worked on my bare breasts and the needles of water stirred my palpitations. A heavy carnal swell. My happy thighs trembled with the steady flow of pleasure from the leathern muscles of my assailants. My body was in a spin, my sex was a yo-yo. Suddenly the swarm abandoned me and headed for the sea. I felt dreadfully naked.

I strode off across the beach again, propelled by the memory of a blue towel.

It was nightfall when I woke with my hair full of sand, my towel over my breasts. The American was near me, cooking fish over a fire. Bright *braseros* were burning as far as the eye could see. There had been a miraculous draught that afternoon, fishermen had come from miles around and were still filling their nets with stray fish. Their boats were parading out there on the black water. I wrapped my tired body in my blue towel. My friend began wolfing his grilled catch, reminiscing about another shoal of fish led astray by deceptive currents off the coast of Mexico, under a full moon. I put my hand on his bare thigh and stroked it. He pressed his knees together slightly and for a second the little fish in his hand hung suspended in mid-air. Carefree, light as a feather, I laughed and did not remove my hand. He smiled, relaxed and took a big bite of the white flesh. I lay my head on his knees and opened my mouth. With perfect aim, he dropped little bits of fish into it. As I chewed, I was buzzing with life.

samson and Delilah

⤳

JACQUELINE SILK

SOPHIE TOOK A STEP BACK AND SURVEYED THE PAINTING, putting the brush between her teeth so that she could tighten the ponytail that held her hair.

Not bad, she thought. *Not bad at all.* She leaned toward it again, using the brush to touch up a piece of skin on the man's back. She had got the color just right. Not too dark, not too pink. The flesh smooth and gleaming, like polished bronze. The muscles rippling beneath.

The contrast with the paler skin of the woman worked well, she thought.

The man was kneeling in front of her, one leg raised, his huge hands clasping her hips. She stood tall and straight, her head thrown back to the sky. She was naked, as he was, her body white but pure as a pearl, almost luminescent. She cupped her breasts in her hands, tilting them upward, their nipples a fragile, flowering pink.

Sophie liked the way the eye was drawn upward, yet the

meeting of their two bodies was happening below. The man leaning forward, his broad back disguising the whole lower half of her body, except in the place where his dark head met her thighs. Just the suggestion of her pubic hair, above the blacker curls of his hair. And her legs, from calf to foot, appearing either side, from where he had pushed them apart. He was eating her.

Sophie rested her brush across the bottom of the easel and, with one swift movement, pulled her T-shirt over her head. Then she dropped it to the floor and stretched her arms upward for a moment, marveling at the feel of the breeze on her naked flesh. The door to her studio was propped open. She could hear the birds worrying the bird feeder at the top of her garden and, in the distance, the muted complaining of sheep. She took a deep breath, tilting her large breasts upward, her ribs suddenly more prominent, her jeans slipping down over her narrow hips to reveal a smooth belly.

She loved the smell of the Welsh countryside. It was only early March, but the first daffodils had already arrived—and the newly grown grass, pushing up with sticky fingers, was so earthy, so sweet. She closed her eyes and reached down to cup her hands around her breasts, echoing the pose of the woman in her painting. As she shifted her weight, she felt the moistness between her thighs, and rocked her hips slightly, just to feel the delicious pull of the jeans against her clitoris.

Lately, she liked to take off all of her clothes to paint. No one could see her here, in her studio at the top of the garden. Around her were a few trees and then open fields backing onto hills. That was why she had chosen this place, this small cottage in the heart of North Wales. There were no other houses around. And it had been easy to convert the cluster of outbuildings into a studio. She loved the isolation and the security. Loved the paintings that this tranquil life made her produce. She had never painted like this before. Never translated her longing so perfectly onto canvas.

Sophie tweaked her nipples, pinching them between finger and thumb. She felt a sharp, reverberating pleasure below, as if it were connected, as if she were an instrument being strummed. Still with her eyes closed, she dropped a hand down to the waistband of her jeans, then slowly slipped it inside. Her cunt was deliciously wet, had been getting that way for most of the morning. Opening her legs slightly, she slid a finger inside and left it there, feeling herself tighten around it. She could practically come like that. Just a slight movement, a gentle swaying of the hips. She opened her eyes and stared again at the broad expanse of the man's back.

He was an Adonis. She had deliberately painted him that way. None of the wiriness and intensity of the men she had known in London. He was half animal. You could tell by the thickness of his calves, the large bulldog head. His hands were more like paws and each shoulder was as wide as the woman's whole body.

Sophie shifted her gaze to the back of his head. Black hair and thickly curled. How would it feel to bury her hands in it as he knelt in front of her, twine it around her fingers to pull his mouth closer? Would he pant as he ate her? Make thick, animal noises in his throat?

She began to move her finger gently in and out of her cunt. The sensation was almost unbearable. With her other hand, she undid the buttons on her fly and pushed her jeans down until they fell around her feet, then she stepped out of them.

She could feel the air on the whole of her body now. It circled around her waist, stroked at her bottom, whispered through the gap in her legs. A chair was placed to the right of her easel. She reached for the back of it and leaned over, pushing her buttocks high into the air. Her finger was still working between her legs; she felt it caressed by the breeze coming through the door. With each movement, the heel of her hand nudged her clitoris. Widening her legs even more, she leaned further forward, until she was fully exposed. Then she inserted another finger and began to move her hand more quickly, frenziedly, the sensation collecting in her clitoris as tightly as the flowers in an unopened bud. A trickle of moisture slid down the inside of her thigh.

She imagined the man from her painting watching her, kneeling behind, enormous hands placed gently under the swell of her buttocks, easing back the skin on either side. She couldn't see his face, because she hadn't painted it yet. But she felt his warm breath against the lips of her labia, so close, so hot. She came urgently, her hips jerking down to meet the very ends of her thrusting fingers, her forehead resting on the edge of the chair and her cunt cooled by the air from the open door.

• • •

That afternoon, Sophie headed for the lane that led up into the hills. Her dog—a Border collie named Marley—trotted happily beside her. He was the only thing that she had brought with her from London that didn't seem incongruous, here in the Welsh hills. He had settled into the lifestyle quickly, loving the fresh air and the freedom to wander and behave more or less as he liked. He was getting quite old now—less energetic. He stayed by her side, his tongue lolling merrily, his eyes, when he looked at her, almost cross-eyed with eager anticipation of their walk.

The trees began to thicken and form a canopy above their heads. Sophie could hear the familiar trickle of water from the stream at the bottom of the gully. A rabbit dashed across the road in front of them and Marley pricked up his ears for a moment, standing still and watching as it disappeared into the bracken at the other side. Then he trotted on.

I could be the only person in the world, Sophie thought. *How lonely it is.*

She glanced to her right, where the branches of the trees looked like twisted arms groping through the green-tinted sunlight. On some of the larger trees the roots were exposed and they seemed to creep, too—pointed fingers scraping back the earth.

Sophie smiled. Perhaps she was so desperate for company that she was perceiving everything anthropomorphically. That morning, she had even made a painting come alive. She dug her hands deeper into the back of her jeans and thought again of the fantasy she had weaved. What a shame the man didn't really exist. She felt an ache, deep in her chest. It was so strong, she had to stop and take a deep breath. Then she recognized what the sensation was: longing. She closed her eyes, feeling the sun's warmth on her upturned face as it broke through a cloud and pierced through the trees. *If only,* she thought. Like a child.

A droning, spluttering noise broke the silence and Sophie reached for Marley's collar and pulled him over to the grassy verge. They waited, listening to the sound getting closer. At last, a tractor appeared from the direction in which they had come, towing a trailer loaded with hay. Sophie nodded at the driver as he passed and he raised a hand, his expression inscrutable below the pulled-down brim of his cap.

The road climbed steadily. On one side, the gully with its

gurgling stream; on the other, the trees giving way to the bald side of a hill. As they rounded the next corner, the trees disappeared completely and the road flattened. They emerged into bright sunlight and Sophie went to sit on the wall of a small bridge that formed this part of the road. The stream rushed under it, glinting between the spiky blades of grass. A few sheep were chewing nonchalantly on the bank beside the stream. When they noticed Sophie and Marley, they began to edge away, some of them trotting quickly up the steep slope to rejoin their companions on the hillside beyond.

Sophie turned and rested her stomach on the cold stone, tossing a stick into the water and watching as it bobbed along then disappeared under the bridge. She could no longer hear the tractor. She guessed it had stopped somewhere over the brow of the hill, just out of sight. She turned back around to face the sun and slid herself down until her back was leaning against the bridge. Then she closed her eyes. *I'll just rest them for a minute,* she thought.

When she opened them, the fields seemed very green, the gorse on the hillside more golden than brown. The sky, when she looked up, was more like a summer sky—powder blue, with the occasional puffy white clouds, like sheep set out to pasture. But there were no sheep on the hills. They had disappeared. The landscape seemed deserted without them and there was something else missing. Sophie stood up and turned a full circle, shading her eyes with a hand. Marley was nowhere to be seen. She called his name, several times. Nothing. Then she noticed the hole in the fence that led down to the stream.

She scrambled over the rusty gate. Although it was private property, she and Marley often trespassed when there were no sheep around so that he could play in the water. But he had never ventured off on his own before. When she got to the bank she looked up and down and even under the bridge. No sign.

Sophie began to feel worried. He was an old dog. They had only been in the house for a couple of months. Would he be able to find his way back? She decided to climb the hill so that she could get a better view. Perhaps she would be able to see him from there.

At the top of the hill, she realized where all the sheep had disappeared to. They were gathered around two bales of hay in the field below. Feeding time. The tractor that had passed them earlier was parked just inside the gate. At first, she couldn't see the driver, but then she spotted him. Kneeling with his back to her, fastening something at the back of the trailer.

Sophie's heart missed a beat. Even from that distance, she could make out the huge width of his back beneath the shirt. His neck was bent, revealing black, curly hair beneath his cap. The muscles on his forearms were straining against the restrictive material of his rolled-up shirtsleeves.

It's him, she thought. Then, *turn round. Let me see your face.*

As if on command, he stood up. He was very tall. His legs well-muscled, his bottom tight. Sophie held her breath as he reached up and lifted his cap to smooth a forearm across his brow, wiping off the sweat. There was something indescribably sexy about his movements. Graceful despite his size. He replaced his cap and turned to look over at the sheep. They were making a lot of noise.

Sophie studied his profile: straight nose, full mouth, wide jaw. The eyes were slightly hooded, set in deeply beneath heavy brows.

Or perhaps he was frowning. She looked across to where the sheep had been eating peacefully. Now there was mayhem. Most of them had dispersed to the edges of the field, huddled in groups and moaning pitifully. Only a few remained by the food, unaware of the creature that stalked them, a dark shadow which, even now, was creeping craftily forward, his large ears pricked in gleeful anticipation.

Sophie recognized Marley immediately. She began to run down the hill, shouting his name. But her voice was drowned out by the baying of the sheep. The man had moved to the front of his tractor and was reaching in to get something. When he turned around, Sophie stopped in her tracks.

He was carrying a rifle. She watched in shock as he lifted it to his shoulder and began to aim it in Marley's direction.

"Stop! No!" she shouted. She began to run again, waving frantically at the man. But she was still too far away. She stumbled over a small rock and fell to her knees. He was about to pull the trigger, she was sure of it. She lifted the rock and threw it as hard as she could. It hit him squarely on the side of his head, knocking off his cap. He lowered his rifle in surprise.

She knelt panting in the grass. Two legs appeared in front of her. She looked up — a long way it seemed — to the furious face that scowled above them. It didn't seem so attractive, now.

"What the hell do you think you're doing?" it said.

"You were going to shoot my dog!"

As if on cue, Marley arrived and began to lick her face. She grabbed him by the collar and stood up, reaching in her pocket for the lead.

"So, he's yours, is he?" he grunted.

"Yes. And you nearly killed him!"

"He shouldn't have been bothering my sheep. Anyway..." he reached up a hand to where a lump was already beginning to swell on the side of his head, "you nearly killed me."

"Serves you right." Sophie tugged at Marley's lead and began to turn around. But the man reached out and grabbed her arm.

"Where do you think you're going?" he asked.

She looked down at his hand. Huge fingers. Just one of them could wrap itself completely around her wrist. She shrugged it off. "I'm going home."

"Not that way you're not. This is private property." He nodded toward the gate at the other end of the field. "The road's that way."

She stared at him. "But it'll add at least another mile."

He shrugged, then folded his arms. Huge arms, they were. Enormous biceps. Sophie scolded herself inwardly. The man behaved like a brute. What did it matter that he was built like one, too? She pushed past him and, with as much dignity as she could muster, began picking her way through the mud to the road.

• • •

After about ten minutes, the skies opened as they often did in this part of the country — without warning and without letting up for a full half hour. The rain stung the back of Sophie's neck, flattened her hair to her head until it clung in sodden tendrils around her face. The thin shirt she had worn was soaked through. Her breasts were clearly visible beneath, the nipples erect and rosy pink. She hugged her arms around her chest, shivering. Marley lollopped beside her, his fur sodden with the rain. Every now and then, he looked across at her, hoping for forgiveness. She had been scolding him all the way home.

The noise of an engine made them both turn around. It was loud enough to be heard above the rain. Sophie scowled when she saw the tractor. Scowled even more when it slowed right down and

43

she saw the man lean over from the driver's seat.

"Get in," he said. "I'll give you a lift."

"No thanks," she said, turning her cheek resolutely back to face the road.

"It's a long walk," he said.

She stopped and looked across at him, placing her hands on her hips. "I know," she said, meaningfully. But the sarcasm seemed to be lost on him. He was staring at her breasts where they were molded against the wet material of her shirt. Angrily, she covered them up again with her arms.

"Well, if you're sure." He revved the engine, sending a splattering of mud up from the back wheels as he moved off. It hit Sophie just above the knees. She stood with her mouth open, staring after him.

"*Da boch chi!*" he shouted, lifting an arm into the air. *May it go well with you.* She had learned enough Welsh to interpret that particular piece of mockery.

• • •

When Sophie got home, she ran herself a hot bath. But despite lying in it until the skin on her hands and feet wrinkled, she couldn't relax. She still felt cross about the man's behavior. He had been so rude. And she was angry with herself for having found him physically attractive. His resemblance to the man in her painting had been uncanny, particularly given the wistful mood she had been in when she set out on the walk. It was almost as if she had conjured him up. But the magic stopped there. The joke was on her. In personality, this rough farmer had nothing in common with the man she imagined. He was insolent where the man in her painting was worshipful. He looked at her as if she were a peasant; the other man knelt, as if the woman above him were a queen.

At last, Sophie stepped angrily from the bath. She wrapped herself up in her dressing gown and went into the kitchen to pour herself a drink. But when she reached for the bottle of whisky, she suddenly remembered that she had finished the last of it off a few nights previously.

"Damn!" she muttered. She looked at her watch. Eight o'clock. And the rain had eased off, enough for a short walk down the hill. She didn't stop long enough to change her mind.

Ten minutes later, she was pushing open the door of the village pub.

She had been in a couple of times before. Enough for her entrance not to cause too much of a stir. She noted the landlord's raised eyebrows, however, and the way the conversation at the bar changed smoothly into Welsh. A couple of elderly men sat up on stools, huddled over their pints. She ordered a beer and started to make her way over to a table by the fire, but then thought better of it and dragged up another stool to sit at the bar. She could feel the men casting her curious glances as they sipped at their beer. The one immediately to her right started to stare so hard that, eventually, she had to turn toward him. When she did, he immediately swiveled his beady eyes away from hers. The expression in them was crafty — like two rats caught in a cage.

The landlord leaned forward from the other side of the bar, a tea towel draped over his shoulder. "So, how are you getting on?"

"Fine."

"You're settling in?"

"I think so."

She could sense the other men listening.

"Beautiful day, today."

She sighed. "Apart from that sudden downpour about four o'clock."

He nodded, pulling off the tea towel to polish the top of one of the pumps. "Got caught in it, did you?"

"Yes, I did." She stared at the top of his bald head. It was nearly as polished as the brass. He lifted it and caught her gaze, then smiled at her. His eyes were so kind, she suddenly wanted to confide in him. Though, perhaps it was the beer, warming her stomach. "I had quite a nasty experience, actually."

He stopped polishing the pump and leaned in closer.

"Someone tried to shoot Marley — my dog."

"No." His face was a picture of concern.

"We were out walking and Marley ran off. I know I should have had him on a lead.... It was my fault. When I found him he was bothering the sheep. This man in a tractor got out a gun. There was no need for that."

The landlord shook his head. "Of course not. No need at all." He paused, casting a quick glance at the other men who were both

45

sitting with their heads down, suspiciously quiet. "Where was this?"

"In one of the fields at the top of the hill. The one that backs onto the road at the other side of the stream."

"Ah, yes." He nodded. "I know it."

"I don't know what he was doing with a gun."

He shrugged. "We do a lot of shooting round here. It was probably an air rifle."

"I suppose it might have been."

He leaned in much closer to her. "Was it a burly fellow? Black, curly hair? Youngish?"

She nodded. "Yes, do you know him?"

He shook his head. "Not really." Then he went over to the other side of the bar.

Sophie stared after him, bewildered. Then lowered her head to stare at her fingers.

"New here, are you?"

The question surprised her. It came from the old man beside her. But he wasn't even looking at her as he spoke. She stared at his profile; the bulbous nose, slightly reddened at the tip, the bushy eyebrows curling to the side of his head like huge, wiry question marks.

"Not really," she said. "I've been here a few months."

"New here," he said, nodding into his beer.

She took a sip of her drink, trying not to feel offended.

"You in Glenwyn, then?"

She smiled weakly. "How did you know?"

He looked at her. "Small village, isn't it? Not a lot happens that we don't know."

She saw the other man nodding behind him. It was her turn to look away. Did the whole village know her business?

"And you're a painter, now?"

She looked back at him. "How did you know that?"

He shot her another quick glance, a small smile curling his mouth. "Saw them carrying the stuff in."

Of course, she thought. He'd seen the removal men. But even so, it made her feel slightly uneasy. She took another sip of her drink.

The man leaned back a little from the bar, swelling his chest and lifting his head. He was obviously beginning to enjoy himself.

"And you like it here, do you?"

"What? Here? Oh, yes." His eyes narrowed and focused on her face. She felt that she should say something more. "Especially the house. I love the house…and the garden."

He lifted his pint and took a long gulp without removing his eyes from hers. "Backing onto fields, isn't it?"

"Yes. Yes, it is."

"Nice views I should imagine."

She nodded.

"You've heard about the building plans, I suppose?"

"What?" So far, they had been conducting their conversation sideways on. Now she turned her body around to face him. "Building plans? What building plans?"

He lifted his drink again, taking another gulp that was agonizingly slow. She watched the Adam's apple bob in his throat. At last he put his glass down.

"Arwell Jones. He owns the farmland at the back. He's got big plans for it, you see. Wants to put up some new barns, maybe keep some pigs." He glanced at her out of the corner of his eye. "Of course, he'll need your permission."

It was the first Sophie had heard of any such plans. She hadn't even met the farmer who owned the fields at the back of her land. She folded her arms across her chest and fixed the man with one of her coldest stares. "Well, he might have to wait a very long time."

"Thought you might say that," he chirruped, smiling smugly into his beer.

• • •

Sophie hadn't planned to stay longer than half an hour but for some inexplicable reason she found herself unable to leave the pub and was still sitting there two hours later when *he* walked in. She'd been bought one drink after another, first by the man who had spoken to her — who introduced himself as Yal — then by his friend. Even the landlord had given her a drink on the house — "to make up for your bad day," he had said. So when the tall figure swung through the door, she wondered at first if the drink was making her see things. But then he leaned across her to order his beer and she noticed the large bruise swelling on the side of his head. He glanced down at her and froze, his money held aloft, his eyes fixed on hers.

She knew that he had recognized her as she had recognized him.

"God, it's the woman with the dog," he said, as if to himself.

She shot him a withering glance, but it was lost on him. As he reached for his beer, his face relaxed and he suddenly grinned at her. She couldn't help noticing how attractive he was when he smiled like that. His eyes were a warm brown, the irises flecked with gold.

She tried to retain some dignity, however. "I don't think it's particularly funny," she said.

"Don't you?" He gazed at her over the top of his drink, a small foam moustache collecting above his upper lip. He licked it off with his tongue.

Sophie shivered. "Perhaps I should send you my cleaning bill."

"Cleaning bill?" he laughed. "For an old pair of jeans and a flimsy shirt?" His eyes moved down to her chest and lingered on her cleavage. "Then again, you did look pretty in it."

She blushed, remembering how see-through the shirt had been. "You're very rude," she said.

"Am I?" He looked around the bar, noticing the others for the first time. They were making no secret of the fact that they were listening. He gave Yal an exaggerated wink. "She's not from round here, is she?" he asked, his eyes returning to tease hers.

"She's just moved here from London," Yal said. "She's a painter."

"A painter? I see. That explains it." He smirked.

Sophie winced. She didn't like being talked about as if she weren't there. She felt as if they were assessing her on criteria she didn't understand. "What do you mean?"

He laughed. "Well, you certainly don't seem to know much about farming."

"What makes you think that?"

"Everyone knows that if you let a dog loose in the fields during lambing season you shouldn't expect to see it return."

"It was an accident."

"We don't have room for those around here." He narrowed his eyes and spoke more quietly. "You're lucky nothing happened to your dog. Or to you." He looked her up and down again. She was very aware of the threat he was making.

"You really are the most insolent man I've ever met," she spluttered.

He laughed, turning his back to her and picking up his drink.

Sophie grabbed her purse and got up to go.

The landlord reached over and nudged her tormentor in the ribs, nodding toward Sophie.

"Whoa!" He turned and put a hand on her shoulder. "I'm only teasing you. It's just a game. Let me buy you a drink."

His hand was burning a hole in her skin. She hated the way her body betrayed her, thrilling to his touch. Summoning all of her strength, she shrugged his hand off and gave him one of her most scathing looks. "No, thanks." She pushed past him and made her way to the door. It swung closed behind her, the cold air hitting her full in the face.

She stood for a moment, sheltering in the porch.

What arrogance! She had never met anyone like that before. None of the men she had known in London would have dared speak to her like that. It was just a game, he had said. But surely he had known that the cards were stacked against her. She was the stranger, after all. She didn't know the rules.

She began to button up her coat. The conversation had begun again inside the pub. They were talking about her, she supposed. About what a fool she had been. She should have known not to confide in the others. They had known the man she talked about all along.

Sophie took a step out of the porch, but her feet stopped, refusing to move any further. She felt a sudden return of the ache she had felt that afternoon. A nagging pain; a longing. But what was she longing for?

She heard Yal's voice raised above the others. "But you see, Arwell. You can't win them all. It's all just a question of timing, isn't it?"

Arwell. The name rang a bell. She thought back to her conversation with Yal earlier that evening. And then she remembered. The farmer. It was the name of the farmer who wanted to build at the back of her land. Perhaps she'd been given a decent hand in this game after all.

They all went very quiet when she walked back in. Arwell had his back to her. He was the last to turn around and meet her gaze.

He lowered his pint very carefully back to the bar.

She walked straight up to him. "Arwell?" she asked, softly. "Are you Arwell Jones?"

He nodded, a spark of interest lighting up his eyes.

She reached out a hand and he took it. "Let me introduce myself. My name's Sophie. I've just moved into Glenwyn. You know it?" She waited a second for realization to dawn in his eyes. "It's the house with land that backs onto your field." She paused. His eyes really were lovely close up. "I believe you need my consent to build on that field?"

A small smile began to curve his lower lip, but it didn't quite reach his eyes.

She squeezed the hand that she still held in hers. "What a shame," she said. And she turned on her heel and walked away.

As she left the pub for the second time she could hear them all laughing, but this time she knew it wasn't directed at her. *One all*, she thought, jubilantly. She tried not to skip down the road. *It's a draw, that's all*, she told herself. *This game has only just begun.*

• • •

Over the next few weeks, Sophie visited the pub quite regularly. When she saw Arwell, he did his best to woo her, offering to buy her drinks that she steadfastly refused. Sometimes, she saw him from a distance in his tractor. He always raised a hand to wave, looking rather sheepish. She only nodded in return.

But she couldn't help the thrill that ran through her each time she saw him. She began to have sexual dreams in which he featured. He appeared in all of her paintings — the same naked man making love to the woman. Only now she could put a face to the glorious body.

She didn't know how to feel about her attraction to him. It was becoming something of an obsession. This annoyed her. She suspected that Arwell was used to getting his own way with women. One thing she knew: even if, as she suspected, he was also attracted to her, she would never give in to him on his terms.

• • •

One morning in late April, Sophie and Marley had stopped by the side of the stream. There were no sheep about so she let him play in the water. The sun was really hot that day and Sophie lay back in the warm grass, letting it caress her bare arms and face. A few minutes later, she felt a shadow fall across her body. When she looked up, she saw Arwell standing above her, his huge arms folded across his chest, his shoulders so large, they blocked out the sun.

"Morning, Sophie."

"Arwell." She sat up. He was looking particularly serious, she thought.

"I think it's time we sorted this out."

"Do you?" She couldn't help smiling a little. "Those building plans must be quite important to you."

He shrugged.

"Sit down," she said, patting the ground next to her.

She watched as he stretched out his long legs. She tried not to look at his crotch. She had an overwhelming desire to reach out and touch him, to feel the hardness of his body beneath the thick material of his jeans. She folded her hands in her lap, interlocking the fingers.

"We got off to a bad start," he said.

"We did."

"I had no idea you'd take me so seriously."

"Oh, come on, Arwell. You treated me like a dolt."

He looked at her. His eyes were sparkling beneath their heavy brows. "You behaved like…"

"No!" she interjected. "Don't say it."

He laughed. "I'm just a farmer," he said. "I've been a farmer all my life. You can't expect me to have much patience with city girls."

"You shouldn't put people in a box. It makes them feel worthless."

He put a hand under her chin and tilted it toward him. "I wouldn't want to do that. I don't think you're worthless, Sophie." He let his eyes fall down to her mouth, then let them travel the line of her neck to where her breasts were just visible beneath the open neck of her shirt.

She pushed his hand away. "Don't do that!"

He frowned. "Why? You should be flattered that I want you."

"But you're so certain that I'll want you in return."

"Don't you?"

"No. Yes. But not like this. I can't stand your arrogance…it's…" she paused, then set her mouth in a firm line. "It's demeaning."

He stared at her, obviously shocked. "I'm not one to paint a pretty picture, Sophie. I like to tell it how it is."

She sighed. "You just like to be in control."

"Do you think so?" He was looking at her so earnestly that it made her wonder. "OK." He reached across and took her hands in his. "What can I do to make it up to you?"

Sophie raised her shoulders in a small shrug.

He widened his eyes in mock astonishment. "You mean there's nothing? Nothing at all?"

She laughed. He still had hold of her hands, capturing their heat. She felt a stirring in the pit of her stomach. "Well," she said. "Maybe there is something."

"Go on."

"But you might not like it."

He grinned, showing his white teeth. "Try me."

• • •

The sun burned through the glass, falling on the back of her neck and her bare shoulders where the straps of her top had slipped down. The door was slightly open, but there was only a small breeze. It stirred the tops of the daffodils that grew just outside her studio door.

"So, what do you want me to do?" he asked, hands on hips.

He seemed much bigger in the confines of her studio. His head nearly touched the roof.

Sophie cleared her throat. "Take your clothes off," she said.

He glanced at the half-finished composition on her easel. Most of it had been painted from memory. Perhaps he recognized himself. Sophie felt herself grow hot as he walked into the center of the room and began to unbuckle his belt. He pulled it from his trousers and dropped it, with a clatter, to the floor. Then he unbuttoned his shirt. She was not disappointed when he cast it aside to reveal a deeply tanned upper torso. The muscles bulged around his arms and chest, the jeans slipping down to reveal a taut stomach and the large bones of his hips, a thick tuft of black hair snaking its way toward his crotch.

She licked her lips. "And the trousers," she whispered.

He smiled at her and started to undo them. She couldn't take her eyes off his huge hands, the thick fingers and wide cuticles.

Then the jeans were dropping to the floor and she held her breath as they revealed the black bush of hair and swollen penis. It wasn't just his upper torso that was huge.

"You're not wearing any underwear," she said.

He smiled. "Neither are you."

She wanted to ask him how he knew that, but, instead, she turned to the easel and picked up her paintbrush, wiping it clean with a tissue.

"Any particular pose you want me to adopt?"

She couldn't believe how relaxed he was. As if he had done this before.

"Could you lie down?"

He stepped back onto the rug and stretched himself out, supporting his weight on an elbow. Then he gazed at her, a tranquil expression on his face.

She couldn't concentrate with him looking at her like that. "Perhaps if you closed your eyes," she said.

He immediately complied and she was able to study his body in detail. Everything about him was perfect, from the thick hair on his head to the dark strands curling around his toes. Sophie breathed in deeply, then let the breath out in a shuddering sigh. She was going to have to show a lot of self-control if she was ever going to finish this painting.

• • •

An hour and a half later, she stepped back, lifting her elbows to massage her stiff neck. The painting was finished. And it was good. A man's naked body, stretched out on a red, velvet rug, as if he were some succulent fruit being offered to the woman who stood above him. She hovered like a dark priestess, her white body partially hidden by a purple cloak, her eyes as slanted as a cat's guarding its prey.

Sophie glanced across to where Arwell still lay with his eyes closed. She guessed that he was asleep. His breathing had become very deep. She stared at his body, not with a painter's eye this time, but with a very human one. She wondered what it would feel like to be touched by those hands, have those hips thrusting against hers. Her hand began to reach for the zip on her jeans and she slowly pulled it down, slipping a finger inside where the cool air met her hot skin, pushing it downward until it met the juicy opening of her cunt. Her clitoris was very erect. She began to gently rub at it, all the time keeping her eyes on his face in case he should wake up. Her other hand slipped inside her shirt and cupped her naked breast, pinching the nipple in time with her other finger's rubbing until she whimpered with pleasure.

"I see that you've finished."

Her eyes shot open. She had only shut them for a minute. She dragged her hand out of her jeans and began to pull up the zip with a shaky hand. He was sitting up, staring intently at her flushed cheeks. She noticed that his penis was fully erect.

"You should let me help with that," he said.

She turned her back to him, blushing even more. She could see his reflection in the window. He got up and made his way over toward her. Then she felt his hands slip under her shirt, his chin resting on the top of her head. He cupped her breasts in his hands, gently pushing them up and rubbing at the nipples with his thumbs. She gasped but she couldn't pull away. It was as if he knew. He pulled the shirt up over her head and dropped it to the floor. Then he reached forward to unzip her jeans.

Sophie could see herself in the window. It was like the hazy reflection of a siren. She leaned forward, placing her arms on the window ledge, and let him push down her jeans, stepping out of them as they crumpled to the floor. She felt his hands momentarily on her hips, then one arm encircling her waist as the other hand slipped over her naked buttocks and gently parted her legs. His fingers were at the entrance to her cunt, teasing the swollen lips. She cried out as he suddenly pushed his thumb inside her, slowly drawing it back out only to thrust it back in. Arching her back, she urged him to go deeper, her nipples pressed against the glass. She felt his lips on her neck, his rough stubble scraping the soft skin at her shoulder. Then he drew his thumb out and rested his hand on her waist, still sticky from her.

"No" she moaned. "Don't stop!" She pressed her forehead against the cold glass.

"Wait there."

She watched his reflection step back and reach for something in his trouser pocket. He was rolling on a condom, his penis so huge in the window that she couldn't take her eyes off it. He placed a hand on the small of her back, encouraging her forward again. She opened her legs wider without being asked. He could see all of her now. She wanted him to see.

For an agonizing moment, she felt nothing. She raised her head and met the reflection of his eyes in the glass. Then his hand returned to her waist and she felt him enter her slowly, inch by inch, the walls of her cunt clinging to him as he moved further in. She stretched back her neck and moaned, pushing her hips back against his. He laughed deep in his throat, starting to thrust a little harder. With one hand she reached behind and found the tautened muscles of his thigh. She clutched at the skin, feeling it tighten and release with each jerk of his hips. "God," she moaned. "Fuck." She didn't think she could take anymore. Everything inside her was begging for release. But he pulled out again, leaving her almost crying with frustration, her legs shaking as they tried to support her weight.

"That's not fair," she said. "You can't do that!"

But he was kneeling down behind her, sliding his hands slowly up the backs of her legs until they reached the swell of her buttocks. She felt his warm breath on her exposed flesh as he pushed her buttocks further apart.

"God, yes!" she cried. "Do that!"

She didn't think she could open her legs any wider. She felt the first quick dart of his tongue. It flicked at her clitoris, then dragged along the entrance to her cunt. She pushed against him, sure that she would come then and there. He reached up and parted her lips between his thumb and index finger. She felt his tongue again, flicking up, then darting inside, strong and firm, hard. It tunneled inside her, twisting against the vibrating flesh. His other hand reached forward to massage her clitoris. She closed a hand over his, reveling in his fingers' stickiness, moving them faster up and down until she couldn't stand it anymore and she exploded against his mouth, reaching her sopping fingers back to twist them in the curls of his hair.

• • •

Later, they stood together in front of the painting. He held her from behind, wrapping his arms around her waist.

"How do you feel?" she asked.

"Unmanned."

She turned around to face him. "Really?"

He nodded. She had taken him in her mouth, let him watch the semen slip from between her pink lips.

She frowned. "I hope you don't think this means you can build on that land. We still need to talk about that."

"Forget about the land," he said. "I have."

She grinned, reaching up a hand to pull at the curls at the side of his jaw.

"It looks like me," he said, nodding toward the painting. "Only the hair's a bit shorter. What are you going to call it anyway?"

She turned back to gaze at the canvas. "I'm not sure, yet," she said. Though a title was already forming in her mind.

She reached forward and smudged at a dark spot of paint next to the man's head. If she tried, she could make it look like severed hair.

Yes. She would paint in the scissors later.

seven cups of water

ॐ

MARY ANNE MOHANRAJ

MY BROTHER'S WEDDING DAY. The feasting lasted long past dark, and I went to bed exhausted. I first peeled off my sweat-soaked sari, rinsing my body with cool well water before changing into the white sari I wore to sleep. The old women had consulted the horoscopes of my brother and his young bride, and had pronounced that this day, in this month, would be luckiest, in fact the only day that would not bring down a thousand curses on the young couple—never mind that it was also one of the hottest days of the year. There was no flesh left on the old women's bones, nothing that could drip sweat; I am sure they enjoyed making the young ones miserable.

I thought that for once, I would be able to sleep. I'd been allowed a little of my father's whiskey, to celebrate Suneel's wedding; I had danced with the other unmarried girls. My sisters' friends giggled and preened as they danced, flashing their dark eyes and slim brown bellies at the young men who lounged by the door, drinking. I just danced; I had no interest in catching a man. Not that any would have spared a glance for me, too-tall, dark Medha with coarse hair and flat chest. I danced for myself, not for them. I danced until my feet were aching, until my arms and legs were lead weights. I danced until Suneel and his lovely Sushila were escorted to his bedroom, until the last piece of rich wedding cake was eaten, and the last guest had gone. Only then did I bathe and change, only then did I lie down on my bamboo mat, a few feet from my peacefully sleeping sisters. And still I could not sleep.

It might have been the heat. Our house is near the ocean, and usually cool breezes fill the small rooms, but that night it was so hot that it was hard to breathe. I kept thinking it would get cooler, but instead it got hotter and hotter. Sweat dripped in uncomfortable trickles from my neck to my throat, from my breasts to the hollow between them, pooling in my navel. My mouth was dry as dead leaves, and I finally rose to get some water.

The house was silent. I left my sisters sleeping, passed my parents' room, and my brother's. I passed the main room, where dying flowers and bits of colored foil testified to the day's happy event, and finally entered my mother's huge kitchen. We weren't rich, but we did have one of the largest houses in the village. We needed it; I was the youngest of eight, and cooking enough food for all of us took many hands and pots in the kitchen. The moonlight streamed in the window, illuminating the rickety table where my mother chopped, the baskets of onions and garlic and ginger and chilies, the pitcher of water that was always kept filled. It was one of my mother's rules—if you drank from the pitcher, you refilled it from the well. With five daughters and three sons, she needed many rules to keep peace in the house. Not that we always obeyed them.

I stepped over to the pitcher, took a tin cup from the shelf and poured myself a cupful. Then I saw her. Sushila huddled in the far corner of the kitchen, her back pressed flat against the baked mud walls, her red wedding sari pulled tight around her, so tight that the heavy silk seemed to cut into her fair skin. Folds of fabric were wrapped around her fists, and those in turn were pressed tight against her open mouth. She looked as if she were trying not to scream, but she didn't move, or make a single sound.

I stepped toward her. "Sushila?" I knelt at her feet. Her knees were pulled up tight against her chest, and I rested a hand on one.

"Are you all right?" It was a silly question, and after a moment I understood that I didn't deserve an answer. The cup was still in my other hand; at last I stretched it out to her. "Would you like a cup of water?"

She nodded, and slowly lowered her fists. I raised the cup to her lips, and tilted it so that she could drink. Sushila took a deep gulp, draining half the cup. Her whole body shivered then, though the water couldn't have been cooler than lukewarm, after sitting all night. She shivered again, and again, her arms now hanging loose at her sides, her eyes wide.

I didn't want to ask my next question, but I had to. "Did Suneel...did he hurt you?" The words almost choked in my throat. My second sister had married a brute who beat her; she came home crying every week to show us the bruises, and then turned right around and went back to him. I knew that there were men like that in the world; it was part of the reason I never wanted to marry. But Suneel—he had always been the gentlest of us all. He had converted to Buddhism a year ago, had turned vegetarian and mourned every time he accidentally stepped on an insect. He never teased me like the others had; he'd protected me from the worst of my oldest sisters' rages. My favorite brother—I didn't want to believe that he could have hurt Sushila, but there she was, shaking before me....

Sushila shook her head. *No.* After a moment, the word came up and out of her throat—"No." I was almost as glad to hear the sound of the word as the sense of it; there was a crippled child who lived in the alley nearby who could not speak at all. I raised the cup again, and she drained it in another gulp. I put it down, not sure what to do next.

She was still shaking. I leaned forward, pulled her into my arms. When she was completely enclosed in my arms, the white of my sari covering the red of hers, she turned her head, so that her mouth was against my ear. Her breath was hot against my neck as she whispered, "I'm bleeding...." Before I could speak, she reached up and took my right arm, her fingers sliding down to my hand and pulling it down between us, under the sari to the space between her thighs. Her legs were wet, and when I brought my hand up, the tips of my fingers were stained red. When Sushila saw the blood, she started to cry.

I wrapped my arms around her and held her tightly, letting her cry against me. My second sister had shared every detail of her wedding night with us; she seemed to enjoy our shock and fascination. I knew that Sushila was the oldest daughter in her family, that her mother had died years ago of a fever. But didn't she have any aunts? I stroked her hair, so soft and fine, and told her softly, "It's all right…shhh…." Her shaking eased, slowly, though the tears still fell hot against my neck, sliding down my chest and mixing with my sweat, an indistinguishable mix of salty waters. I held her, and rubbed her smooth back, and whispered the words, over and over, until she understood.

• • •

I asked her at breakfast the next day if she had slept well. Everyone laughed, and Suneel's face reddened. He had inherited my mother's pale skin, and every emotion showed through. Sushila smiled demurely, and assured me that she had. I was glad for her, but I hadn't slept at all.

I had drunk cup after cup of water after she'd left, then refilled the pitcher from the well. A breeze had finally picked up, and the ocean's salt air filled the rooms, caressing my body stretched out on its mat—but still, I couldn't sleep. I kept remembering how she had felt, her small body huddled in my arms, remembering the sweet trembling, the softness of her cheek against mine. I had held my sisters and countless cousins, of course, but this had been different. And at breakfast and lunch and dinner, throughout the day, I watched Sushila. She was slender and fair, a perfect foil to tall Suneel, and she moved as if she were dancing. She was clever too, telling small jokes that made everyone laugh. If I could only look like her, talk like her…well. Might as well wish for Krishna to come down and carry me off.

That night, I dozed for a few hours, but in the deepest hours I woke, sweaty and damp. I wanted some water. I got up and walked down the hall.

She was standing near the kitchen window, drenched in moonlight.

"I thought you might be awake," she said, turning as I came in.

My tongue stumbled, but I managed to say, "I just woke up."

"Thank you for last night." She was blushing, but her voice

was firm and clear. There was no sign of the trembling girl I'd held in my arms; Sushila held herself straight and poised. "You must think I'm very silly."

"You're welcome. I don't think you're silly." The moonlight shaded the planes of her face, the delicate curves; it was almost like looking at a statue. I could have stood there, watching her, for hours. "Shouldn't you be in bed...with your husband?" My brother.

"I was thirsty. I often get thirsty at night." She was wearing white, a thin gauze sari that barely covered her limbs. Sushila's small arms and legs made her look almost like a child, but I knew she was sixteen, almost as old as me. "I came for some water, but I couldn't find a cup."

The cups were in plain sight; perhaps the shelf was a little high for her. I reached up, pulling down the same one I'd used the night before. It had a small notch in one side, and you had to drink carefully or you might scratch yourself. It was different from all the others, and my favorite. I lifted the pitcher, and found that it was almost empty. Someone hadn't refilled it. I poured what water was left into the cup, and held it out to her. As she stepped forward to take it from me, she stumbled, and her outstretched hand knocked against mine, spilling the water over both our hands, splashing onto the dirt floor.

"Sorry!" She seemed frightened for a moment, though it was only water.

"It's all right. But that was all the water." I could draw some more from the well, of course.

Sushila sighed. I could see her breasts move under the thin fabric of her blouse. "I'm really very thirsty." She lifted her dripping hand to her mouth then and started to lick the water from it. Her tongue was small, too, and licked very delicately, with determination. She licked away every drop, slowly, as I watched.

"Still thirsty?" I asked. Sushila hesitated, and then nodded. I could have drawn more water, but instead I took a small step forward, bringing my wet hand up to her slowly opening mouth. She reached out a hand and gripped my wrist, surprisingly tight. She took the cup out of my hand and set it on the table. And then she brought my hand to her mouth and started to lick.

I started shivering then.

When she finished, having carefully licked first the back of my hand, then the palm, and then taken each finger into her mouth, she let go of my wrist. My arm dropped limply to my side. Sushila's eyes were wide and still, her head cocked to its side like a little startled bird. She bit her lip, and then said, "Thank you. That's much better."

I didn't know what to say. The wrong thing, and I knew this would be destroyed, might as well not have happened. I wanted to take her damp fingers in mine, and lick them, but when I opened my mouth, these were the words that came out: "Suneel might miss you."

Sushila took a quick breath, then nodded. "Now that I've finished my cup of water, I'd better go back to bed." Sushila turned away and stepped quickly and quietly down the hall. I heard her pushing aside the curtain that covered their doorway, and then it fell back into place behind her. I picked up the pitcher and went out to the well.

• • •

The third night, I didn't even try to sleep. I had napped a little during the day, and my mother had called me a lazybones. It didn't matter. They were only staying a few more days, just three more days and then they were getting on a train, leaving the north, going down to the capitol where Suneel had secured a government job. The tickets were bought; plans had been made. This night, and then three more — that was all.

After everyone else had gone to bed, I went to the kitchen and waited. I watched the moonlight travel across the room. I counted the cracks in the ceiling, and the lizards that lived in the cracks. I listened to the wind moving through the coconut palms, and when I couldn't sit still any longer I went outside and picked shoeflowers from the garden. Their soft crimson would look lovely in her hair. I arranged them in circles on the table, and in the center of the circle, I placed the filled tin cup. I was bent over them, straightening a crooked flower, when I heard her step behind me. I stood up straight, but didn't turn around. Her arms slid around my waist, and Sushila rested her head against my back. She started to whisper: "It's dry in that room. It's so dry. My mouth and skin are dry. The air is like breathing chalk. The heat is outside and inside and burning. It hurts to breathe."

Did she know what she was doing to me? She must have known. I said nothing, just listening, just feeling her slim arms around my too-solid waist, the unbearable warmth of her against my sweating back. My blouse covered so little, and her cheek lay against my naked skin, her belly was hot against my lower back.

"Medha," she whispered, "I'm thirsty."

I took the cup of water from the table, and turned to face her, still enclosed in the circle of her arms, so that now her belly pressed against mine. I raised the cup to her lips, but Sushila shook her head, keeping her lips tightly closed until I lowered the cup, confused.

She smiled. "Aren't you thirsty?" she asked.

Oh. Of course I was. Desperately thirsty. My hands, curved around the cup, had turned to ice, but my mouth was burning. I raised the cup to my lips.

I filled my mouth with water, soaking the dry roof of my mouth, my parched tongue. Then she raised up on her toes and opened her mouth; I bent down, and placing my lips on hers, I gave her water to drink. Sushila took it from me, sucking the water deep down her throat. She swallowed, and I felt the motion in my own lips. Then she pulled back, and for a moment my chest tightened with fear...but she only said, "More."

I fed her the water from my lips, making each mouthful smaller and smaller, each transfer taking longer and longer. Finally, the cup was empty, and not just empty, but dry. She released me then, and stepped back. She said the words, formally, the ones I knew she was about to say.

"Thank you for the cup of water. I should return to my husband."

I nodded, and Sushila disappeared down the hall. Of course she had to return. This was impossible, so impossible that it wasn't even explicitly forbidden—but if I didn't think about it too hard, maybe it would be all right. Three more nights.

• • •

On the fourth night, as I poured her cup, I pointed out that the well was full of water. If we left the kitchen, if we went behind the house, to where the well stood, shaded by a large banyan tree—there were many shadows near the well, and there was much water within it.

"I shouldn't be away that long," she said. "Just long enough for a cup of water."

I wanted to protest, but didn't. If I did, she might decide she wasn't that thirsty after all; she might simply go back to Suneel. It would be so much safer that way.

I have always loved my sweet brother.

The fourth night, she took the cup away from me. Sushila dipped her small finger into it, and then traced a line along my arm. She bent down and licked up the water. Then it was a line from my throat to the top hook of my blouse, and her tongue dipped briefly beneath the line of fabric to chase a drop of water. Then she knelt to draw a circle on my belly, a spiral ending in my navel, where she lingered, sucking gently, then not so gently.

I tried to take the cup, to at least dip a finger in myself, but she pulled it back. Her eyes were laughing, though her voice was clear and firm.

"I'm sorry, but I'm really very thirsty tonight. I need to drink it all."

Sushila pulled me down to my knees and turned me, to drip water along my back. She seemed especially fond of the back of my neck, and I brought my hand to my mouth to stifle the moans that I could not keep down. Thank the gods that my father snores so loudly. You can hear him from the kitchen, his snores regular as the ticking of his prized gold watch. If he found us like this....

Half a cup gone when she turned me back around, and she paused a moment, staring at me. Her eyes were large and wide and dark, her lips so full they seemed bruised, bitten. I leaned forward, my own mouth slightly open, hoping that she might choose to put her wet finger inside it, and then follow it with her mouth, but instead she reached up and pulled down my sari, so that the sheer fabric fell to my waist, leaving my upper body dressed only in my blouse. The blouse fabric was thicker than the sari, but I felt naked. She smiled then, and scooping up fully half the remaining water in her palm, she drenched my left breast.

She put her mouth to the fabric, sucking the moisture from it, the water mixed with my own sweat. I raised my hand to my mouth again, teeth closing down on flesh. Sushila started with the underside of my small breast, and then circled up and around. Spirals again, circling closer and closer until finally her mouth closed on the center and I bit down hard on the web of skin between thumb and forefinger, breaking the skin, drawing bitter blood. She sucked harder and harder, pausing at times to lick or bite, sucking as if she meant to draw milk out of my breasts, enough milk to finally quench her thirst. Eventually, she gave up the attempt. She released my sore breast, lifted her mouth away, and smiled when she saw my bleeding hand. Her eyes danced, daring me to let her continue. I could stop this at any time. I could smother the fire and walk away.

What would she think of me if I backed away? I could guess, and could not bear the thought of it. If I backed away, she would only return to her husband. He would have her for the rest of his life. Her body would lie under his, and he would bend to taste her breast.

I nodded acquiescence. She poured the rest of the cup's water onto my right breast and lowered her head again.

• • •

Fifth night, and one more to go. When Sushila came into the kitchen, I opened my mouth to speak, but she laid a soft finger against my lips.

"You seem very thirsty," she said. "You should drink the water." She filled my tin cup, filled it to the brim, and then handed it carefully to me.

"I am thirsty," I answered. "I'm burning up." I waited, but she just smiled. The next move was entirely mine. I hadn't slept—I'd been thinking all day and all night of how to make Sushila burn. I needed to match her ingenuity, her ideas, to push the game forward. I needed her to understand that this was more than just a game. We couldn't stop here, or even slow down.

I put my hand on her shoulder and pushed down gently; she obediently sank to sit cross-legged on the floor. She seemed so patient; Sushila could wait forever, unmoved. I needed to move her. The words pulsed through me — *one more night one more night*. I didn't have time to be patient. I needed her burning, the way I was, a burn that spread from her center to her heart and tongue and brain; a fever that kept her from thinking, from playing, from leaving. I pushed down again; her eyes widened, but Sushila obediently lay down, stretching her legs out straight, with arms at her sides, her sari stark and white in the moonlight, against the dark dirt floor.

I touched her eyelids, and she closed them. I stood and picked up my mother's chopping knife, cold and heavy in my hand. I had always been clumsy; I had dropped it many times, and had cut myself as I chopped. But tonight I would be careful.

I pulled over a basket and, lifting out a handful of chilies, began to chop, as quietly as I could. The wind whistled through the palm trees, and my father snored, but still.... I chopped the chilies finely, minced them the way my mother could never get me to do when it was only for cooking. I minced them until they were oil and ground bits, almost paste. Then I scooped them into a tin bowl, my fingers covered in hot oil and slowly starting to burn.

I knelt beside Sushila and placed the bowl and cup by her still body. I pulled loose the sari fabric, pulled it down so that her upper body was only covered by her blouse, as mine had been the night before. Then I started to unhook her blouse.

I expected her to protest, but she said nothing, didn't move. I don't know what I would have done if she had tried to stop me; stopped, I suppose. But she didn't, and so I unhooked each clasp. I peeled back the fabric, baring her breasts. They were ripe and perfect, large dark mangoes bursting with juice. I was so thirsty. I let down my sari and undid my own blouse, freeing my small breasts. If we were interrupted now, there could be no innocent excuse...and yet it wasn't enough. *One more night.* I smeared the chili paste in a weaving line, starting with her navel, curving up over her belly, looping and swirling until I reached her breasts, then circling in as she had done, circling to the centers.

Chilies don't burn at once, on the skin. They take time. To Sushila it must have just felt like some slightly gritty jam. Perhaps she thought I planned to lick it off—but there was a whole cup of water to use up, and first, I wanted her burning. When I finished drawing my patterns, I put down the bowl. I sat back on my heels, and waited.

She felt it first on her belly, the slight, growing burn. Sushila shifted a little, uncomfortably. I watched. Her eyes started to open, and I placed a hand, the clean one, over them. She kept her arms at her sides, but her body began to twist, to rise up from the floor, to arch. It was useless. Her belly was heated, her breasts. They were

66

getting hotter and hotter. Soon it would be unbearable.

"Please...." The word broke from her lips. I took the tin cup. I started with her navel, started rinsing the chili paste away, caressing the skin with wet fingers, relieving the pain. But there wasn't very much water in the cup. I could only dilute the chili essence, soften the intensity, and by the time I reached her breasts, the water was more than half gone. And there just wasn't enough water left to do her nipples, their darkness crowned by fiery red paste. I let Sushila open her eyes then, raised the cup and showed her its emptiness.

There were tears in her eyes, but her arms stayed perfectly still at her sides. I smiled down at her.

"Do you want to go back to your husband now?" The water was gone.

"I'm burning, Medha. I'm burning up."

My heart thumped. I lay down beside her, moved my head to her breast and took the fire into my mouth. I have never been able to eat very hot food. I swirled the chili paste on my tongue; I savored the burning flavor of it, mixed with her sweat. My tongue had been stabbed by millions of tiny pins. I wanted to suffer for her.

I suckled at her right breast, feeling her body shifting against mine, hearing her whimpers. I was afraid we would be heard. I moved to the left breast, and her hand came up to tangle in my hair, to keep me there. Her leg slid between mine, and I began to suckle again, rocking our bodies together as I did. Her breath left her in a tiny sigh, and at the sound, my chest exploded.

I went to bed that night knowing that small traces of oil undoubtedly lingered on her body, that she lay beside Suneel still burning for me.

One more night.

• • •

They planned to leave the next morning. I had been thinking all day, and when she came to me that night, I was ready with my arguments.

I took her hands in mine, caressing her soft skin under my rough fingers. When she smiled, I spoke. "Come away with me."

"What?" Sushila tried to pull away, but I held on tight. Her eyes were suddenly wide and frightened, and I held her fingers as tight as I could, trying to reassure her.

"Come away. Take the tickets; we can trade them for another day and then leave together. We can go to the city; I can find work." I was whispering, but I willed her to hear how much I meant what I was saying.

Her mouth twisted in a way I had never seen before. "Work? Doing what? What can we do?" Her voice was low as well, but scornful. "Should we end up washing someone's filthy clothes? Lose caste, lose family — lose the future?" She did pull away then, sharply.

I wrapped my arms tightly around my body, trying to slow my thumping heart.

"*You* are my future!" I wanted to shout the words, and keeping them quiet was almost more than I could stand. "It doesn't matter what we do to survive. Nothing matters but that you come away with me. I'm burning, Sushila."

"You're being foolish." Her eyes were disgusted, and my chest hurt. "I can't leave Suneel — you have nothing and I have nothing. I have the jewelry your family gave me; would you have me sell that so that we can buy rice and lentils?"

"Yes!" I was passionate; I was convinced. "It's not fair that we should be separated. It's not right, Sushila!" I reached for her hand, but she pulled away. She walked to the window and stared out as she spoke. Her voice had grown so soft that I could barely hear her.

"It's not right to leave, Medha. The jewelry, even my saris, belong to him, not to me. I belong to him. Would you have me abandon Suneel, leave him alone and shamed, without wife or the hope of children? Does he deserve that? Is that fair? It's not right to leave him. I have to go with Suneel."

What had happened to my Sushila, who had burned for me last night? She sounded so calm, so cold.

"It doesn't matter what's right or wrong. What's *really* wrong is that you should leave with him, that you should leave me here, alone." I didn't know if I was making any sense — I just knew that I was desperate to say something, anything that would keep her. But she wasn't listening to me.

Sushila turned back to face me. "It won't work. I'm sorry." She sounded like the statue I had once thought her, as if she were built of stone.

"But I love you! I love you!" My heart was breaking. It had broken and she was crushing the pieces under her heel. "Don't you care for me at all?"

Sushila's voice gentled, a little. "I do care for you. But if they found us, they'd drag us back in shame. They might do worse. I had a friend — her husband died and they said she'd poisoned him with bad cooking...they burned her. They burned her alive."

I sucked in my breath, shocked that she would think.... "My family wouldn't..." She cut me off before I could finish.

"No, you're probably right. They probably wouldn't. But Medha, it won't work. You know it won't. My place is with Suneel. There's no place for us out there. Just here, in the kitchen, without words. Just for these six nights. Just you, and me, and the cup full of water." Her voice had turned soft, persuasive, but I would not be persuaded. I wanted to surrender to her, but there was no time for that now.

"The cup! Is that what matters to you? The cup is *nothing*, Sushila. The cup is just a game, it's *your* game. It doesn't matter. You just want to play your game and then go off, safe in the arms of your husband, leaving me here." Leaving me alone.

"Safe? You think I'm safe with Suneel?" Passion was finally in her voice — but not the kind I'd wanted.

"He'd never hurt you." I was sure of that, at least.

She closed her eyes, squeezed them tight for a long moment, then opened them again. "Oh no. He's sweet, and gentle, and kind. He will try to be a good husband to me, and I will try to be a good wife to him. We will have children, if the gods are kind." There was the pain I felt, there in her voice. But it wasn't for me. "And after ten or twenty or thirty years of that, I will have all the juices sucked out of me; I will be dry as dust. I will die of my thirst and blow away on the wind. And that's the way it is; that's the way it always is. You're the lucky one, Medha." Sushila meant it, I could hear it, but I didn't know why.

"Lucky?" I didn't understand her, didn't know her. Who was this woman with flat eyes, speaking of dust?

"At least you are still free, for a little longer. Take what pleasure you can of it. That's all we can do, Medha. Take a little pleasure when we can."

Sushila fell silent, and I did too, still thinking that there must be some other argument, some persuasion I could offer. I didn't believe what she was saying—I couldn't believe that was all there was for us. But I thought for too long.

"Come," she said softly, "take up the cup." It waited, full, on the table. I knew that she was trying to save what she could; it was our last night, the very last. But I couldn't do it. I grabbed the cup, held it in my shaking hands.

Then I turned it over, spilling every drop of water to the floor.

I didn't know what she'd do, if she'd rage and shout, if she'd drag me to the ground. But Sushila just turned, and walked away.

I let her go, let her walk down the hall and disappear into his room. I had lost her entirely, and lost our last night too. I had wasted a cup of water, for nothing.

• • •

I slept like the dead that night. Perhaps I didn't want to face the morning, hoped that she would just slip away without my having to face her again. My mother shook me awake.

"What, are you sick too? Get up, Medha—I need your help. Sushila's sick and they can't leave today. I need you to take care of her today."

I dressed quickly. Not gone yet! Not leaving today! I rushed to Suneel's room, to find him standing over his wife, his cheeks pulled in. Sushila's eyes were closed, and she did look pale.

"Medha, she's nauseated. She's been throwing up all morning. Stay with her, will you? I need to go change our tickets."

I nodded, and he bent to give her a kiss and then left the room. Once he'd gone, her eyes opened, and she motioned for me to bend down. I did, and she whispered in my ear, "I made myself throw up. I decided to give you one more chance." When I pulled back, Sushila was smiling, and I was too. Perhaps I looked too happy, because all too soon she was saying, "Just one more night. Suneel and I will leave tomorrow."

"But..." I had visions of persuading her, if only she would stay a few more nights, a week, two....

"No, Medha. It's too dangerous."

My eyes were stinging, but I knew she was right. Each night we'd gone further, each night we'd taken more risks. If we kept this up, we would be caught, and if she wouldn't leave with me...then

70

it was this, or nothing. I finally nodded agreement. Just tonight.

I stayed with her through the day; we didn't touch. We could perhaps have held hands, or stolen a few kisses…but that would have been going outside the game, and the game had kept us safe so far.

It was an eternity until nightfall.

When I arrived in the kitchen, she was waiting. Something was different. The tin cup sat on the table, and the pitcher, but something else as well—a stone. It was my mother's sharpening stone that she used for her knives.

"Help me," she said. She picked up the cup and ran the stone along the jagged edge. I thought at first she was dulling it, making it safer—but after a few strokes, I realized she was making it sharper. Sushila handed it to me, and I stroked it to greater sharpness. We passed the two items back and forth, the cup and stone, sharpening the edge to match that of a blade…and still I didn't know why. It didn't matter, though. I trusted her. Finally, she put down the stone and called the cup done. Three-quarters of the rim was still that of a cup, safe and dull. But one quarter had a sheen of sharpness to it, and it seemed more than just a cup.

"Pull up your sari," she said. I was startled, but obeyed, pulling it up past my ankle, my calf, my knee until almost all of my thigh was visible— "Stop." I stopped, obediently, and watched her do the same with her sari. Her legs were so smooth and fragile; for a moment, I felt like a great, hairy cow. But the moment passed. We were past that now.

"Cut me." She pointed to her thigh, and, suddenly understanding, I took the cup in my hand. I reached out, pressed it against her soft flesh, bit my lip, and sliced down. A short, sharp cut, barely half the length of my palm. She had exhaled once, sharply, but made no other sound. She took the cup from my hand and, with a swift motion, made an identical cut in my thigh. The beads of blood welled bright, shining in the moonlight, and for a moment I was so dizzy I thought I would faint. But then I steadied, and when she leaned forward and pressed the cuts together, blending our blood, I held firm. She kissed me then, and the world spun around us.

"Pour the water." I poured the water into the cup with my left hand, spilling some onto the table. It didn't matter. I poured until the cup was full. She took it then, and carefully sluiced some onto our joined legs, pulling away as she did. The bright blood ran down, mixing with the water, diluting.

"Don't pour it all!" I trusted her, but I couldn't keep the words from coming out. When the water was finished, so were we....

"I haven't. See?" She showed me the water left in the cup, barely a mouthful.

"Good." I looked at our legs, at the cuts that would turn into scars that we would carry forever. Forever! She wouldn't forget me, and I would never forget her. But we had a problem. "If we let the fabric go, the saris will be stained. People will wonder."

She nodded, smiling. "We'd better just take them off, then."

It was so risky; it was the last time.

We carefully removed our clothes, holding them away from the now-trickling blood. We piled the fabric on the table and then, carefully, eased to the floor. My leg hurt, but as she bent her head to kiss me, the pain mingled with pleasure.

My hand found her breast, and her arms wrapped around me. We lingered over our pleasure until the sky began to lighten, and then we shared the last mouthful of water. By the time the household wakened I was back in my room, embracing the ache in my leg, trying very hard to remember everything.

• • •

When she left, she reached up to my ear one last time. In full sight of everyone, she whispered, "It's for the best, Medha. You'll be married soon, and you must try to be happy. I will always care for you."

I didn't say anything out loud, but I knew that I would never marry, and I swore in my heart that I would never love anyone as I had loved her.

• • •

The scar faded into nothing within a year, and I cried when the last trace of it disappeared.

Sushila....

virgencita

꒰

Myriam Gurba

I.

THE FINAL SUMMER OF MY *ABUELITA'S* LIFE, I earned a
nickname that still makes my cheeks burn when I think of it. That
summer baptized me as *Gringita Macha*—macho American girl.
When my mother and I talk about that summer now, my mother
recalls it first and foremost as a strange and sad time. It was
undoubtedly the most humid summer the city had ever seen. The
air was hot but thick and it clung to the body with a deliberate, slow
and wet heaviness. I filled this summer, a seasonal exile from Los
Angeles, with the laziest pastimes I could find: rolling and smoking
my own cigarettes, eating fruit so soft it had to be cut with a delicate
hand, and listening to the sound of my grandmother's caged birds
from my languid perch—a stone bench on her front patio. I sat
there a lot that summer, barefoot and heavy lidded, weighted down
by the tropical gravity, watching Guadalajara go by in a haze of
tobacco smoke, wishing I were at home.

We had traveled to Mexico because my grandmother's weekly letters had stopped arriving. It had been my grandmother's habit to write my mother each Sunday and my mother had taken those letters for granted. Each week the mailbox had held a letter documenting the last six days of my *abuelita's* life, the smallest microcosms of an existence happening half a continent away. No detail had been too small to omit from the letters: whether she had gone to the butcher shop or the bakery that week, the condition of the stray dogs and birds she had taken in, whether she had eaten papaya or mangos for breakfast—these were the goings-on that had filled her letters. Sometimes short, sometimes long, the letters had always been very clear and played like a silent movie of my *abuelita's* solitary life.

Then one day, the letters stopped coming. At first, my mother had thought they were just late. Maybe they had accidentally been delivered to our neighbors or maybe the mail was just slow. After three weeks of making excuses and repeating "Maybe…" scenarios in her head, my mother finally realized that the letters were not going to arrive. With this realization, she flew into an angry panic because her only option was to telephone my *abuelita*. Telephoning my *abuelita* was one step short of total uselessness. My mother dialed and the phone rang and rang but my *abuelita* either couldn't or wouldn't answer it. See, my *abuelita* had grudgingly given in to the installation of a phone but only as a convenience to others. She hated the telephone and never answered it. She swore that the only people who had ever even touched her phone were the few guests who had set foot in her home. The last straw came when my mother went to check on the monthly money wire that she sent to her mother each month. The money, which my grandmother used to buy her groceries, had gone unretrieved.

In light of my grandmother's disappearance, my mother decided that a voyage to Mexico to find out for herself what was going on was the final solution. I was to be her companion. Shy, skinny and seventeen, I didn't mind. The last time I had been to Mexico had been before my father died and those memories were mostly a blur. The week of our departure, my mother spoke with her employer, with our neighbors and the garbage collector. She arranged for the roses to be watered in her absence, for the mail and newspapers to be collected daily, and for the dogs to be walked and fed. We packed our things and left our small house in East Los Angeles and boarded a train at Union Station, bound for Tijuana. My mother and I rode to the border in silence, I with my sketchpad, doodling parrots and toucans and other exotic birds and my mother worriedly biting her lip, trying to read. As we rode, I tried to remember my grandmother but the only memories of Mexico I could recall were of my father, holding my hand as we hiked up the small pyramids that lay on the outskirts of Guadalajara while he told me about the Indians who had built them.

II.

After two transfers and a minor delay, we finally arrived in Tijuana. There, we took a taxi to a bus station where we boarded a rickety old bus that we rode for the last stretch of the journey. I hated this leg of the trip. The bus rattled and shook as it rode through the states of Sonora, Sinaloa, Zacatecas and Nayarit, finally arriving in Jalisco. The road to Guadalajara was dirt in some places and paved in others. Some parts were even cobblestone but no matter where we were there was the constant presence of potholes. At each town we stopped in, I made a beeline to the pharmacy and purchased the strongest bottle of cough syrup I could find. Half a bottle of it would usually dull my senses enough to put me to sleep so that I didn't have to feel my teeth rattling in my head as we drove across Mexico.

When we finally arrived, I had lost several days to sleep but I didn't care. I had my land legs back and we were at last in Guadalajara. We took a cab to my *abuelita's* house, passing Plaza Patria and El Mercado de San Juan de Dios. My mother and I rode in silence and I could tell that she was mentally preparing herself for whatever the very near future held in store.

I recognized her tiny sky-blue house almost immediately. It was small but pretty with a garden patio in front. A large wrought-iron fence surrounded the house and was slowly being overgrown by the lush vegetation that filled the space. There were flowers, small shrubs and a plant with long tendrils that looped its way around a trellis propped against a window. That was my grandmother's window.

We made our way to the front door and knocked. Nobody came to the door. No sounds came from within. My mother rattled the doorknob and found it unlocked. She gently pushed open the door and we heard the scattering of roaches tapping against the floor. The air smelled stagnant and stale and I turned to look at my mother's face. It was expressionless. My mother walked past the small sitting room piled high with newspapers, and approached an open door. I followed slowly behind her. My grandmother was there, on the bed, in a white nightgown. She looked asleep and I could not tell if she was breathing. My mother took a few steps to her bed and knelt down beside it, placing her hand on my grandmother's cheek, feeling for warmth. I saw my mother smile. My grandmother opened her eyes and stared up at my mother. Death already dominated her gaze and I knew to leave at that moment. I took a few steps backward and shut the door. I went to the front hall and picked up our suitcases. I opened the door to the other bedroom, the one adjacent to my grandmother's and began to unpack our things. I arranged the room and then, sitting down on the bed, realized I was exhausted. I lay down on the naked mattress and fell asleep to the sound of whispers coming from the wall that separated the rooms.

When I later awoke, it was already night. My mother was seated at the foot of my bed.

"*Gracias m'ija,*" my mother said to me.

"*¿Porqué?*" I asked.

"*Porqué nos diste la intimidad que necesitabamos. Viste en sus ojos que Mamá no estara con nosotros por mucho más. Vamos a permanecer con ella hasta su día final y ese día está muy cercano.*" My mother thanked me for giving her the privacy that she needed to be alone with her mother. These were to be my grandmother's final days and we would stay here with her until she took her last breath. Judging from what my mother said, it could be a few days or a few months. Either way, I prepared myself to spend long days alone, wandering the streets of the city or seated in the shade, drawing, giving my mother and her mother the privacy they needed during their last days together.

III.

The next day, I began my wanderings. I walked through *el zócalo*, downtown, past the cathedrals and churches and religious shops. With sketchbook in hand, I explored the colonial district, staring up at the sprawling old estates, imagining the spiral staircases, the big, old-fashioned kitchens, the gaudiness that must have filled the spaces beyond those walls. September 16 was also in a few weeks, Mexican Independence Day, and there were banners hanging from balconies and in the marketplaces. A stage had been erected near the cathedral and there was a group of women, *tapatias*, performing *bailes folclóricos*. I stood and watched as their skirts twirled and their thin ankles moved and tapped and kicked in the air to the accompaniment of *mariachis*. They were all sweating as they danced and their necks glistened with the sweat matting their hair in wet tendrils to their skin.

I walked to the cathedral for shade and sat inside for a short while, enjoying the comfort of the coolness. I stared up at the icon of the *virgen* that hung behind the altar and blushed. She and I had something in common. After I had cooled down, I got up to leave. On my way out, I stared at the body of a saint, held by a glass box. Her body was covered in wax and I looked at her. She must have been my age when she died. And innocent. Walking home, I passed through the colonial district again and past the Mercado de San Juan de Dios. You can buy and sell anything there and the peddlers perk up at the sight of an American. My clothes said American before I even opened my mouth and I heard shouts of broken English, "Hey joo, American boy, joo wanna buy leder, nice leder belt, leder boots? No? I gib joo good deal American boy."

I smiled to myself hearing this. They could see that I was *gringo* from a mile away but the true nature of my body was wrapped in disguise, baggy boyish clothes that my slender hips and almost-flat chest swam in. My face was young, soft, plain and framed by a baseball cap. To Guadalajara, I was just a green-eyed American boy.

IV.

After a few weeks, the heat became almost unbearable and I would silently perch myself on the stone bench in front of my grandmother's house, sketching and watching the city go by on Avenida de Niños Heroes. My baggy clothes and ball cap became oppressive in the heat and I soon ditched them. My uniform of choice became cotton boxer shorts, shirtsleeves, and a thin cotton bathrobe. I would walk barefoot and squish my feet in the warm dirt of my grandmother's garden. Before long the ground became littered with my cigarette butts and I came to know the patterns of the street: what time housewives made their daily trips to the market, when the schoolgirls walked home from school, when old men walked their dogs. I sat there in my shorts, smoking, drawing, stretching my long legs out, a smooth-looking boy save for the most subtle suggestion of a breast and no Adam's apple. I could tell I confused most of the people who walked past and happened to meet my gaze. I could see their thoughts through their expressions, "A strange-looking boy...." Eventually, some of the women got wise to me. If I'm standing in just the right position, the light hits the angles of my face in such a way that you can see the woman I really am starting to emerge. These women saw. I could see them become flustered when they'd come to this realization, not knowing what to do with this surprising new knowledge. Some would start accompanying their daughters home from school instead of allowing them to walk down the avenue alone. I admit that did make me laugh.

But it wasn't these people who held my attention. They were just average pedestrians, people from *la vida diaria* who blended into the cityscape and were interchangeable with the rest of the urban scenery. They were the kind of people that a fly on the wall of any city would have seen. That was, until *they* came along. They were a group of women, not like any I'd ever seen in Guadalajara or anywhere else for that matter. They were loud and boisterous, with slick lips painted with a heavy gloss and long golden streaks in their hair. They stood at least six or seven inches taller, some as much as a foot, than the rest of the women who passed me daily. That owed in part to the high heels they wore, sandals with tight ankle straps binding their feet, making them tower over ordinary women. But these women also walked tall, carrying their spines straight, chests thrust forward, emanating a certain feminine pride absent from the others I had observed. They bantered and laughed good hearty laughs that came from deep within. Sometimes they would strut and shake their hips, their heavy golden hoop earrings jangling to the rhythm of their strut. Their clothing was always tight and made of thin materials: long sleek dresses that looked more like slips, and sheer skirts and sleeveless blouses. There was one who was always with them and she was the only one who sometimes wore boots, which went all the way up to her knees, even in this hot weather — it didn't seem to matter to her. The heat had to have been bothering her — her legs encased in snakeskin knee-high boots — but she never let on.

The others varied from day to day and there were usually four, sometimes five. I almost dropped my cigarette the first time I saw them and I know the one with the boots caught this out of the corner of her eye. This made me more nervous than I already was and I fumbled with my cigarette, trying to keep from burning my bare arms and legs. After that first time, I'd wait for them every day and they'd pass like clockwork at three-thirty, probably on their way home from dinner, Mexican time. The one that I most looked forward to seeing was the tallest one, the one with the boots. Her skin was darker than the rest and her eyes were hazel. She spoke with a deep and husky voice like mine, a smoker's voice.

These women from the avenue began appearing in my dreams. I would go down to the corner for dinner around ten, my eating schedule still running on American time, and wolf down a few tacos and a bottle of Coke. Then I'd go back to my grandmother's. I'd go directly to the room I was sharing with my mother and switch on the tiny black-and-white TV and watch whatever happened to be on *Televisión Azteca*. I knew that there was death in the house, sitting in the halls, waiting and watching, but it didn't bother me. In Mexico, death is always there, watching and waiting, as natural and ever-present as the air you breathe. It was just another element like the fire or water that I accepted as a part of that country's universe. It was natural. And so, it didn't bother me.

I would watch the small TV until my eyes felt heavy and I'd doze off to sleep, the women from the avenue appearing in my dreams, beckoning to me from beyond my grandmother's wrought-iron gate, taunting me like sirens as they made my skin burn, so hot that it became dangerous to touch.

V.

Instead of the usual underclothes that had become a lazy uniform, I dressed myself one morning in jeans and a T-shirt. I fished some pomade out of my toiletry bag and greased my hair back. I looped a thick black belt around my waist to hold my jeans up over my slender hips. I wore a heavy silver chain around my neck and polished my black boots. I would be wearing them out that day. Underneath, I wore a men's undershirt and boys' underwear. I had been thinking about this and I had made up my mind. I would sit at my perch and wait for them today and this time I would not just watch them go by. I would watch, wait and follow.

I took my bag of tobacco, a mango, a knife and my rolling papers and waited for three-thirty. When the appointed time finally came, I had just finished the mango, its juice dripping from my fingers and landing in small drops on the dirt below. I licked my fingers with anticipation and heard them coming. She was laughing, a deep laugh that came from the bottom of her throat, and I felt my breath catch. She was coming. Their long legs emerged and then the rest of them appeared and I watched, taking in the color and the smell of the women. My favorite was wearing her boots and her hair was swept into a ponytail, held in place by a knot of her own hair. She wore a dress that tied behind her neck, leaving her back exposed. I could see the bones of her ribcage, a tiny mole on the left side of her spinal cord. Her breasts bounced as she walked and her nipples were small, firm and strained against the fabric of her cream-colored dress. She turned as if to speak to one of her friends but for just a second, I thought her gaze had met with mine. As they passed the garden, I stood up from my bench and followed behind them, pressing my body against the gate. They walked for about two blocks until turning a corner and then I let myself out of the garden, determined to see where they were going. I followed from about thirty or forty yards behind, cautiously, slowing down when I thought it seemed that they had begun to suspect they were being followed.

After many twists and turns, we were miles away from the avenue in an old part of the city I had not yet explored. The streets were lined with old estates, palatial homes from the colonial period with lush gardens filled by banana trees and hibiscus. They approached one of these homes, the smallest on its block but by no means small, and turned onto the path leading up to the front door. I watched as they walked up the path to the front steps of the house and a servant held the door open for them. They entered the house one by one. My favorite was the last to enter. I stood at their fence watching when she turned around and looked at me. My stomach sank with the fear that I had been caught. But then she smiled at me and motioned for me to follow. I was confused and excited at the same time. I hurried up the front steps as the servant held the door open for me and I took a deep breath.

Inside, I followed the servant to a sitting room with a high glass ceiling and filled with light. There were four tall palm trees emerging from heavy clay pots and pillows strewn about floor. There were settees and divans for reclining, covered in brocade, and there were heavy tapestries framing the windows. At first I wasn't sure where I was but soon it all became very clear to me. The servant motioned for me to be seated and I sat in silence waiting.

I heard the clicking of heels on a tiled floor and turned to see my favorite emerging from a hallway. Her voice was deeper and huskier than I had realized and she spoke to me in lightly accented English.

"You know we could have you arrested for following us," she said. "I could easily tell the police that you were harassing my sisters and me. The police owe us some favors and I doubt you would like to spend the night in a Guadalajara jail. They are nothing like American jails. And never mind that the charge wouldn't be true. The justice system in Mexico doesn't really care about the truth. No, instead it takes into account the balance of power and the favors it creates in return."

My palms began to sweat and I could feel my heart racing. I should never have followed these women.

She smiled and continued. "But we don't want to have to involve the police. Instead, I am going to close the house this afternoon to resolve this matter. Closing will cost us, but we know that we'll be compensated in return if you deliver according to my request.

"As you've already figured out this is a house of prostitution. But it is not an ordinary house of prostitution, just as you are not an ordinary boy."

These words made me blush.

"No, this is one of the most expensive houses in Mexico, maybe even the world, because we serve people discreetly. We have been conducting business for over one hundred and fifty years. We are a tradition, a Mexican institution, ourselves and our sisters before us paying our fees and serving everyone from governors and presidents to bishops and priests. Also, we serve special needs for people who don't want to sacrifice quality for their perversions. We cater to many perversions here but we hold one in common, one that the rest of the world considers a perversion but that we consider to be of the purest nature. We all became women by choice. And we are better women than most who are born that way. We look better, we feel better, and we love better."

I stared at her wide-eyed.

"*Gringita Macha*, the reason that I allowed you to follow us here, the reason that my sisters and I picked you up is because I am tired and I need release. Whores need tricks too and make no mistake about it you are the trick. You aren't very good at hiding your feelings and I know that you want this opportunity — to fuck us and especially to fuck me."

I sat in amazement after hearing her last words, realizing the effect that her speech had worked upon my body. My pussy had begun to throb slowly, beating with blood and heat as she spoke, and now I could feel its wetness beginning to soak my legs and underpants. She continued smiling and took several steps toward me and sat down on a divan directly in front of mine. I stood up to walk toward her but she stopped me immediately.

"Sit down," she said. "First, before you can touch me I want to see how you touch yourself. Perform for me. I want to watch you touch yourself. I want to see you come."

At her command, I sat back down and stared at her mouth. I focused on her lips as I slowly began to unbutton my pants, imagining that her fingers were pulling down my zipper and reaching in for my penis, the cock I sometimes felt that I truly had. I focused on the glossiness of her lips, on how wet and slippery they would feel as they wrapped themselves around my imagined shaft and how powerfully she would be able to suck it, swallowing and devouring me like a ripe fruit. I touched my clit as I thought of these things, pumping it slowly at first, building a steady rhythm of sex. I slowly pulled my hand from my pants and brought it to my mouth. I licked my palm and fingers, giving myself extra lubrication, and stuck it back down my pants. I began pumping harder with an increased pace of blood flow to the vessels in my crotch, igniting nerve endings, sending electric jolts of heat through my pelvis. I was slick with wetness and could feel my clit enlarging, engorged by the attention it was receiving, getting hotter and hotter as I came closer to coming. I clenched my hand into a fist and began rubbing, jerking myself off with my fist, banging against my clit in simulation of a boy jerking off his young cock. As the speed of my arm increased, so did the breath of the woman sitting across from me. I rolled my head back and closed my eyes, focusing purely on the sensation, and imagined it was her tongue, her pussy touching mine and that was what did it, sent a quake through my body, made me explode, made me shake until the orgasm had finished rocking my body and left my pants a sticky mess.

I sat there, slowly catching my breath. I opened my eyes and stared at her. Without a word, she emerged from her seat and approached me. I stayed seated, sensing her dominance and not wanting to make the same mistake I had the last time I had approached her. With one hand, she pushed me back and climbed onto the settee with me. Her legs were spread as she straddled me and she pulled her dress up over her head, leaving her naked except for her large gold earrings and boots. Her breasts were small and high and her waist was so small, I could probably have circled it with my hands had I tried. Her hips flared delicately into an ass that was shaped like a valentine heart turned upside down. Her nipples were so hard and I longed to suck on them, to have them feed me. Given the opportunity, I knew I would tear at them like a hungry child. She smiled a half smile and then lunged at me, grabbing both of my hands and pinning them above my head. She was much stronger than I had imagined. I lay there helpless and immobile as she stared into my eyes and then gently whispered into my ear, "*Gringita Macha*, you're mine now. I'm going to fuck you so hard you'll feel as though you were never alive before this moment." The hair on my neck stood straight up and she bit into my neck with such intensity that I almost let out a shriek. I absorbed the pain, allowing it to mix with the pleasure, both emotions and sensations folding into one. She worked her way toward my face and kissed my cheeks, then slowly eased her tongue into my mouth, licking the insides of my cheeks and savoring my flavor. She sucked at my lower lip like it was a piece of orange and then slowly pulled back, releasing my hands from her grip. She pulled my T-shirt and undershirt up over my shoulders and dropped them to the floor. She traced my ribcage with her fingertips and ran her nails down my chest, their sharp edges leaving scratches that began to rise as pink, inflamed welts. She traced her way up to my right nipple and flicked it with her nail, teasing me like that for what could have been several seconds or several minutes—I had become oblivious to time.

She then began to pinch my nipples, taking one between her fingertips and turning it with sadistic glee. She tugged at it, pulling hard, away from the skin, making me burn with pain, which only increased my wetness and my need for her to fuck me. She leaned over, mouth open, and took turns licking each breast, sucking them, and bringing me to the edge of a cliff that I was ready to fall over. She then began to buck against me and I looked down at her pussy, the small mound of hair where her two long golden legs met, and bucked up to meet her, helping her to come. We fucked against each other like this, with her head tilted back, my brow covered in sweat and her face moist with perspiration. She came quickly and violently with a shudder that made her bolt upright, an unseen current of electricity holding her back erect. She looked down at me and smiled again and then she slid herself between my legs and crouched down, her hands on my belt buckle. She undid the buckle and pulled my pants down around my hips, past my knees and ankles. She then pulled off my underwear and stuck a finger into the hot wetness. She wiped this finger down my chest and then licked my glistening come from my torso.

"Turn over," she commanded me. "I'm going to fuck you like a boy...like you're a boy. That's what you want isn't it...to be a boy?"

"Yes," I answered.

"Put your ass in the air," she commanded.

I did as I was told and felt her hand slap me, bruising my exposed ass. She reached around and clamped a hand over my mouth as I felt something enter me from behind, something small, like a finger. It was wet and it pushed in gently at first and I wanted so badly for her to make me come. The finger pumped inside of me, loosening my asshole until it was ready to take another finger. She slid in a second and then a third finger and at three I stopped counting. I knelt, concentrating on the tight pleasure of a hand gently tucked inside my ass, pumping inside me, pushing against my female sex organs, churning my glands, banging my insides, bringing me close to coming. I began to move in sync with her fist as she fucked away my virginity. The pain of constriction and of being completely full was almost unbearable and I began to move like an animal, impaled on her forearm, writhing to climax. We moved that way, together, until my muscles clenched and I came, my eyes rolling back in my head and all movement ceasing. Waves of calm passed over me and I slowly came back down from wherever it was I had gone. Slowly, she removed her hand from me.

We lay side by side, my eyes closed, her arms embracing me. I breathed quietly, silently, still as death. I didn't want to open my eyes. I did not want this to end. I was afraid that if I opened my eyes, I would find that it had all just been a dream. But it was not a dream. It was real and I was born again that day. I became a boy and I became tainted, no longer a saint covered by thin wax. I was free.

Bill and Ted's other Excellent Adventure

ॐ

MELANIE HANNAM

THE YELLOW MOTORCYCLE WAS HEADING NORTH ON VINE. It signaled and took a right. Ted pursued it first onto Franklin then left at the junction with Beachwood. Gripping the vinyl steering wheel, her hands looked tiny against the backdrop of dials and meters and glossy fake walnut. She felt her palms dampen with anticipation and a frisson of terror at what she was doing. Ted clipped the curb as she turned, spraying the windscreen with road chippings. The hire car was a leviathan, a beached white whale with a dinged front end where she had tried to squeeze it into a compact bay in an underground lot off Wilshire.

That had been their first quarrel of the trip. Bill was supposed to be watching Ted drive in safely but let herself get distracted by a girl with candyfloss hair asking for money. Ted had watched it happen in the wing mirror: squinting in the gloom, the girl prettily pushed a ratted pink lock out of her eyes as she spun Bill some line. Ted caught "...from Seattle to party...some jackass...empty tank..." Seattle alone would have been enough to sucker her. For Bill it was a mythic place, a Xanadu of extravagant coffee and girls with obscene slogans lipsticked over soft, white stomachs. When Bill reached for her purse, Ted completed the parking maneuver with a tooth-grinding clang and jumped out of the car in time to stop her friend from naively handing over a whole day's budget. Bill had a weakness for all things Seattle: Ted had a soft spot for LA, and an actor by the name of Keanu Reeves.

Bill and Ted had taken a bungalow for the week on West Cahuenga Boulevard, just by the Hollywood Bowl. The place was full of athletic blondes flashing flesh over the Ping-Pong table but there were fewer cars sporting bullet holes than down on Sunset, and fewer bat-faced boys thrusting out their hips on street corners. Bill had completely missed the point of Los Angeles, beyond asking a sweaty tourist in Velcro sandals and nylon socks to snap a picture of them posing by Marilyn Monroe's petrified handprints and dragging Ted to a couple of worthy museums. "We could stay by the sea somewhere," Bill had suggested. "Wake up hearing the ocean break, feel the spindrift on our faces. Smell the redwoods, get brown and watch pelicans..."

Ted had smiled serenely, setting a small picture of Keanu — wetsuit, Point Break circa 1991 — against her travel alarm clock. "Not yet. You said this was *my* week, remember?"

That was supposed to be the compromise; first week Ted's, second Bill's but they seemed to have been forced into small secondary compromises every day since they left England. Bill would want to picnic at the Bowl, listen to the LA Phil rehearse; Ted to eat somewhere you'd actually want to be seen eating. Yesterday, they had settled for an outside table at Caffe Luna, on Melrose. "Think they're talking about a movie?" Ted had jiggled her cherry-red ringlets toward three middle-aged men engaged in conversation a few tables away. Their polished demeanor, not to mention polished skin, bore the patina of bona fide player status.

"Probably," said Bill. "It *is* Los Angeles, for fuck's sake." She might have added that the woman in drooping, pee-stained stockings who'd jabbed Ted's delicate, braceletted ankles with a shopping cart of dirty plastic bottles had also been muttering about the motion picture industry. "And by the way, Theodora, nobody uses the word 'movie'. Surprised your no-brainer celebrity mags didn't tell you that?"

While Ted had bristled at the slighting reference to her chosen reading matter—she considered it vital research for her future happiness—she didn't bite. She knew her friend was only sulking. Bill was itching to get to Seattle to hear some raucous grrl band called Devil's Playground but Ted had an agenda of her own. She had come to Los Angeles fully intending to meet the man of her dreams and on this point, she would be accepting no compromise.

The hire car juddered as she put her foot down to keep the motorbike in sight, a couple of vehicles ahead. The delivery van in front turned off into the Beachwood supermarket parking lot leaving only a road-hugging convertible in between. The biker was slung low over his machine too, the deep curve of his back wrapped in tight leather that looked as pliable and black as the best licorice. Yummy; Ted felt her mouth start to water as she watched his dark, collar-length hair whip about the requisite safety helmet. The bike made a left onto Ledgewood. She signaled her intention to follow suit and stole a quick glance at the hand-drawn map fluttering on the dash, only her *Speed* key ring (doctored to show Theodora Bennett, not Sandra Bullock, snuggled up to Keanu) preventing the fan from blowing it into the car's cavernous interior. The directions had been scribbled on the back of somebody's resume; the heavy off-white paper dog-eared and soft already where she had folded and refolded it all morning, trying to make up her mind. Her already thumping heartbeat seemed to go up an impossible gear; they were definitely heading in the right direction.

Last night at the Whisky-A-Go-Go, Ted had paid some guy — who claimed to know a friend of the drummer in Keanu's band — seventy-five bucks for the directions to the actor's house in the Hollywood Hills. He had wanted a hundred originally; Ted daren't bid lower, they'd been in town three days already and all she had achieved was inserting a hitherto unheard-of distance between herself and her best friend. "All this because you want to fuck an actor?" Bill had been beyond incredulous as she gestured around the heaving club. The heavy sarcasm was blunted by the fact she had to shout to make herself heard over a girl in a blue glitter bikini shrieking-singing against guitars repetitively grinding three simple chords. "This place is full of actors. He *must* be one, there's another.

Gosh, I think I saw him being resuscitated on 'Baywatch.' Ted, why don't you start with someone who actually knows you exist? Someone who..."

"Not just any actor, Bill. I'm his..."

"You're his biggest fan? Oh, for Christ's sake, sweetie. Would you grow up already? Sure, Keanu makes a fine eye job but you don't know anything about him and if you think he's just waiting for his English Rose to show up..."

"I know he rides a yellow Norton motorcycle. There can't be many British bikes around here."

"True," Bill was forced to admit, rolling her kohl-rimmed eyes. Half the men in the room knew Bill existed and Bill didn't care. A couple of days before they left home, Sarah Billingshurst had taken a pair of dressmaking scissors and lopped off her raven tresses to chin level. She carried eyeliner, Carmex lip balm and a credit card. Ted's shoulder bag contained approximately half her makeup collection, a set of gas-powered curling tongs, an Evian water spray and *The Fame Magazine's Guide to Star Shagging*. Ted couldn't remember when Bill last dated but it clearly didn't worry her. It was more than eight months since Ted had sex and the fact frequently made her howl like a cat. Unfortunately, every man who'd crossed her path in that time had left her cold — except Keanu, who accompanied her to bed each night, watching from the ceiling with eyes bottomless, black and mysterious as the La Brea tar pits Bill had insisted they visit the previous day. Under this gentle gaze, Ted slept alone on her chilly, lumpy futon, one hand protectively cupping her lonely, tangled crotch while she dreamed that certain parts of her were beginning to fossilize. "You know what?" Bill shook Ted's shoulder. "You want to waste your holiday getting lost in the Hollywood Hills, feel free, Theodora. Tomorrow, I'm going to Disneyland. I might as well enjoy someone else's bizarre fantasy world." True to her word, after breakfasting on the Dunkin' Donuts supplied in the lobby, Bill had tied her blue-black hair in a bandana and boarded a tour bus to Anaheim with the Ping-Pong playing Swedes.

Ted was pursuing the yellow motorcycle above the nicotine-colored smog now. She peered anxiously through the tree cover, trying to estimate the drop but not disliking the rare sensation of being on the edge. She was not accustomed to driving alone. Since she and Bill became best friends almost a year ago, Ted was unused to doing much on her own. The name Ted was rarely mentioned without the name Bill but now this was Ted alone, Ted in pursuit of Keanu. The very thought gave her butterflies. When she looked at the road again, the yellow motorcycle had vanished from sight. The butterflies grew agitated. Ted took a deep breath and put her foot down hard, the car's big engine responding gratifyingly. No way was she going to lose him now.

Before the Norton first appeared in her rearview mirror, she had already driven fruitless loops along snaking roads that seemed to lead nowhere much; past exclusive housing enclaves and deadly looking escarpments that were scarred with the remains of old road accidents. The directions seemed to get vaguer the more she looked at them. Frustration, and a little motion sickness, got the better of her and Ted had indulged in a brief crying tantrum. She had been heading back along Cahuenga Boulevard to repair the water damage to her face when she'd caught sight of the yellow motorcycle preparing to overtake. It couldn't be, could it? Ted had hung back a little to let it pass her. There had been something undeniably familiar about the rider's tight, hard-bodied physique and she felt her inner thighs automatically warm up a degree. "Somebody down there recognizes you," she'd whispered a touch lasciviously, and accelerated after it. The biker seemed to be out for a leisurely drive—enjoying his powerful machine as it hugged the twists and turns of these canyon roads. Ted had carefully maintained the close tail ever since, growing increasingly proud of her driving skills.

She caught up with the Norton again when it was forced to slow for a sharp bend on Mulholland Drive. The hire car squealed when she took it around a little too fast. She continued to pursue the bike up the winding slope of the Hollywood Hills, her ears popping, tires kicking up dirt. There was other traffic, of course. Tourists trying to find the best view of the Hollywood sign, seeking out the mansions of the rich and famous, but for Ted, there was just one car and one motorcycle. She bounced the elongated car over the crests of hills; hand on horn, cut off other motorists and sprayed the occasional dog walker with gravel. He must have known she was there, it was a game of cat and mouse. This was high-speed foreplay and increasingly, nothing else mattered.

Ted was scarcely aware the light was starting to fail around them and the heady glow of the LA skyline beginning to emerge through the purple dusk. She was incapable of comprehending that she was hopelessly lost and the needle on the fuel gauge hovered dangerously over the red. For the first time in her life, she was making love without a condom and her cheeks burned uncontrollably in spite of the nuclear winter belted out by the air conditioner. The world was imploding. Even the chase — even Keanu — mattered less than what she was experiencing. Ted was suddenly hyper-aware of the power of the car's engine, of the almost painful juddering beneath her as, losing her concentration again, she swerved in then out of the loose gravel at the side of the road. She might as well have been riding the motorcycle herself, legs akimbo over 850 cc's of vibrating horsepower, and her pussy began to spontaneously ring like a piece of fine crystal. When the hire car went into a second minor skid, Ted realized she was actually driving the thing one-handed and, admitting defeat, she flicked on the indicator and pulled off the road into a cutaway.

She paused, then restarted the vehicle, letting it chug a couple of yards off the blacktop surface until it was protected from the road by a screen of lush green branches. The engine was very close to overheating, she could hear the internal fan whir frantically, trying to placate it. Ted slid herself forward easily on the hot vinyl seat, the fabric at the back of her skirt quite wet now where it had bunched up underneath her. She arched her back, relieving the strain of being bucketed in the driving seat for such a long stretch. One hand still gripping the clammy wheel, Ted let the other burrow urgently under her skirt until the first two trembling fingers arrived at the roughness of slightly frilled, knicker elastic. The elastic was chafing between her legs. It felt alien against the organic warmth of her skin but before she could do much about removing it, her hand froze. The fan underneath the car's stretched hood had stopped turning but, besides the delirious white noise in Ted's ears, there was another sound. It was the sound of a second engine.

Ted was way beyond removing her hand at this point. Her skin grew deliciously slick as the motorcycle eased into the cutaway and coasted to a standstill next to the passenger window. The dusk was full now; a couple of insects threw themselves mesmerized against the single headlamp. Ted watched the rider swing one impossibly long leg across the seat and kick the metal stand into place, leather pants moving like the seductive but deadly surface of an oil slick. He tapped once on the glass. With her free hand, Ted flipped off the central locking. The biker opened the passenger door, letting in a puff of hot, fragrant air and the chirruping sound of cicadas.

"Keanu?" she whispered, but the name was irrelevant now. Her body felt like double cream, whipped into peaks and fantastical icing shapes to be explored by sticky fingers or hungry, sugar-starved mouths. The name might as well have been Kenny or Mike or…

"Bill?" Ted watched wide-eyed as the biker removed the yellow full-face crash helmet with both gloved hands, shaking out a mass of silky black hair. The same hair that had licked the collar of the leather jacket with paintbrush-blunt ends all afternoon.

"I can be Keanu if you want me to be," the biker replied softly.

"You?"

"Me."

"All this time?"

"Forever, sweetie."

"Bill, I didn't know you could ride a motorbike."

"Here," said Bill, folding herself coltishly into the passenger seat and reaching into Ted's lap to take her now violently trembling hand from her damp cotton underwear. She held the hand for a second or two then put Ted's fingers against her mouth, letting her lips part wide enough for a little taste. Her voice shook slightly too. "Here, let me do that for you. You will let me do that, Ted? I'll be Keanu for you, honey. I'll be whoever you want."

"Screw Keanu," said Theodora, and she peeled off the black motorcycle glove, marveling at its soft-as-butter texture, the warmth of its inside turned out. It's Bill-ness. She inhaled the scent of the glove as Bill slipped one finger under the harsh elastic of her underpants, then another.

"Screw Seattle," said Bill.

Like a honeybee to a source of sweetness, Bill's first finger was drawn to Ted's soft, fleshy mons. Playfully it buzzed her clit; the bee stung momentarily and Ted inhaled sharply. A second finger began to trace tight circles around her pussy, like someone trying to make the rim of a drinking glass sing. Bill squeezed her free arm behind Ted, the leather sleeve squeaking against the seat back. She slid her forward and with a hand under the girl's ass, tilted her pelvis slightly; the finger slid easily inside and the drinking glass burst hesitantly into song. For a second, Ted even wondered if someone had switched on the car radio softly. There was definitely music but to her surprise, it wasn't nearly loud enough. She finally released her grip on the steering wheel and reached over to run a hand through Bill's glossy hair until her fingers encountered the warm boniness of the back of her friend's neck. Her hand seemed clumsy and bloodless; in contrast, Bill's delicate bones felt like the spine of a frail stegosaur. Carefully, Ted pulled her over the cleft between the driver and passenger seats, Bill's red-hot cheek coming to rest against her own busy hand.

"Fill me up now," Ted whispered urgently.

She felt Bill nod and briefly she experienced a cool, vaguely medicinal sensation she could only imagine to be Carmex lip balm, which vanished as the girl flurried hot kisses around her vulva. Bill began to lap studiously at her, pausing as if to register each fresh texture, each new taste. Every pass of her tongue seemed to tug at Ted's skin until she felt as inside out as Bill's motorcycle glove, abandoned on the floor with their crumpled road map and half-empty bottle of flat Calistoga water. Bill eased out the finger, leaving it to butter Ted's clitoris with her own copious juices. For maybe half a second, Theodora Bennett felt emptier than she'd ever been on her loneliest, horniest night, and she groaned, bereft, until the tip of Bill's tongue pried between those poverty-stricken lips and began to dart in and out like a scrap of stiff velvet ribbon. Raspberry tongue on raspberry tissue, a flash of teeth. Dazed, Ted recalled Bill's now-astonishing tongue doing such ordinary things as licking postage stamps or wrapping innocently around an ice lolly in their lunch hour. Now Bill seemed to want to crawl inside her headfirst, to wear her like a second skin. Ted felt the muscles of her abdomen tighten warningly. She feared her pussy might drown them both, but greedily, Bill licked up all the bowl of cream then sucked until Ted came some more. A joyful scream built up inside her but Ted decided to hang onto it, just in case this miracle was never to happen again.

• • •

The whole city of angels is spread out before them like a carpet of stars. It looks like you could walk on it: if you wanted to, if you could make yourself get out of the fleshy, Bill and Ted redolent interior of a steamy, far-too-big hire car whose very walls appear in the darkness to be pink and quivering vaginal walls. Somewhere out in the LA night, one coyote yips, then another. Together they raise up a howl; it sounds plaintive, not dangerous.

"Listen?" says Bill. "They're calling out the dogs."

"Huh?" Ted raises her head, dreamily. Her makeup is lopsided, she looks like a happy Easter egg. At some point they have swapped places, neither of them can remember when exactly. The motorcycle's single headlamp has dimmed, the battery is failing. There is just enough light to illuminate the flushed pink blotches on Ted's chest and shoulders; Bill's serene, luminescent face.

"The coyotes are calling the pampered lapdogs outside. The pekes and the poodles, and the pussycats too."

"What're they saying?"

"Not the truth," Bill tells her. "Saying *I'm going to eat you up* never lured anybody anywhere."

"Oh, I don't know about that," says Ted softly. "I'm going to eat you up, Bill." And her cherry-red ringlets, a little wilted now, disappear once more.

Hostale coelho

᠊ᢒ

ARABELLA LAINTON

I.

THE MAN FROM GRANADA SMOKED A JOINT AT THE OTHER end of the bar and stared at her through red slits. A beaded curtain kept the sun and a few of the flies out in the street. He was small and dark and she could smell on him, even from the other end of the bar, that he wanted to fuck. It was too much, the stench of it, sweet and fungal; it stirred around her, filling her nostrils and finding its way into the pores of her skin. He was motionless, but for the joint passing to and from his lips, and the quick black eyes inside his lazy eyelids. She could feel his stare pulling at her. There was something brutal about him. She refused to look at him, yet she was aware of nothing in the room but him. She got up from her seat, drained her bottle of beer and went back up to her room. The Granadan went outside.

It seemed the more Alice tried to expel sex from her thoughts, the more insistent it became. She had begun to find it everywhere, in things and places it had never been before, in the soft salty texture of a mussel in her mouth, in the delicate unfurling of a rosebud in bloom, in the pungent sweetness of a passing man's sweat. Everything in this place — in the sea that it edged, in the sky that it stretched under — conspired in erotic seduction.

Later that night, as she watched the sunset blaze orange and pink across the purple sky, she couldn't get his black eyes out of her head. The night rolled into the village, and still the air was heavy with heat and dust. She turned off the light, and in the dark sat on the edge of her bed to unbuckle her sandals. The moon rose over the purple hills outside. That Granadan with the black stare was probably still out there, she thought. She began to unbutton her blouse, but stopped, walked across the room and turned the light back on. Slowly pulling off the blouse she moved in front of the window and pushed the lace curtains open a little more. It was dark outside and the light above her head made it impossible to see anything out there but blackness. She unhooked her bra and her pale nipples brushed the lace of the curtains. Bending forward, she slipped out of her skirt and stood in the window letting her nakedness gleam out across the countryside. On her face she bore an expression of sweet distraction, as if her perfectly placed, spotlit exposure was nothing but unwitting. A minute passed, then another, until suddenly hot with embarrassment and regret, Alice turned off the light and lay down on her bed. Outside under the fig tree the Granadan stubbed out his joint and headed back inside.

II.

"Coelho?" The coach driver had twisted in his seat and from astonishingly green eyes, flashed her a look that said "you must be mistaken."

"*Sin*, Hostale Coelho," Alice repeated, holding out several *escudos* in her upturned palm.

"Coelho?" He said it again, louder this time, and twisted further in his seat, jamming his shoulder against the steering wheel. He seemed to be convinced that she was wrong and that she didn't in fact want to go to Hostale Coelho, but somewhere entirely different.

"*Sin, sin*, Coelho." She pushed the *escudos* toward him for emphasis. He raised his eyebrows and a slow smile spread across his thick mouth. He took the money and, running his gaze over her body, waved her into the seat behind him.

The coach pulled out from Sintra's train station and wound down the hill toward the coast road. Villas of cinnamon and pale green appeared among the fir trees with every bend, geraniums and bougainvillea crawling over their cracked walls and iron balconies. Above them, Sintra's pink palace rose from the treetops. Two elderly sisters sat behind Alice. They were pilgrims to the Capelinha das Aparicoes, the holy shrine in the town of Fatima where, in 1917, the Virgin had appeared to three young shepherds. Behind them sat a young man, a tray of cheese tarts beside him in a seat of their own.

Sintra disappeared and the coach driver picked up speed. A lot of speed. Soon he was hurtling through tiny villages of three or four shops, bouncing over speed bumps, churning up dust and stones. The young man clutched his cheese tarts and Alice held the edge of her seat as the lush terraces fell away from the blurred edge of the road. The driver's green eyes hung before her in his rearview mirror. She couldn't escape them as every minute or so he flicked her a look, shaking his shoulders with the samba pulsing from the radio he had taped to the side of his driver's box. By the time they passed through Collares, she knew they were nearing the sea. Salt mist had infiltrated the spaces between the eucalyptuses that crowded the roadside, and through the ragged rows of grapevines the sun shone hazily.

The driver pulled up at a junction marked with a small shrine to Our Lady, three geraniums in a glass jar at her tiny feet. And as Alice was struggling into her backpack, he turned to her and said simply, "Husband?" When she said no he pressed his lips together and offered his steering wheel a rueful shake of the head. He opened the doors and pointed north along the dusty road, closed the wheezing doors and rattled off toward the east.

Alice walked until she came to the dirty white cube that was Hostale Coelho. A rampant marrow vine wound through the overgrown lawn and out the front and a fig tree dropped ripe fruit to the cement below. To the north was the tiny fishing village of Azenhas do Mar and to the south the garish resort town of Praia de Macas. The *hostale*, it seemed, belonged to neither place, it just sat there alone, exiled to no-man's-land on the cliff-top road of Portugal's Atlantic coast.

"I'm sorry but the beer is warm. The power has failed again." Without bothering to look at her, the landlady of the Hostale Coelho put the bottle on the bar and returned to her conversation. The fans were idle, the fridges silent, and the heat thick and heavy. The landlady leaned on the bar with her bum high in the air and laughed with a white-haired man, another customer, whose green tattoos bled into the loose skin of his forearms. The room was dim and the smell of *bacalhau* fritters and sweet rotting figs hung heavily.

Alice shook off her backpack and pulled a plastic stool up to the bar. She had the beer at her lips when she realized the landlady and her white-haired friend had stopped talking.

"Oh, I'll just go and sit down over there…" her words trailed off and the pair at the bar resumed their conversation. The white-haired man said something and the landlady cackled rustily as Alice took a seat by a lifeless pinball machine. She looked at the Portuguese national football team on the wall and blindly eavesdropped. They spoke that odd mix of rolling Latin consonants and swallowed Slavic vowels that was Portuguese. She liked the sound of it; it wasn't like any other language she'd ever heard.

The lights in the bar flickered. The landlady, her friend and Alice all froze, and looked up at the naked bulb expectantly. But nothing happened, it just flickered and died. The heat was rising and there was sweat collecting under the backs of Alice's thighs. She peeled one leg and then the other off the plastic stool. The lights flickered again. They all looked up and two seconds later the room was blazing with light and sound. The pinball machine jumped and sang, the fridges started up a busy hum, the fly-exterminator crackled and zapped, the fans creaked into action, and the landlady and her friend cheered. Alice smiled. The return of the electricity seemed to make the woman more amenable to strangers, or maybe she just warmed to Alice because she had been there at that momentous instant when it had surged back through the wires. Either way, she suddenly felt inclined to direct a question at her.

"Where's your husband?" she called across the room, her chin jabbing the air. The white-haired man turned on his stool.

"Oh…no, no husband," Alice answered. No husband, no boyfriend, no sex full stop. That was the plan anyway. She didn't want to think about it while she was here. She wanted a sex-free, stress-free holiday. As she'd watched the coach disappear in a cloud of dust and looked out at the blue smudge of sea beyond the hills ahead, she decided there were going to be no awkward courtships over cocktail umbrellas, no running out of town to get away from some over-ardent holiday lover. Not this time. It was just more trouble than it was worth and this time she wanted nothing but relaxation.

"No husband." The landlady raised her eyebrows and nodded at her friend. Alice had obviously given the right answer, because they were suddenly friendly, inviting her back up to the bar, pulling the stool in close and cracking her another beer.

"Ah. I've got just the man for you." The landlady leaned conspiratorially across the bar.

Her friend sighed: "Whatever you want: a lover for the night, the week, a month or a lifetime, she will find him for you." He pointed at the woman, who smiled and closed her eyes with proud satisfaction. She was from Lisbon, but a devastating love affair had propelled her from the city, and she had sworn never to step foot inside its borders again. She had bought herself a deserted *hostale* four miles from the ocean and settled down to a bit of peace and quiet. There were some in the nearby villages who didn't like her city ways, her tight skirts and swinging hips. But they tolerated her and some had even become her friends. Everybody knew what went on in that *hostale* and, to each other, they complained that it wasn't right.

The landlady was indeed a matchmaker. Her own affair had ended so dismally that she sought solace in the affairs of others. She liked her *hostale* to be filled with the sighs of lovemaking, liked to feel it rock in the night. And, though they would never admit it, the villagers liked it too. Wandering home with sherry on their breath, they would somehow always end up detouring past her place. They'd peer through the grimy windows, past the lace curtains, listening out for the noises of pleasure, and then sighing they'd follow the moon all the way home.

"I just want a bit of peace actually. I don't want to meet anyone, not for any length of time. But thanks anyway."

The two of them continued to talk in Portuguese, and every now and then they smiled at Alice.

III.

Even in the bathroom there was no escaping it. *How many orgasms can one woman have?* thought Alice, as she tried to cool her body against the tiled walls. From here, at the other end of the corridor, it sounded like several women, their cries flying around one another in the darkness, echoing through the *hostale*. And it seemed that Alice was the only one being tortured by it. She hadn't seen any of the other guests, except of course the man from Granada. The noises stopped. Alice wiped her face and neck with a damp towel and went back to her room. But no sooner had her head hit the pillow than the noises began again, just breathing at first, long and heavy, falling through the ceiling, and then the slow creaking of springs. Her skin burned. She tried to ignore it, but the louder the noises became, the more mutinous were the images in her head: fine hairs across the small of the back; glistening trails of saliva; a soft, open mouth; fingers sliding over swollen pink; a cock hard in her hand; hot jets of come streaking her belly. She was sure her bed had begun to sway as the house shuddered and shook, its roof threatening to shatter with the force of the passion it contained. She put a pillow over her head and tried to ignore the unbearable heat spreading from between her legs.

IV.

"If you meet someone, you can push the two beds together." The landlady opened the conversation brusquely as Alice came down the stairs from her room.

"Oh no, it's OK, really. I don't think I'll be meeting anyone. Too much trouble," said Alice as she combed her wet hair at the bar.

"Won't meet someone? Of course you'll meet someone." She disinterestedly popped a *bacalhau* fritter in her mouth and waved a fly from the *pastel de nata*, stale now so long past breakfast.

"There are many handsome men in these villages. Fishermen who can charm the sardine to swim right into the net, surfing men with smooth salty skin. And of course there are many tourists— English, French, Germans…. You know what?" Something had occurred to her and it was so exciting she was up off the bar, her black-rimmed eyes flashing. "There is a Spaniard here, right here in the *hostale*," she said, waving her long thin arms. "I think you would like him. He is small, but not bad looking." She settled forward again with her elbows on the bar and studied Alice for a reaction.

"No, I don't think so. I'm quite all right. Thanks though." Alice sensed this lady wasn't going to let it go. She'd taken a shine to her and, it seemed, was determined to jam a bit of love into her life.

Alice walked over pebbles, through stubble and scrub and along scalding bitumen roads; she counted the rose-scattered shrines to the Virgin carved from the rock, their smooth plastered walls painted Madonna blue, until finally she came to the edge of the land. Praia Grande, the *hostale's* nearest beach, stretched magnificently below her. She stood on the cliff and looked down. Boys half peeled from their wetsuits crisscrossed the sand, surfboards under their arms. A small corrugated iron shack perched precariously at the top of the track. Smoke puffed from a crooked tin chimney and a cache of surfboards rested against one side. The shack was open to the road and inside a man hacked chunks from a mountain of white dough. The man's hair was a mass of chaotic black curls and he wore nothing but a pair of board-shorts and a guitar across his naked chest. He held the guitar's neck with one hand and with the other he rolled the floury dough around hunks of *chorizo,* then threw them into the hot mouth of the oven that fairly filled the shack.

A woman leaned in from the road. The high rump jutting unashamedly toward the sky was unmistakable. The landlady. She was out for the day in high-heeled sandals and a spotted dress that showed her tanned shoulder blades. She was talking to the man inside from beneath her questioningly raised eyebrows. He chopped at the dough with his machete and nodded at the landlady. Then she spotted Alice.

"Ae-lice. Come try a *chorizo* bun," she called to her, looking her over through narrowed eyes. The man rolled his dough and stared.

"Maybe later. I'm going down for a swim." Alice tried to avert her gaze from the sure hands as they massaged and kneaded; there was something about the weight in the heel of his palm, his muscular fingers, which stirred her. Silently he watched her watching him and with strong, firm strokes continued to work the dough. She waved and headed down the beach track. The landlady reached in and gripped the man's arm. Her rough, rapid-fire Portuguese drifted down the track behind her as Alice approached the beach.

There were people sprawled over every inch of the sand and surfers skidded across the glassy lip of the waves as they rolled in, one after the other. Alice walked the length of the beach and kept walking. She headed for the white lighthouse of Cabo de Gata, Europe's westernmost point, quivering in the heat haze further up the coast. There was nothing at Cabo de Gata but a single stall selling seashells, and though waves smashed violently against its rocks, there was, Alice had been told, a string of tiny sheltered coves just to the south.

She waded out through the wash to get around a particularly sharp edge of cliff. There were only three people on the tiny beach. A woman on her own, reading under a striped umbrella, and a young couple lying beside each other, their long naked bodies stretched in the sun. If they were naked, she was going to go naked too, Alice thought. She sat down, pulled off her bathing costume and lay back on the wet sand. The sun's hot rays began to insinuate their way between the curled strands of the hair between her legs. She closed her eyes. The insistent rays found their way to her naked lips, burning unbearably, deliciously. She parted her legs and let the heat find its way to the pink edge of her naked pussy. She could feel herself swelling and opening up to the sun, despite her best efforts to keep her focus elsewhere. She got up, took a deep breath and tumbled into the whitewash. The Atlantic Ocean was freezing. And rough. It threw her about, pounding her body, but it was exhilarating. She crawled out exhausted and knelt on her knees and elbows on the glossy sand to catch her breath. Through the wet curtain of her hair, something caught her eye, some movement farther up the beach. The man and woman were no longer lying side by side. She was lying over him, her long black hair on his face. His hands were on her hips. Alice dropped to the sand and turned her head to watch them. The woman began to move herself slowly against the man's hips; as his hands gripped her tighter, she moved faster, grinding into him. Alice couldn't believe it. She looked at the woman under the striped umbrella, but she just turned the page of her book and adjusted her crossed legs, completely unaware, while not two hundred meters away, the woman with the long black hair arched her back and the man beneath her bit hungrily at her throat. The cold water had made Alice's skin tighten with goose bumps, it had forced her breath from her, but it had done little to alleviate the torture of the throbbing between her legs. She'd barely slept for the interminable fucking in her *hostale*. She couldn't keep the entwined naked limbs, the flicking tongues and brushing fingertips out of her head. The more she tried to push the images away, the more the moans and guttural groans pushed them at her and forced her hand between her legs. And now this.

She pulled her bathing costume up over her legs, picked up

her towel and headed across the beach to the rocky way back to the *hostale*. She walked and walked until she saw the smoke of the *chorizo* shack, and then its chimney, but before she saw the shack itself she heard the music sailing down the cliff on the sea breeze. The surfboards had gone and so had the afternoon customers. The dough man stood inside, by the oven, practicing scales, and every now and then he indulged himself with a little embellishment, a doleful shred of melody. Alice was transfixed. There was magic in that man's fingers, those long agile fingers. She couldn't take her eyes off them. She stood, her towel dangling from her hand, and watched him.

V.

The Granadan is at the bar again. Staring again. Alice pulls across the beaded curtain and stands in the doorway with her back to him. She can feel his black eyes crawling across her shoulder blades, along the small of her back, circling the cheeks of her arse. With a deafening rattle, the grocer across the street pulls down his steel shutter. Night comes creeping in and the streetlights flutter.

Alice locks her door. She takes off her clothes and lies on her bed. She stares at the hills beyond her window for a minute then reaches over to the key in the door and turns it until it clicks open. The heat is unbearable tonight and the open window makes little difference. She turns off the lamp and drifts in and out of sleep, dreaming of *chorizo*, black eyes, and weeping guitars.

Midnight approaches. There is no noise in the *hostale* tonight and when the door handle turns, its squeak screams in the tiny room. It's probably just the landlady checking to see if she's asleep, or a guest wandering lost into the wrong room. Alice lies still. The door opens and a second later closes again. *They've gone*, Alice thinks, and closes her eyes. But there's another noise, a heavy footfall. Her eyes spring open but it's dark and she can't see a thing. She flicks the lamp switch but nothing happens. It's dead. She tries the overhead light. Dead. She edges back under her sheet and lies still. Rough fingertips brush her cheek. Adrenaline stiffens her limbs but still she doesn't move. She feels the sheet slipping from her naked body. The smell of rotting figs rises from the ground outside. Her eyes are wide in the blackness, every hair stands on end, but for some reason she doesn't make a sound. Suddenly the stranger's mouth is at her ear, his hot breath rasps on the tiny hairs of her delicate lobes. He doesn't speak, just breathes hotly. He moves his mouth down her neck, brushing her skin with his lips, flicking the tip of his tongue in the shallow pools of her collarbone. He seeks her breast. Alice inhales sharply and her nipple hardens against his teeth. While he sucks, his hand finds her other breast. The palm is coarse and moist with sweat. He pinches her nipple hard and bites her with his teeth. Still she doesn't move. She should scream, or at least push him away, but she's stuck to the bed, unable to move with terrified excitement. She can't see him, she doesn't know who he is, but his touch is electric and all she can do is lie still and let him stroke her, lick and suck her. The mouth leaves her breast. She smells tobacco on his breath. He pushes his tongue into her mouth, hard, fills her with it, stifling her tiny sigh.

His odor is strong, sweet with musky sweat. He pushes her into the mattress, and forces her thighs apart. She lies back against the pillow, her hands by her side. She doesn't touch him but lets him touch her. He's drinking from her, lapping at her, his rough whiskers grazing the delicate folds of her lips. She lifts her pelvis to meet his mouth. She's moaning now, softly, the pleasure is unbearable. His mouth and tongue swirl over her, inside her; she moves her hips off the bed pushing into his face, but he doesn't like that and he stops and pushes her back down into the mattress. She wants to touch him, wants to feel his cock in her hand, wants to guide it inside herself. But she doesn't. There's rustling beside the bed and she gasps as suddenly her wrists are seized and pushed above her head. He makes no noise but for the harsh breath in his throat. A heavy cord wraps around her wrists and ankles, tighter and tighter, it binds her to the bed. She doesn't resist. His head is between her thighs again and his hands knead her breasts roughly. A dog whines in the street outside while inside the room there's nothing but the greedy sucking of his mouth at her cunt.

He pulls his head away, and she groans in frustration. The loud clack of his belt unbuckling is deafening in the tiny room. A momentary current of fear runs through her body, only to be subsumed by unbearable desire. Seconds later his naked cock is nudging against her. She tries to move her hips toward him, to engulf him; she's aching for it, but he moves away. He comes closer again and slides the hard end of his cock all over her wet and open lips. His coarse hair is against her cheek, his teeth at her throat. She smells soap and tobacco. She wants it so much but it's he who'll decide when he'll give it to her. She lies back defeated and as she does so he lunges into her, sinking in until his public bone grinds against hers. She cries out. The room is filled with the wet noises of his cock moving inside her.

He fucks her, harder and harder, the base of his swollen cock pushing against her clit, until she is screaming. She feels the orgasm sweeping over her, rising from the pit of her belly, gathering power like a swelling wave, but just as it's about to break he pulls out of her, dribbling warm come over her heaving belly. Oh God, she's desperate for him now. She can't see him, she can't hear him, but she has to have him. There's nothing she can do, she's bound to the bed, the cord cutting into her wrists. She doesn't dare speak.

She hears coins jangling in his pockets as he pulls on his trousers. She can't believe he's leaving her like that, dangling on the edge of orgasm, lashed to the bed. She lies still, closes her eyes to the breeze cooling the sweat on her naked and splayed body. She waits for him to untie her, but the door creaks open and his footsteps disappear up the corridor.

Alice is verging on panic. It's the middle of the night and she is bound to the bed, naked, unable to move. She's exhausted and her limbs are aching. She's boiling with anger and frustration when, less than an hour later, the door squeaks open again. He's back. She still can't see. She hears his footsteps coming toward her. She holds her breath. She can feel his breath on her face. His hands stroke her wrists but he doesn't untie her. She feels his breath move down her belly. He holds her thighs and runs his tongue along her clit and inside her lips. She shudders and feels the blood surge again under her skin. He is sucking her, sucking out the come he left pooled in her aching cunt. She feels herself cascading again toward orgasm, and he can feel her vaginal muscles ripple in anticipation. He takes his mouth away and she groans. Every time she's about to come he pulls away. His puts his lips against hers, softly, slowly. She opens her mouth and licks the salty drops from his tongue. He's gentle now. Calmed. Delicate fingertips stroke her thighs, her stomach, the space between her breasts, the inside of her arms. With his thighs either side of her, he kneels above her, unties the cord around her wrists, and kissing her grazed skin, gently lifts her off the bed. She relaxes into his arms and inhales his scent. Still there is no sound but the scraping of his feet on the linoleum. The porcelain of the sink is cold against her naked buttocks. He slides his finger inside her, and her cunt sucks at it. Gently he moves his thigh between her knees, pushing them apart, wider and wider. He fucks her, slowly and gently, relentlessly. And this time he lets her come; he doesn't stop even as her orgasm rips through her body.

VI.

When his footsteps disappear somewhere in the *hostale*, Alice tries the light again. Still dead. Another power failure, she thinks. She sinks into the mattress, dozing fitfully until dawn breaks over the mountains. She opens her eyes to the faintest light of blue and in a T-shirt opens her still-unlocked door and heads for the bathroom. She pulls the light cord, but of course, nothing. Water splutters from the tap. She hangs her sleepy head over the basin and dips her face in a sinkful of cold water. She's dazed from sleep and the lack of it and stands absently inspecting the layers of flaking paint on the mirror frame. Tiny tributaries of water split and branch down her chest and shoulders and fall from the bruised and tender tips of her nipples. Hoarse whispers in Portuguese rouse her from her half-sleep. She's surprised to hear people awake; it must be no later than 5 a.m., and the sun is yet to fully rise.

With careful, quiet steps she goes to the top of the stairs on her way back to her room. The whispering is coming from the dark shaft of the stairwell. She leans over the banister and in the gray below sees the landlady's nightgown-clad arse. Her head is in the *hostale's* fuse box and by her feet, sitting side by side on the bottom step are the Granadan and the man from the *chorizo* shack. The landlady's head emerges and with a grin she flicks a switch and the corridor is flooded with the light from Alice's room.

Alice checks the coach timetable and packs her backpack. The landlady kisses her and says she must come back. The man from Granada smokes at the bar and the man from the shack plays his guitar at a table by the window. Without a glance, Alice walks past them into the sun, leaving the beaded curtain swinging in her wake.

perfect touches

༥

DEBRA HYDE

EVERY TIME HE TOUCHED CHRISTIANA, CARL MELTED.
The warmth of her skin and the substance of her flesh were like
magic to him, and touching her satisfied his every longing, no
matter how urgently it came upon him.

Now, as Christiana slept next to him, the sight of her once
again encouraged his tactile desire for contact. Rather than disturb
her sleep, he gently contoured his body to hers. Spooning her, Carl
draped his arm around her waist and lightly kissed her shoulder.
He felt the quiet rise and fall of her breathing ripple through her
body and across his lips. She was breathing easily, sleeping without
strain. Finally.

He rested his head on her shoulder, wondering how he
managed to get so lucky. All his life, he had used touch to make
sense of the world and when he had found someone who accepted
his touch with a welcoming patience that never discouraged, life
became perfect. Christiana never twisted away from him, whether

it was in the middle of the night or in the middle of loading the dishwasher. If anything, she came alive at his touch. Even she marveled at how arousing his touch could be.

Even an orgasm, she had told him repeatedly, *is better with your fingers, not mine.*

Carl gazed across the room to the window and terrace door. Both were open and a lazy breeze teased the curtains into the rise and fall of a dance as gentle as Christiana's breathing. The air smelled clean and uncomplicated here, far from the pollution that had not so long ago invaded their lives.

The breeze rushed across his naked body, sweet and gentle, and he remembered how it had felt to wake to that breeze the last time they were here, some twenty years ago. Then, he had watched Christiana's nipples go tight as the air whispered over her body, and it had made his dick ache with fullness. Then, they'd been simple newlyweds. Now, as he felt her sleep in his arms, he knew that time and circumstances had changed them. Things weren't uncomplicated anymore. He closed his eyes, his head still upon her shoulder, thankful to have his wife next to him.

Despite his best effort, Carl's tenderness woke Christiana. She rolled over to greet him by snuggling into him. She brought her lips to his and kissed him, once, twice, and on the third kiss, slipped her tongue into his mouth.

Carl sucked in his breath at the sensation of her tongue seeking his and wrapped his arms tighter around his wife. If all she offered was her embrace or her kiss, Carl would've been satisfied, but when she rolled onto her back and offered herself to him, he smiled in unabashed morning glee. Some things, he realized, were still as uncomplicated as they appeared to be, and Carl knew better than to second-guess his wife's invitation. He climbed onto her and brushed his hard cock across the lips of her pussy. Christiana shuddered.

"Don't make me wait," she whispered.

Carl played at entering her. He expected resistance and began reaching for the lube when, to his surprise, he slipped into her. Christiana was slick with welcome and her wet, lush grip made him shudder. Rarely was it like that anymore.

As Carl pulled back and pushed into her again, he reached down to her clit, intent on sharing his good fortune. Christiana responded immediately, bucking at his touch, and in no time their quiet morning lovemaking spiraled into a heated, wild fuck. They lost themselves in each other, in the sensations that one body imparted to the other as the morning breeze rippled through the window and over their naked, twined bodies.

They fed off of each other and came, Christiana first, Carl later, and, as husband collapsed onto wife, they remained embracing as Carl's cock waned and slipped from Christiana's luscious depths.

• • •

When the breeze brushed through Christiana's hair as she stood on the veranda, Carl couldn't help himself. He had to join her there. He came up behind her, wrapped his arms around her and kissed the back of her head lightly. "Where do you want to go today?" he asked.

Christiana sighed as she watched the clouds move across the ocean's horizon. "I don't know. It all looks so inviting."

In the bright light of day, Bermuda was a balm for her. Its verdant hills were dotted with so many pastel houses that it looked like an impressionist's dreamscape. The site brought as much warmth to Christiana's soul as the sun did to her body. Colorful, it was a welcome change from the dreary winter she and Carl had come through just months before, a winter made bleak not only in the barrenness of the land, but by the dull, listless walls of the treatment center and in the overwhelming weariness that had gripped Christiana every time she visited that place.

All that had slowly evaporated when she had, in the doctors' lexicon, "achieved a successful outcome." The *been there, done that* crowd within her support group encouraged her and Carl to get away and reclaim their lives. "A cruise," they recommended. "You need to start living again."

But they didn't take the advice immediately; they were too cautious to move far from their new fortune, from Christiana's all-too-fresh reprieve. It took time for them to regain their trust. When they did, they were ready enough for sunshine and ocean breezes that they opted for a fast airline over a leisurely cruise line.

That brought them to Bermuda, site of their first honeymoon some two decades prior. The island remained as clear and crisp as ever. Hamilton's storefronts still sported bright facades while their interiors remained dark and filled with treasures from the British

Isles. Saint Georges still proclaimed its history in its fortress walls. The Botanical Gardens still made for a lush stroll where human voices hushed themselves, deferring to the cacophony of birdsong. Ice cream in the afternoon still tasted rich and extravagant under the thick canopy of a giant rubber tree.

"How about a glass-bottom boat ride?" Carl asked. His hand wandered from her waist to her breast. He cupped its soft fullness and squeezed gently. When he felt her nipple grow hard in his hand, Carl couldn't help but become aroused.

Christiana felt his dick twitch and press into her backside. "Are you *really* telling me you'd rather stay in this morning?" she teased.

Carl laughed. "No. But you might have to walk in front of me until my cock becomes suitable for polite company."

Christiana leaned her head back against Carl. "No boat ride," she decided. "If there's anything I can skip this vacation, it's any reminder of nausea."

Carl understood and tenderly kissed the back of her head again. Silently, he resisted the urge to cup the other side in his hand, the one void of fullness. Although he loved it as much as its counterpart, now was not the time.

"How about the lighthouse?" he suggested. "Remember how it was closed last time?"

They had bused their way across the island to see the solid, cast-iron structure, only to find it undergoing a paint job. It was the only major site that had turned them away.

"Yes, let's do the lighthouse," she decided and, with Carl's erection still prodding her, suggested, "Maybe we should skip our underwear."

Purring, she added, "You never know what we might do there."

· · ·

From the narrow platform of the lighthouse, Christiana noticed how the coral reefs interrupted the blue waters of the ocean with their dark-green presence. She gazed at the craggy rocks that jutted from the beach below and wondered how something so roughhewn could coexist with the delicate, fine sands of the beach. How could such direct opposites come together? But then she realized it was much like her body, rendered asymmetrical by lifesaving necessity.

No matter where she went or what she did, that necessity always came into play in her experiences and observations. It had redefined her existence and she wondered if she would ever learn to take it for granted. *Perhaps when I'm declared a survivor,* she decided.

Christiana surveyed Southampton Parish from on high and tried to push the thoughts from her mind. Scanning the distance, she loved how Bermuda's bright rooftops fought thick treetops for visibility while ships' masts crowded over the blue waters of various landings. To the north, the island stretched flat and indistinct. At its end lay the fort of Saint George, complete with pillories, Shetland sweaters, and enough lemonade to ease one's midafternoon heat frustration.

Nearby, Carl muttered to himself and she could tell by the tone of it that he was annoyed with something.

"Problem?" she inquired.

"I forgot the other memory card," he said, holding up the camera. "We're out of pictures for now."

Christiana shrugged. "So put the camera away. You can do other things, you know."

From the sly look on her face, Carl knew what she had in mind. "Here?"

"Maybe. But we won't know if you don't try."

As Carl embraced and kissed Christiana, he marveled yet again at how perfect she felt to him: how she melded into him, how his arms seemed to mold themselves around her, how her body seemed to mesh with his. Like two pieces in a jigsaw puzzle.

Their tongues played as they kissed, seeking, darting and connecting. Their breathing grew hurried as flesh against flesh created a heat far stronger than the late-morning sun. When Carl moaned and pulled her even closer, Christiana felt his erection at her thighs.

Christiana loved his hard dick. It told her in complete certainty that the absence made more than the heart grow fonder. Once, she had been terrified that she'd lose Carl's attraction to her, but the first time he curled up next to her in bed, she knew by the enthusiasm of his touch that everything would be OK. The first time he caressed her and they had both become aroused, she knew that this part of her life would go on.

Carl, however, was stuck in the here and now. He wondered how they'd consummate their little act of public sex. The platform was narrow—too narrow for a quickie. Perhaps Christiana would drop to her knees. Perhaps he would. But before he could find out, a sudden gust of wind swept over the lighthouse and stole Christiana's hat from her head, whisking it away. Still in mid-kiss, they felt the unmistakable sway that made this lighthouse famous.

Carl pulled away first. "You still move me," he joked.

As suddenly as the gust had come upon them, voices rose from within the cast-iron lighthouse. People were coming and from the tenor of the crowd, they knew it was a family with children.

"Maybe we'll have better luck at the beach," Christiana suggested. "And I'll go first so people won't see how much you enjoyed yourself here."

Christiana stepped in front of her husband and brought his veranda prediction to fruition.

• • •

South Shore Beach was much as Carl and Christiana remembered it: amenities at the start of its length, giving way to private, secluded spots the farther one walked. Fine sand underfoot, the warm sun on their backs, and craggy rocks all around—remnants of ancient coral reefs—made for a perfect stroll. Around them, the ocean's rhythms lapped against land as the wind rustled the trees just beyond the rocky crags. They scanned the beach's width, looking for that one spot that might work better than their last, too-brief stolen moment.

They quickly realized that finding a seductive spot would be easy, but finding one secluded enough to avoid the notice of others would not. People dotted the length of the beach and a trail of hoof prints suggested that horseback riders passed by regularly. As they explored one beautiful rock outcropping after another, they found them all too peopled. What they'd need, they realized, was a spot so homely no one would ever consider it for a Kodak moment. It took them the better part of an hour to find it.

"There," Carl said, pointing to the innermost reaches of an ugly outcropping. "Let's go there."

The rock was dark and cool, shielded from the afternoon sun. The sand was cool underfoot. The spot spoke of hidden things,

things to be discovered.

Carl's discovery came first: he sported an urgent erection the moment he pulled Christiana to him, kissed her, and maneuvered her up against the rocks. He loved pushing her up against hard things, and putting her quite literally between a rock and his hard place felt dominant and lusty. In the old days, he would've pulled her hair to hold her in place, but he'd lost the heart to do so once he'd seen it thin. Now, tenderness was a more satisfying approach.

As they kissed, he pulled her hands above her head and held them there. He transferred them to one hand and began to surf her body with his free hand. Her breast felt taut, nipple hardened. Her ribs rose and fell as he caressed her. When his hand dipped between her legs and found her warm crevice, she shuddered.

He broke their kiss just as he parted her labia and pushed a finger in. Her cunt felt dry and unyielding, but if her panting meant anything, it meant she found his probing arousing. His cock lurched in agreement. Unexpectedly, they moaned in unison and the sound of their matching desires made them all the more aroused.

Carl pulled his finger from Christiana and turned her around. He placed her hands on the rocks. "Keep an eye out," he ordered her. "Watch."

Reaching into his pocket, he brought out a small tube of lubricant. Deftly, he freed his cock and flipped open the tube. He squeezed a small portion of the lube onto the head of his cock.

Christiana knew Carl was prepping himself. She spread her legs and tilted her rump just enough to make her cunt an easy on-ramp. As she looked at the rock before her, she noticed it held tiny seashells, little snails fossilized in stone, frozen in time. When she felt the head of Carl's cock at her cunt lips, she groaned and dug her nails into the rock. She loved feeling his cock there and no matter what had been taken from her, she was glad she hadn't been robbed of her appreciation for penetration.

Carl slipped inside her with ease. Slowly, he worked his cock in and out, luxuriating in the tight feel of her cunt. Hers was a wonderful spot, with just enough friction to hug his dick, just enough depth to welcome him wholly. Who needed a scenic grotto literally when you could have one as figuratively splendid as Christiana's?

At that, he started in on her, fast and greedy.

Christiana loved how Carl took her and used her. She

welcomed the edginess of outdoor sex with all its uncertainties. She welcomed his selfish enjoyment of her. She welcomed letting go of all the times he had had to care for her and cater to her. Now, she reveled in the rawness of the moment.

As Carl rammed her from behind, she fought to keep her eyes scanning the edge of their fuck place. Having to keep watch while he used her made for a strange objectification. From below the waist, she was a pleasure toy being put to good use. Above, she was a sentry on duty. Together, they were enough to make her moan.

Fucking Christiana was less poetic for Carl. He was hard, horny, and wanted to get off. His dick was working a lush hole of delight. His balls were clenching, ready to let go. Hurriedly, in the vernacular of the quickie, Carl looked for the fastest way out.

He reached forward and found Christiana's nipple. He squeezed it through her dress. The sensation made her groan and buck. Her reaction made him roar. Instantly, his orgasm overtook him, shot from inside him and into that wet grotto that held his dick. For Carl, ecstasy came and went in five, hot spurts.

For Christiana, ecstasy was being held in his grip, in Carl pinching her nipple, in the determined, focused way he fucked her, in the ferocity of his orgasm. Ecstasy was in being human and alive and vibrant, under the afternoon sun with the sea around you and your lover behind you.

For the moment at any rate. As Carl pulled himself away from his wife and stood up, Christiana pulled away from the outcropping. Her nails tore two shells from the rock as she dropped to her knees and took Carl's withering cock into her mouth. Blissfully, she cleaned it of their juices, sweet tastes to her tongue.

But she had also spied the shells as they fell to the ground, and once she had tucked his dick into his pants, she plucked them from the sand before rising.

Again, Carl pulled her to him and kissed her deeply. His hand went to her breast and cupped it tenderly, with love, in gratitude, and as he kissed and caressed her, Christiana held tightly to the shells, as though they were too special, too magical to lose.

With those two tiny shells buried in her hand, Christiana prayed that Carl's touch would last her a lifetime—and a generous lifetime at that.

• • •

Carl watched trees and houses zip by as the taxi headed for the airport. The chatter and laughter that Christiana shared with their cab driver should've delighted him—he appreciated his wife's ability to find common ground with almost anyone on the face of the earth—but he was preoccupied on this morning of their departure. Before sleeping last night, Christiana had complained about tightness in her chest just as a prolonged coughing spell overtook her. The memory of that cough made the hackles rise on his neck. It felt wrong, suspicious. Like a bad omen.

More than anything, he wanted to reach inside his wife and, through his touch, make sure everything was all right, that there was nothing to dread, nothing a change in inhalers couldn't remedy. But magic powers he lacked, and he'd have to live with anxiety and uncertainty until they got home. Until they saw her doctors again.

Christiana tore Carl from his distraction by linking her arm in his and pulling herself closer to him. As he gazed at her, the bright smile on her face and the joy in her eyes soothed him. And when she spoke to him, she shattered his every worry.

"Touch me," she whispered. It was the perfect invitation, the perfect culmination to a splendid week.

Carl brought his hand to his wife's cheek. Softly, he stroked her face. His inner fears quieted and he relaxed, thankful for his wife's invitation. Regardless of what that cough had meant, as long as his fingers touched her skin, everything in his world made sense.

room with a view

ﾉﾉ

CATHERINE LUNDOFF

YOU STAND AT THE WINDOW, WATCHING FLORENCE'S glorious merchant palaces spread their pale orange wings on the other side of the Arno. I get up to lean against you, wrapping my body around yours, my hand reaching down of its own accord to ease its way under your blouse. I can't help myself.

"Stop." You breathe the word like a sigh, like you don't mean it. It's as though you want to hear what it sounds like to say "no." But your eyes are still fixed on the green Arno and the centuries-old palaces turned hotels and restaurants and trendy boutiques on the opposite bank so I continue my exploration.

My hand finds the silky skin between your bra and skirt and I lean over to take the lobe of one ear between my teeth. I work the tender flesh with my tongue, rejoicing at the quickening of your breath. My fingers find and close on a hardened nipple and you squirm against me. "Stop," you hiss the word insistently between gasps.

All right, I will. My fingers reluctantly loosening, I step back with a courtier's bow. But you'll beg me for it later. I can see it in your eyes when you turn around. You know it, too. I grin down at you, my smile more a baring of frustrated fangs than anything else.

"C'mon, don't pout. Let's go look at something. I don't want this to be one of those trips where we never leave the hotel room." Your lower lip thrusts out slightly with the words as though I'm going to deprive you of a treat. I almost expect you to stamp your foot for emphasis.

As if I could deprive you of anything. Instead with an ironic "After you, *signorina*," I wave you toward the door. After a minute, you grab your bag.

"And don't you look so smug. I know every centimeter below the waist aches right now." You smile triumphantly, narrow red lips framing white American teeth. I smile back, knowing it's true for you as well. I can see it in your eyes, in the rapid rise and fall of your breasts. It's a game we have played before; all I have to do is wait you out.

But for now, since you want to play tourist, play tourist we shall. And we do. There's the Academy of Art with its giant *David* in all its splendid marble glory. Michelangelo's masterpiece towers some forty feet above us in its own dome and we gaze upward in awe. Renaissance man at the height of his glory and power, illuminated by the glowing eyes of a hundred tourists. It dominates the room, crowding out the other sculptures as though they were invisible.

Eventually, though, the crowds sweep us out and on to the Convento di San Marco and then to the great Cathedral, the Duomo. We look our fill upon Fra Angelico paintings in the austere cells of the monks and at the glory of the Catholic Church at the height of its power. I am a blur of dying saints and marble faces, annunciations and gold-trimmed ceilings.

We wander the piazzas and winding stone streets, gaping up at red tile roofs and tiny flower-lined balconies. I almost forget you are with me at times, until you brush up against me and take my arm like Italian women do with each other. I pull you close, wrap myself in the scent of your shampoo, in the warm curve of your arm in mine. I revel in the opportunity to feel protective, possessive, resisting the temptation to gaze fiercely at passersby to reinforce my claim.

But our feet hurt. This inescapable fact sends us into a bar for the ubiquitous *paninni*, the all-purpose ham and cheese sandwich, beloved by both locals and tourists. There, I devour my lunch so I can watch you pick more daintily at yours. My eyes dwell on the line of your throat with each swallow, the tip of your pink tongue clearing red lips with each bite. I rush to buy you *gelatti* and watch enviously as a tiny drop of ice-cold chocolate drips down between your breasts.

My tongue longs to follow it, to bury my face in your ample flesh until only the need for air can force me upward to the surface. You giggle and grin up at me as your hand dips a napkin into your cleavage, reading my thoughts until I look away, ashamed at being so predictable. We wander on to the Uffizi, the grandest museum in Florence, with its riot of painted ceilings and gold-framed Marys and Christs. You admire the Raphaels, I the Botticellis, though his Venus seems distant and coy.

It is in one of these rooms I find Titian's *Venere di Urbino*, the Venus of Urbino, and fall in love. I read somewhere that she was a famous courtesan of her time and meeting her come-hither gaze, I can believe it. She reclines nude, one hand gently covering her mons, face tilted as she looks sidelong at the viewer. Titian must have loved her. The sheer erotic power of this woman burns across the centuries after her death and I get wet just meeting her eyes.

You see my look of longing and you fidget, trying to draw me on to yet another Madonna, another crucifixion, more bloody yet unbowed saints. I look into the eyes of the painted woman and I know you are right to be jealous. I dream for a moment about painting this Venus, capturing her rounded form for the eyes of a Medici, a Sforza. I imagine myself lovingly applying each stroke, outlying her rounded flesh, the fall of her ringlets. But how to capture that look, the soft sweetness of her cheek? She seduces me with her gaze and the upturned tilt of her mouth. I want desperately to kiss her, to taste her flesh. But she is long gone.

And you are here tugging at my arm. I smile down at you as my thoughts return reluctantly to the present. The moment is gone but my resigned glance still lingers on her as we move on. I wonder what her name was and state the thought aloud. "That I don't know, but if she was still alive and caught your attention like she does on canvas, I wouldn't be too happy." You glance back with a speculative look on your face then smile back at me.

You are more attentive now, pressing your body against mine at every opportunity as if by accident until I become more aware of you, leaving the glowing painted beauty behind. Your breast caresses my arm and you smile longingly up at me and lick your lips. I think of steering you toward the WC and savoring the promise in your eyes but the lines are too long. In the crowds, you contrive to stand in front of me and grind your soft ass against my hips. I manage not to respond, but only just barely.

"Perhaps we've seen enough art for one day?" I place the words carefully before you, an offering redolent with desire.

"Maybe. But I can think of a few more pieces I'd like to see." Your grin turns impish as you pull me back toward the hotel. Outside the Uffizi, we pass people frozen in place like statues, waiting for the permission of coins deposited in the boxes before them to enact a small performance. For a euro, a gold-painted man bows and extends a golden rose to you. You giggle happily at the novelty of it and he winks at me over your head before freezing back into position.

The sun catches the gold flecks buried in your hazel eyes as you laugh up at me and I forget the painted Venus in their glow. We walk on through the Piazza della Signoria, through a tide of tourists and locals and vendors. You stand before the statues and for an instant, I contemplate taking you on the ledge beneath the fake *David*. I have no trouble imagining your soft thighs opening to the insistent thrust of my hand, the strokes of my tongue.

I picture the tourists all capturing the moment, something to show the folks back home in Peoria or Tokyo. Pity you'd never agree. Still, I manage to cup your ass and squeeze, my fingers just under the hem of your skirt. You gasp and glance around wildly as if I'd let someone else touch you like this. We stand waiting for an opening in the crowds and I ease my fingers further up your skirt, reaching up between your thighs, but not far enough to touch what I really want. Just enough to remind you that I'm here. You make a small strangled moan and your hip rubs sweetly against mine.

The crowds part and I remove my hand, using it instead to steer you away across the uneven cobbles. I wonder if I could pull you down a deserted side street, press you up against a wall like a medieval lord with his mistress. I imagine pulling up your heavy skirts and sinking into your wet, welcoming warmth. My pants are hot and moist at the thought of thrusting my way inside you, your carmined lips parting in a torrent of Italian that begs me not to stop.

Looking at the ancient stones, I choose not to remember the religious wars that made these very same streets run with blood. Or Savoranola, the mad monk with his bonfires of the vanities that consumed so many books, so much art. No, instead I dream tourist dreams of beauty and sophistication, poetry and love, and forget the ugliness of the past. And for now, since the crowds are unrelenting and there are no deserted streets, my medieval lord is a story for another time.

The hotel, however, is conveniently nearby. I tow you forward and you follow unresisting, your lips pursed in a small smile as we wind our way down several short streets to get to the right one. It is a yellow brick building on the Arno, probably a merchant palace in its time and when I look up, I can see the balcony of our room. Good. I have plans for it. We smile charmingly at the desk clerk on our way past and she smiles back around her cell phone.

It is only when we reach our room that you pull back, removing your arm from mine. "Give me a couple of minutes, hon. It'll be worth the wait, I promise." And with that you're gone, vanished into the shower down the hall. I am left to sit like a neglected puppy, soda in hand, waiting for your return.

It seems like hours. You stroll back in and toss me the bathroom keys. "Your turn." It's more of a command than a request and I want to ignore it. But I can see that it will get me nowhere and there are places I want desperately to be. The shower is not one of them, but I force myself to think of the lukewarm water as a brief intermission. I am showered, dried and back down the hall in less than fifteen minutes. I pause at our door, nipples erect with expectation, then I swing it open to see if the delay has, in fact, been worth it.

You are lying on the bed, nude except for the thin red leather jacket we bought you in Milan three days ago. You lounge backward, head tilted and hand covering your pussy in conscious imitation of the Venus of Urbino. You gaze at me sidelong, calling me to you without a word until I bow my head in conscious acknowledgment that you have very nearly mastered her look. That you are here, warm and breathing while she is an ideal frozen in time.

Now I can see your fingers dip downward to seek your clit while I shut the door behind me. The open jacket slips a little to reveal the snake tattooed on your right breast. I throw the towel aside and tear off my shirt. My eager hands find the fly on my jeans and you smile triumphantly. So, deliberately, I slow down.

Instead of leaping into the bed as I had intended, I take my time and let my eyes rove down your body. Only your fingers move at first, their tips stroking sensitive flesh until your breath leaves your lips in little breathy sighs. I walk slowly around the bed and you watch me hungrily.

I reach down and pull your hand out of your pussy, stopping to lick your juices from your fingertips. Each finger finds its way into my mouth and I suck it slowly, savoring your sweet-sour taste. A moan tears itself from you as I pull you to your feet. For an instant I kiss you, hard, devouring your mouth with mine. My hands roam over your body exploring and savoring what I can never enjoy enough. Then I push you toward the window.

I fling the shutters open to display our balcony, watching with amused desire as your lips part in dismay. I clasp you in my arms again, kissing first your mouth, then your throat and breasts. My teeth find the snake's head coiled near your nipple and they are far sharper than its fangs. Your head is tilted back as my fingers find their way between your thighs. I listen to your gasps and moans as I suck on first one nipple, then the other.

Your eyes are closed when I look up and step back, pushing you against the balcony railing so you lean forward. Now your eyes open wide, startled by the warm breeze and the consciousness that anyone looking up at just the right angle can see you.

I part your thighs and drive my hand inside you. My whole body thrusts with my hand as you spread wide to welcome me. I curl my hand into a fist inside you and your back arches. You push back against me, heavy breasts spilling out of the jacket to rub pebble-hard nipples against the cold iron of the railing. My free hand reaches to find your clit and I wrap myself around you, fist unclenching so I can concentrate on taking you.

You come again and again, shaking, quivering and biting back the moans that will attract attention from the street. You come until your knees buckle and we sink to the floor by the window. Then you wrap yourself around me as you pull my jeans off. With an expert twist, you flip me over so you're on top, crouching between my legs. Then you begin to lick your slow way up my thighs. I groan and shiver with the force of my longing, my clit surrendering to your eager tongue when it finally arrives. Your fingers slip inside me, first two, then three and I close around them, quaking with desire until I can't stand it anymore.

I clasp you fiercely to me then, pulling your lips up to my hungry mouth as we roll farther out onto the little balcony. Below us the streets roar with Vespas and tiny cars, but I hear nothing over the sound of your voice whispering in my ear.

Just for a moment, my thoughts wander back to the beautiful woman in the painting. I wonder if Titian got to taste his Venus. I hope so. The thought of the alternative, of all that unattainable wanting and passion, is more than I can bear and I kiss you harder, wanting to express my passion through my lips alone. A heartbeat later, the crumbling orange and yellow palaces across the Arno watch me kneel to worship at the altar of my Venus.

The shape of cities

꒳

MAXIM JAKUBOWSKI

SHE USED TO COME WITH ME TO FOREIGN CITIES.

The ways of lust were impenetrable; it made us involuntary and uncurious tourists. After all, we couldn't quite spend the whole of every trip barricaded in our hotel room fucking like rabid rabbits, could we?

So, between the hours of sex, we walked, explored. I dived into any bookshop I passed and she bought lingerie (on my credit card); we ate too much, saw movies. The Grand Canal in Venice smelled; maybe it was because we were not in season. In the bay in Monterey the otters were silent. In Amsterdam, we had a *rijstaffel* that made our stomachs churn for hours later. In Barcelona, the Ramblas were overflowing with foreign soccer fans. In Brighton, mecca of dirty weekends, television cameras were everywhere for a forthcoming political party conference, not to capture our sordid exploits in a blue movie. Somehow every city felt the same as it harbored our frantic fucks. They had no shape, just a strange presence dictated by the intensity of sex.

Of course, eventually, she tired of travel, of me.

All I now have left of her is this photograph. Black and white, of a woman naked against a dark background. A hotel room, no doubt. It's not even her, I am ashamed to say. Just an image in a book that somehow reminds me of her. I never had a talent for photography, couldn't even master the simple art of photographing a lover with a Polaroid. Sad, eh?

This is the way she looked as she stripped for me in a hotel room.

Maybe it was in Paris, a hotel on the rue de l'Odeon with wooden beams crisscrossing the rough texture of the walls and ceiling. Or then again it could have been the Gershwin Hotel, just off Fifth Avenue in New York City, where the smile of a Picasso heroine illuminated the wall next to the bed and watched our lovemaking through the walls of darkness. Maybe it was a small hotel in Amsterdam, windows overlooking a murky canal, with the noise of drunk revelers and parking cars keeping us awake at night. Oh yes, we frequented many hotels—those sometimes elegant, often sordid last contemporary refuges of illicit sex. The one in Chicago that was being renovated, where she preferred to sleep in the second bed because I snored too much. (In fact, this was the final hotel that harbored our pathetic affair; maybe the excuse was just an early sign of her fading interest in me.) Or the St. Pierre on Burgundy Street in New Orleans, far enough from the hubbub of Bourbon Street, where I forgot to take her dancing. (She did dance in Chicago, but it was with other men.)

Or the one whose memories I cherished most: our marine and pastel-colored room at the Grand Hotel in Sete, where the balcony looked out on quite another kind of canal, host to local jousts on long boats at the weekend. A coastal port where she took a shine to the limping waiter who served us one evening in a seafood restaurant, and seriously suggested we should invite him back to the room later. Nothing happened, but for months after that I would fantasize wildly of watching her being fucked by another man and even got to the point of lining someone up when we next visited Manhattan, only to have to cancel it because she had her period that same week.

In my dreams I wasn't even jealous to see her in the throes of pleasure as another man's cock slowly entered her. I would listen to her moan and writhe, and watch in sheer fascination as her so-pale blue eyes took on a glazed sheen. After our first time, as I walked her back to the train station, she had told me her partner would know immediately she had been with another because her eyes shined so much. No, I felt no jealousy at the idea of seeing her perform with another. It would be for my pleasure and edification. I would position her on all fours on the bed, her rump facing the door, let my fingers slide across the cleft of her buttocks and dip into her wetness as I introduced the stranger to the beauty, intricacies and secrets of her body. See how hot she is inside, I would say, how that sweet cunt will grip your cock and milk it dry. I would be the director, set it all up, orchestrate their movements, stroke myself as her lips tightened across his thick penis and took him all in, sucking away with the energy of despair. (Haven't I told you how good her blow jobs were? She sucked with frantic energy as if her whole life depended on it, but still retained that amused air of innocence in her eyes as she did so, demonstrating her sheer enjoyment of the art of oral sex — much as I hoped I did when I went down on her, tasting her and shaking while the vibrations of her coming coursed through her whole body and moved onto my tongue, heart, soul, and cock.)

So, she stripped for me in a hotel room. Now she was down to just her stockings. Delicately undulating, thrusting her pelvis out, shaking her delicate breasts, her hands caressing her rump in a parody of sexiness, just like a stripper in a movie. No music, just us in the otherwise empty room. A jolt, a jump, a shimmy, now just like Madonna in that video, just a tad vulgar but sufficiently provocative; now exuberant like Kylie Minogue, but never as frantic as Jennifer Lopez or Destiny's Child.

And I drank in every inch of her body. The pale flesh; the moles and blemishes; the deep sea of those eyes that never reached bottom; the gently swaying breasts; the ash-blonde hair now growing down to her shoulders; the trimmed triangle of darker pubic curls through which I could easily see the gash of her nacreous entrance; the thicker folds of flesh where her labia, lower down, grew ever so meaty and protruding; the square regal expanse of her arse, which looked so good in the thong briefs we purchased together at Victoria's Secret on Broadway.

Then she would look down and see me, no doubt with tongue hanging out and my erection straining against the dark material of my slacks, and she would smile, and my heart would melt. And though I wanted to fuck her right then until we were both raw and out of breath, I also felt strangely full of kindness, a sensation that made me feel like a better man altogether.

I have known this body so intimately that I could describe every minutiae of her sighs, the look in her eyes when she is being entered, the stain on the left side of her left breast, the dozen variations in color of the skin surrounding the puckered entrance of her anus and the hundred shades of red and pink that scream at me when I separate her lower lips and open her up. The memories come running back like a hurricane, rapid, senseless, brutal. Of the good times, and the bad ones too. Of the time we went naked on a beach swept by a cold wind. The visit to the Metropolitan Museum when she felt so turned on by the Indian and Oceanian erotic sculptures that we almost fucked in the nearby restroom. (I was the one who felt it would be too risky and by the time we had reached the hotel again, the mood had evaporated....) The email she sent to tell me she had shaved her pussy and then a few days later another terse communication informing me that she had found a new lover—and my anger at knowing he was the one who could now see her bald mons in all its erotic splendor. The first time she allowed me to fuck her, doggie-style, without a condom, watching myself buried inside her and moving to and fro, our juices commingling. The evening we ate oysters, she for the first time, and she recognized their flavor when she swallowed my come some hours later in the hotel room.

That hotel room where she stripped for my entertainment and amusement, eyes lowered, a sober gold necklace around her slender neck; where once down to her fishnet stockings she slowly moved toward me—I was sitting on the edge of the bed—and, the delicate smell of her cunt just inches away from my face, stepped onto the bed, towered over me and opened her legs wide, the obscene and wonderful vision of her visibly moist gash just a couple of centimeters from my wide-open eyes, teasing me, offering herself, my naked lover, my private stripper, my nude love.

"You like it, mister?" she asks, a giggle stuck in the back of her throat.

I nod approvingly.

She lowers her hand and, digging two opposing fingers into her wetness, she widens herself open.

"You want, sir?" she inquires of me.

I smile with a faint indifference, somehow come up with a relevant joke I can't for the life of me now recall. And she bursts out laughing. Once upon a time, I could make her laugh like no other. I had to warn her to temper her hilarity, reminding her of the time on the Boulevard St. Germain when she had actually peed a little in the convulsions of laughter. She hiccups and lowers herself onto me. The hypnotic warmth of her naked body against me. I am still fully clothed.

All now intolerable memories: of hotels, of jokes that were once funny.

Now, too much has happened since the times we were together and happy in our simple, sexual way, and she wants us to be friends, no longer lovers. There has been a married Dutchman, now divorcing; a Korean with dark skin; and God knows who else. And finally I am jealous as hell. Surely, she insists, we can still have good times together as friends; no sex, it's better that way. How, I ask her, but then I would, wouldn't I? How can we spend days in foreign cities, share a hotel room and ignore the fact her body and her eyes and her smell and her words and her cunt shout out *sex* to me? I know I couldn't accept that ridiculous compact of just friendship anymore.

You can go with other men, I say, and I will not blame you or hold it against you. I understand that I am not always available and that you are young and have needs. But she knows I am lying inside. That I would say anything to have her back.

In hotel rooms.

Stripping for me.

Laughing with me. Laughing at me.

In darkness she moves; I am deaf, I can't hear the music she is dancing so sensually to. Maybe it's blues, a song by Christine McVie or Natalie Merchant. Or "Sing," by Travis. Or maybe it's Sarah McLachlan's "Fumbling Towards Ecstasy" (the Korean man who later abandoned her for a Russian woman, after breaking her fragile heart, had introduced her to that particular music, ironically a man of melodic taste…). Or again that Aimee Mann song from *Magnolia* (we saw the movie together; oh, how she enjoyed seeing movies with me). I hear nothing, can only try and guess the tune from the languorous movements of her body as every piece of clothing is shed to reveal the treasures of her flesh, her intimacy. The crevice of her navel, the darkened tips of her nipples (so devoid of sensitivity, she would always remind me), her throat, the luminosity of her face, her youth, her life.

I open my mouth but I can't even hear myself saying "please" or "come back" or "forgive me."

She dances, my erotic angel, my lost lover.

The silent words in me increase in loudness, but she is lost in the music and no longer even sees her audience. Behind her, the hotel walls are all black and she is frozen like a photograph, her pallor in sharp contrast to the surroundings. Stripper in hotel room. A study in light and darkness.

As in a nightmare, my throat constricts and words fail me totally. I shed a single tear of humid tenderness, all too aware that I will never again be able to afford a private stripper. Let alone a hotel room.

silver cowboy

✤

LESLEY GLAISTER

SHE STANDS IN THE AIRPORT, KEEPING HER EYE OFF THE clock. Everyone else from her flight has gone. There's just her, stuck there alone like some lemon, waiting. *Don't worry,* she tells herself. *Enjoy.* This is her first time in Barcelona. She's hot, headachy—one too many gins on the plane, she never can resist a free drink.

She shrugs her bag off her shoulder, searches through it for the fax: *Meet your flight 2 p.m.. Looking forward. Concita.* She'd ripped it off the machine and looking now sees that she'd ripped off the contact details. *Idiot.* So here she is stuck in Barcelona with no phone number, no address. She speaks no Spanish or Catalan, she has no euros. *Don't panic,* she tells herself. *OK, so Concita's late, people are late, maybe a traffic jam, maybe a mistake with the time.* She makes herself relax, swigs from her water bottle, goes to sit down on a bench. She's too hot, in her stuffy English woolens. Soon as she gets to Concita's she'll shower, put on something cool. Drink more water, take something for her head.

A young couple are kissing. Young sleek skins, fresh lips. Long time since she's been kissed like that. She realizes she's staring and drags her eyes away. She takes out her book and tries to concentrate but her head hurts. She shuts her eyes, supposes that she really should have a plan. Concita *will* come, but if she doesn't she should have a plan.

She opens her eyes and becomes aware of a man standing a little way away, talking into a mobile phone. Long legs in faded jeans, more faded around the crotch, leather jacket, longish fair hair swept back. She does admire men with long legs. He's wearing a great pair of boots, nearly cowboy but not quite. There is something about cowboys.... She finds that she's staring at his boots, his legs, and as her eyes travel up, she snatches them away again—really she is so dazed. She looks back, meets his eyes for a second. He looks back at her coldly. She flushes and looks quickly down at the page of her book.

It's nearly three o'clock. So, the plan: She'll change some money first then—telephone directory? But Concita's only just moved to her flat and is unlikely to be listed. So, think: Concita works for a magazine, what's it called?—she strains her mind back. She needs the toilet. And that means dragging all her stuff with her but she can't sit here bursting, sweating. She must look awful, red in the face, flustered. That last gin was definitely a mistake.

She stands up, shoulders her bag, does not look at the man who is leaning against a wall, keying something into his phone. She uses the toilet, washes her hands, runs them damply through her corkscrew of mad brown curls. Flying brings out the frizz. Her nose is shiny. She looks like shit, she thinks. And what is she to do? She feels like boarding the next flight back to Manchester, having a quiet weekend at home: telly, garden, wine, her own familiar bed.

But back outside, she gives a cry of relief, seeing the familiar figure of Concita. She's looking at the arrivals board, looking at her watch. Cora hurries up: "Concita!"

"Thank God," Concita says, giving her the breath of a swift kiss on each cheek. "Sorry, couldn't get away and then the traffic—" she trails off.

"It's OK," Cora says, "you're here now."

There is an awkward moment. They don't know each other well, met last summer when Concita was staying with a mutual friend in London and hit it off. They had had such a laugh last year, and Concita had given her an open invitation, but now Cora feels uncomfortable. She already feels like a nuisance and with her head thumping away she'll be no company. She feels ridiculously close to tears.

"Come," Concita says. "Let's get back, we're going out to eat tonight with friends and tomorrow a party at my house, then you can meet everyone."

"Great." Cora's heart sinks. What is she doing here? She feels overcome with shyness, a feeling of inadequacy. She should have stayed at home and done the garden. Or visited her mother; she should have done something safe.

She stares out at the streets. It's only March but it is hot. Great gray trees rear their bare limbs against the buildings — something gaudy, must be Gaudi, she giggles, feeling a bit excited despite herself. Back at the apartment, up three musty flights of stairs, Concita opens a bottle of cold greenish wine. Cora remembers that Concita is quite a drinker. Well that's something they have in common. The flat is big and airy, three faded sofas, a balcony overflowing with ferns and lush green trailing things. She sips her wine. Concita puts some music on.

"Why not shower and rest?" she suggests. "I've got a few calls to make. We'll go out in a couple of hours."

The shower is an open corner of the bathroom, floor tiled and sloping to a drain. The sun shafts through yet more ferns, a lovely dusty watery light. Cora pulls off the clothes that have felt so tight and inappropriate from the moment she stepped off the plane. Her skin is marked with the seams of her jeans, the wire of her bra, a wavy elastic pattern is printed on her belly. She stands under the streaming water: *wonderful*. She squeezes some shower gel from a bottle and rubs it over herself — the smell is like mangoes, and something more earthy than that, a little musky.

She shuts her eyes and lets the water stream over her face. She rubs the scented foam over her breasts, which makes them tingle slightly. It wakens her nipples, she feels the way they tweak upward. She cups a breast in each hand and groans. God it is so long since any other hands touched them. Shame, they feel so nice, such a nice gentle weight in her own hands. She squeezes the nipples between her fingers and thumbs and a little shock jumps from there down between her legs. She pours more of the gel into her hand and rubs it down over her belly and into her bush. It foams brightly in the dark hair; she rubs it in, opening her legs a little wider. The foam stings pleasantly; she rubs it between her buttocks, up and around all the creases, a tingle spreading wherever she touches.

Into her mind comes a picture. The man at the airport. Not someone she wants to imagine, he looked so unfriendly when she met his eyes but still—what if? What if this were the story?

He came up to her at the airport.

"You look lost," he said. His English was good.

"My friend is supposed to meet me—but she hasn't shown up."

"Want to use my phone?"

"I don't know her number. Stupid. Didn't bring it. Or her address." Tears came to her eyes.

"Don't cry. Don't say you're stupid. Come back to my place, hey? and have a shower, freshen up. Then, together, we will find her."

His shower was an open corner of the bathroom, tiles sloping down to a drain. Sunlight filtered through ferns, into the steamy air. She stripped off and was washing herself, running her fingers from her nipples to her clit, from her clit to her nipples, eyes closed, lost in the sensation of warm water beating on her skin and the tingly trails of her own fingers when another hand joined hers; long fingers slid suddenly up inside her making her gasp. She opened her eyes, startled, though the feeling of the long cool fingers slipping up inside her was too fantastic for her to object. She was too far gone, lost in sensation. He knelt before her, pressed his head against her belly, then stood up in a swift movement, so tall, gripped her buttocks, the water falling first on his skin and then on hers.

"Wash me," he said. He squeezed a pool of the silvery gel into her palm and she started at his chest, lathering into the fair curling hairs and working down the flat slope of his belly. Almost scared to touch his cock, so thick and long and straining up into the water's rush. She put her hand underneath and cradled his balls, rubbed the coarse hairs into scented froth. It was so big and hot, the weight of his cock bumping her wrist as she scooped underneath and then finally slid her hands up the length, so big and hot and sweet and clean. She stooped to take it in her mouth but he pulled her up, not gently, pushed her against the wall, nudged open her legs with his knee.

The wall was hard against her back, a trickle of water sluicing down between her breasts, between her lips as, bending his knees, pushing her shoulders back against the wall, he put the tip, just the hot purple tip against her clit, just nudged it there a moment, then slid it down, just a bit further.

"Open yourself to me," he said.

She put her hands down and opened herself up to him like a fruit. He pushed the tip of his cock lower, let it slip inside her, only a little. It felt huge. "Want more?" he said. She couldn't speak, could hardly control her desire to pull him right inside her, but only slowly did he slide it in. He was so big she had to open her legs wider apart, could feel herself stretching in a way she'd never stretched before, as he crammed himself up inside her, almost too big for her; she was full and still there were more inches of hard red flesh pulsing between her lips.

He lifted her up. Her legs went around him and he thrust right up into her. She shouted; there was no way she could resist shouting at the huge, hard cock and her almost painful stretching. The water trickled down from him to her across her clit, and he thrust and thrust and forced that last length into her and she came like she'd never come before, so hard and long she almost fainted, clutching and clutching at him, her own muscles amazing her with their voracity.

And then he's gone. The water still pours down. She's alone in the shower — whose shower? *Concita's* shower, alone and very wet and clean and *Oh God* she cringes thinking of the noise she must have made. *Please please* let it have been drowned out by the sound of the water, the music Concita's playing. She dries herself and comes out of the bathroom wrapped in a big white towel.

Concita hands her another glass of wine. "Nice shower, I think?" she says, an amused expression on her face.

Next day Cora visits the half-finished cathedral, La Sargrada Familia, craning her neck up at the rearing peaks, winding up the narrow stone steps to peer dizzily down at the interior where stonemasons are still at work. She visits the Parc Guell, wandering among Gaudi's brilliant tiled curves, which at first she finds crazy, amusing, daring. But it is too hot in the sun and her feet ache. *Too crazy,* she thinks, suddenly sickened by the excess. She finds herself longing for pure lines, cool gray stone, restraint.

She takes a taxi to Placa La Catalunia and stands watching cool water brim over the fountain's lip. Statues of naked women clutching drapes around them seem to writhe as she watches. She shakes her head. *Stupid, just tired.* She walks down La Rambla, sits down at the first café and orders herself a cold *orxata.* She relaxes, sits back to watch the world go by.

There's a stall full of cheeping caged birds; a man selling tiny kites; and nearby, a living statue. She watches him, idly for a while. He's dressed as a cowboy but painted silver all over, hat, face, shirt, spurs. Everything except his eyes. He stands utterly motionless— how can he stand so motionless? Until someone gives money, then he jerks to life, pulls his pistol from his holster, twirls it around his finger, raises it, aims and pretends to fire. Then he shakes the gun, slides it into his holster and freezes back into position.

He's got long slim legs, the creases of his jeans all painted silver, silver wisps of hair visible under his silver hat. As she watches she begins to think he looks familiar. It's difficult to tell under the silver paint but maybe, maybe it's *him,* the man from the airport.

She orders a coffee and some *tapas*—hunks of spicy sausage, crusty bread smeared with tomato—and continues to stare. She is almost sure. When she gets up she goes over and throws a couple of euros and he does the movement again, just for her, points the gun, his eyes meeting hers for a fraction of a second before he sets again like stone.

She'd like to do it again but feels embarrassed and wanders reluctantly off. She buys some red tulips for Concita, a pair of long dangly earrings for herself and takes a taxi back. She is dusty and exhausted.

Concita hands her a cold glass of wine when she gets in, although all she really wants is tea. The room has been transformed for the party, the sofas pushed back, the table moved to make space—presumably—for dancing. There are bottles of wine, bowls of olives, cold meat and cheese, white rings of squid in herb-flecked oil. Concita is cooking a tortilla.

"I expect you'd like to shower?" Concita smiles down into the pan, stirs some eggy potatoes with a wooden spoon.

"Just a quick one," Cora says and in the shower she *is* quick, hardly touching herself although the thought of the man creeps into her head. The more you try not to think, the more you think.... The silver cowboy, the silver gun on his silver finger, the way his eyes met hers. She forces her mind away, switches off the shower and briskly dries herself. No more nonsense.

She dresses for the party in a loose sundress. She ties her hair up in a topknot, puts on the new earrings that tickle her bare collarbone. As she slides on her strappy sandals, her feet ache. Really she would like to put them up, watch TV, have an early night. What a drag she is being, she thinks—though when the first few guests start to arrive, a little of the excitement gets into her.

It's a warm balmy night, the balcony doors are open, the guests are friendly, good-looking people who want to talk to her. She drinks wine, nibbles at the *tapas*, talks to a beautiful dark woman who makes stained glass. And then she turns, and loses her concentration because suddenly he is there. The silver cowboy, right there in Concita's flat. She can hardly believe it. She excuses herself to the stained glass woman and goes up to him by the drinks table.

"I saw you today," she says, but he shrugs, does not speak English. She mimes to him how she threw some money, and whether he understands or not he laughs and does a little demonstration of his act. She would like to touch him. Touch the silver skin, the silver denim—but someone he knows demands his attention and she is edged out. She watches him from across the room. She would like to see him with the clothes off, the silver paint washed off his skin. Is it the same man? It is really hard to tell. Same height, same long legs, same kind of boots.

After a while he raises his hand to her in a friendly salute, and then, kissing Concita on his way out, he goes. She is left feeling flat, disappointed, and suddenly extremely tired. The party is in full swing, voices, laughter, music throbbing in her head. Concita comes over. "You all right?"

"Bit of a headache," she says, "Think I'll lie down for half an hour."

"Not a party animal, hey?"

"Sometimes," Cora says, feeling pathetic. She gets into her bed, pulls a pillow over her head to try and dull the noise. She falls immediately and easily asleep. And then, after she doesn't know how long, she wakes. She wakes because she can feel movement.

She hears a groan, the sound of kissing. No. She's dreaming.

She wakes, half aroused, half amused to feel the movements of two bodies on top of the bed. One of them half rolls onto her, mutters something in Spanish or Catalan, she doesn't know which; she can't understand but it sounds passionate. It's absurd, someone moving against someone else, against her. A deep throaty moaning, "*Si, si, si.*" She should speak. Get up. Say, "Excuse me I'm trying to sleep," say what? It sounds like the stained glass woman with a man and they are making love half on top of her. They will get the shock of their lives if she speaks up, but she can't *not* speak up. She can't lie there half underneath them while they make love, and never say a word.

She moves her head a little from under the pillow. In the mirror she can see them on the bed, see her own face, very red with the heat and the confusion underneath them. The woman is sitting astride the man, whom she can't see, wearing nothing but a green bra. Then they roll over and she can't restrain a gasp. It is him, the silver cowboy, no hat, but his hair is thick silver like strands of mercury, his silver hands are clutched on the woman's olive skin.

The woman sits up and the silver hands reach around to unclip the bra, unloose the heavy breasts. The silver head dips, sucks at the caramel-peaked nipples. The sound of the sucking, of the woman's moan of pleasure sends a sharp electric quiver of desire to Cora's groin. It is ludicrous. What should she do? What is the etiquette for this situation?

She has to push her hand down, just to squeeze the throb that's started, fingers curling inside to hold the ache. She is squashed by the woman suddenly getting up, pushing playful-roughly the man down on the bed. Cora winces as a knee hits hers. Can they really not tell that there's another person in the bed with them? But they are drunk and turned on and so is she turned on.

She watches in the mirror, the woman unbuckling the silver belt, unzipping and pulling down the man's jeans. And underneath he is still silver! His cock reaching up, metallic except for the vivid pink of the tip, shiny straining out of its silver skin. The woman puts her lips around it. Cora can see the bulge of it in her cheek. The woman turns and opens her legs to the man, Cora sees his pink tongue emerge from the silver lips as he licks her, smears of silver appearing on her dark bush of hair.

Cora's fingers are working away now, there is no way she can help it. She can hear the wet sounds of mouth on cock, lips on cunt, hear the groans of the silver cowboy, feel her own hips begin to thrust. There is no way she can help it, maybe too much to drink or maybe the tiredness, but whatever it is, she is so turned on she can't stop and she comes and she can't stop her voice rising into a kind of shriek, a muffled scream. No way they could have failed to hear it.

They do hear it and fall suddenly still and quiet.

One asks the other a question. *Was that you?* she guesses. *No, no,* they both say. She freezes, hand trapped between her legs, clit still throbbing, greedy now. She wants more and more. Her heart is painful against her ribs, her face burns.

The pillow is pulled away. The flushed face of the woman is near her own. She says something. The two stare at her for a moment aghast and then they start to laugh, both of them, then they say a few words to each other. Silver Cowboy puts his face close to Cora and kisses her, so suddenly it takes her breath away. He kisses her deeply, his mouth tasting salty-sweet, tasting of woman. She kisses back, drinking in the taste. But he pulls away and laughs, the silver is smudged. He says something to the woman who leans forward and kisses Cora, a soft female kiss, so different, and she finds herself responding in a different way.

Silver is smudging from one face, one body to another as they roll together, the soft breasts of the woman pressing against her own, the hard cock of the man pressing between her buttocks. Around her, the two of them embrace. She is sandwiched between them and it feels as if the man is making love not to her but to the woman, though, with the other woman's hands on his buttocks, it is Cora he pushes inside, inch by inch, just as big as in her shower imaginings. It must be him, it must.

She grinds herself forward into the softness of the woman, feeling the mingling of their juices, inhaling their smells. The woman kisses her as the man fucks her, soft soft lips and breasts, hard hard cock and he pumps until she comes against the woman, thrusting forward, clit sparking against clit, comes so hard it almost hurts and the woman screams and the man groans and shudders as they all come together. And then lie together, sighing and stroking, wet, hearts thumping and slowing, until she sleeps.

She must have slept. Because when she wakes there's no one

there. Her own sticky fingers still clutched between her thighs. No other smell but hers. She sits up and shivers. Examines her breasts, her thighs for traces of silver, but there are none. She gets up, pulls her dress back on, brushes her hair, goes back to rejoin the party.

Concita looks at her very oddly when she comes out. Someone else turns away to hide a smile.

"You OK now?" Concita asks.

Cora flushes dark red. She nods and accepts a drink, cold wine that she gulps too fast; looks away from Concita around the room where the stained glass woman, fully dressed, cool and poised, is talking to a man, flirting with him, and the silver cowboy is nowhere to be seen.

Next afternoon, Cora settles into her seat on the airplane. She fastens her seatbelt. The only empty seat on the flight is beside her. What luck, she can spread out a bit—but then a final passenger comes down the aisle. A tall passenger, fair hair slicked back. As he reaches up to stow his bag in the overhead locker she looks at the long legs in faded jeans, interestingly more faded and bulgy at the crotch. She looks down at the cowboy boots. He sits down beside her without a word. She opens her book and pretends to read.

As the airplane taxies down the runway, she swallows. She loves the moment of takeoff, when the power of it forces you back into your seat. And when that moment comes, without a word or a look, the man reaches out and runs his long-fingered hand up the inside of her thigh.

smack

ॐ

MARGUERITE COLSON

TIBET IS A GOLD-LEAFED, INCENSE HAZE OF SOFT, YIELDING flesh. It looks like a cliff-top monastery in Lhasa, the highest plateau in the world. This should be a story of brightness where the City of Sun exudes a light so blinding that the reflections from streets and buildings hurt the naked eye. Instead, this is a story about a room, three people, a betrayal and a hunger.

The room…

is tiny. Airless. No natural light. Balanced precariously on a chipped saucer in the center there is an aromatic candle, its flame fighting to penetrate the gloom.

The floor is covered in scratchy, worn rattan squares. There are patches where they do not quite meet and if you should accidentally stumble and shift one of the squares, your feet will be blackened with angry fleas. Beside the candle, there is a peeling, gold-leafed Buddha, about two feet high, its countenance eerily vivid in the shadowy darkness. Its eyes seem to guard a yellowed, fusty, moth-eaten mattress with feathers spilling from its sides.

When you breathe, there is only the odor of incense and ritual and urine filling your lungs with despair. When you speak there is only the muffled sound of your own voice where the world cannot hear, cannot see.

Three people...

sit cross-legged on the floor in the spartan room. I am a mousy nineteen year old with mountain-climbing legs and sun-weathered skin beyond my years. My dark, shoulder-length hair falls in unruly tangles, a protest against perms, river water and three months without a comb. I smile uncertainly as my eyes fixate on the candle flame, trying to escape the moment.

Ariadne sits with her knee touching mine. She is the willowy blonde of television commercials. She is twenty and gay and her long hair hangs in a neat ponytail. We have trekked together for months now because we were both hitching in the same direction one day. Was it China? Or was it India where we met? The foreign voices and hard bunks blur until there are no clear snapshots of our travels, just a vague sense that once there was a time when Ari and I were strangers.

Leaning over the candle is a wizened little man in turmeric-colored robes. The flames dance across his brown-stained leer as he smiles at us with anticipation. He holds a blackened spoon over the flame. An offering and a bribe. He nods at each of us, gestures toward the mattress. The Buddha stares.

Ari rises and stretches high, her impossibly long limbs out of proportion with the minuscule size of the room.

"Please do it," she begs.

Her movements seem calculated, yet there is an edginess beneath the facade. One side of her face twitches when she speaks. Her toes curl tightly when she reaches for her halter-top and removes it with a single, fluid motion.

The old man licks his lips as her breasts spill free, revealing no demarcation line with the rest of her skin. The beaches in Bali have left their golden kiss. With practiced precision, Ari drums her nipples with the tips of her fingers till they extend forth in ruby glory. I look at the floor. Sway uncertainly. I have seen Ari naked. We have shared double bunks. If my flesh had needed hers, my interest would have been piqued by now.

I am sitting in a spartan room with an old, deprived man

and a girl I do not even particularly like. Our paths simply crossed because we were traveling the same way. Now, my soul is for sale.

Ari reaches behind her head, releasing her hair so that it tumbles down and frames her face with an angelic halo. Her hands play up and down her thighs, sliding under the crotch of her shorts. She reaches out, touches my hand. I am repelled by the gentleness of the contact. She clasps my hand tightly, pulls me upright. I stare over her shoulder at a wall I cannot see.

"Please?" she asks again.

She has curled my fingers over the top stud of her shorts. Mechanically, without looking, I unclasp the three studs. She expertly tucks my hands into the waistband and helps me lower her shorts to the floor.

My arm accidentally brushes against her most private patch of hair. My stomach lurches with revulsion. I close my eyes and seek a space where there is laughter and wine and cock. A space that existed before the candle, the Buddha, this windowless milieu.

The betrayal…

happened when we first arrived at the Rooftop of the World. We had stayed in a cheap hostel that had no particular features to distinguish it from any other place we had slept. The aroma of steaming noodles from the street vendor outside wafted through the window. Clamor of traffic and rattle from the ancient ceiling fan made conversation impossible. I welcomed the excuse. My head hummed from the thinness of air and the garish sun.

I had brought him in from the Lhasa night, an off-duty Chinese soldier. Ari had been blessedly absent, wandering the alleys in search of her own respite. He had been standing beside me at an open-air Langma opera, both of us failing to understand the progression of dances, accompanied by high-pitched songs in a language curious to our ears. Both of us strangers in a land suspicious of outsiders. In a day, a week, a month, I would be able to leave and become a stranger elsewhere. He might never go home.

Baoer's champagne skin had the perfect sheen of velvet in the room's harsh, unmuted light. Strong, uncompromising military face. His stilted English made the word *fuck* sound romantic. I tried to melt into him but he held me at arm's length. His white slut. His toy. In his own sweet time.

He held the warm bottle of cheap rice wine to his lips, then to mine. Sweet and acrid, slow burn to the stomach. I had thrown my head back and laughed because of the heady scent of man and the relief from Ari's heavy presence. In my delirium, I stripped and stood brazenly splayed before him. When the bottle was finished, Baoer revealed himself to me, the fine cut of his flesh as carefully crafted as his uniform. Slick, almost hairless body. I had reached for his stomach, felt its iron firmness with my hands before he stepped forward and pressed it against my own more pliant form.

His cock was like no other I had held in my mouth. One shade paler than his skin, its length leapt forth, a separate being. The glistening orb that first touched my lips tasted like barley. I swallowed its pulsating length, grateful my throat was numbed by the rice wine. His wiry pubic patch scratched at my face.

On the thin sheets stamped in indelible ink with the logo of the hostel, I buckled and reared under him as he ran his cock up and down the length of my slit, refusing to push into me. I had wondered about the hundreds of other girls who had lain on this very bunk with unknown men who would disappear into a mysterious dawn. I wondered if they felt the guilt of having betrayed the Tibetan people for mere carnal pleasure. In the end, desire has no politics. A man is just a man. Eventually, when my begging ceased, he slammed into my wetness. Sweat against sweat. Incongruous strains of the Rolling Stones scratched their way into the room. I had gnawed my way to a climax, altering my rhythm between the thumping beat of "Honky Tonk Woman" and the uneven rattle of the fan.

I awoke with a dull headache, my bottom stuck to the sheets in a stale cocktail of lust. The curse and pleasure of the traveler. Intimate sharing of sights, sounds and bodies that last no longer than the train, the bus, the plane to the next city. On the bunk opposite, Ari snored softly in contented stupor.

When I open my eyes, I am still in an airless room with Ari and the old man. My cheesecloth dress lies puddled on the ground. I am standing nipple-to-nipple, hip-to-hip, in a statue freeze-frame with another woman.

The fingers that had drummed her own breasts now caress mine. A goose-bump chill weakens my senses. It is a soothing, worshipping exploration such as I might exact upon myself.

"He wants you to touch as well."

I glance at the man. He is solemn and expectant, still heating the spoon. His robes have been parted to reveal a thin, elongated cock. It seems to lack rigidity. I squirm at the thought of its semi-flaccid length worming its way into my pussy. I say a silent prayer to the Buddha icon that I might be spared this duty. It continues to stare with hollow resolve.

My trembling hands move with sudden determination, encompassing each of Ari's breasts in a desperate clasp. To my surprise, they bounce back, springy and soft against my palms. Her flesh is warm like winter scones. I can feel the steady rhythm of her heart. I press harder, so hard that her breasts are squashed back into her chest, excess flesh squeezing out under her arms. I know it hurts. I look into her eyes. There is a need in them. A blank, bitter need that is separate from me, the man, the room. Her eyes watch the spoon.

Ari's lips embrace one of my nipples, suckling dutifully on my less than abundant offering. I follow suit, contorting my head to the side and pulling one of her heavy breasts upward. I sink my teeth into the pliant mound, shocked by the taste of blood that trickles onto my tongue. Ari registers no hint of pain. I cease to bite and content myself with sucking around the aureole, forming tiny red circles that will eventually ache and bruise.

In my whole life, I cannot remember ever being lifted. Not as a child. Not by a boyfriend. Ari lifts me like I am one of the feathers in the tattered mattress and lays me down on its lumpy softness. My temples throb. Height sickness. The musty room. The nearness of cunt.

With a dizzy intake of breath, I am aware of Ari's fingers in my hole. She has mounted me in a sixty-nine position and I do not want to be the recipient of a kiss from her pungent pussy lips. I have no choice. They grind against my mouth, which I stubbornly keep closed. To my horror, I feel a welcoming slickness that allows Ari's fingers to slide into my hole unabated.

My teeth hurt from the pressure of Ari's body against them and I relent with a small, experimental flick of my tongue. My nose, my mouth, are covered by Ari's pink, dripping slit. My tongue is confused, but not repulsed as it licks at random clefts and mysterious bumps. I reluctantly drink the acrid brine that weeps from her cunt.

I jump when I feel the first wet lash of tongue against my hardened bud. Most of me does not want this. A small part of me now craves to finish it.

This morning at the Jokhang Temple, I felt myself suffocating in the medieval chaos of humanity that juggled and worshipped and bartered around me in a maze of incense clouds. Each individual in the crowd performed with a sense of purpose, as though they understood their role in this intricate design. I wandered in twisted spirals, convinced that I was somehow outside this seething mass, visible only to myself, the only person who had no reason to be here. Outside this room, the devout pray, threadbare mats barely protecting their knees from the cracked cement. They pray for liberation. I search my mind for the same prayer, but my faith is hollow.

There is a chant inside my head. It resonates as though in a tomb, a prolonged reverberation that becomes louder as ten gongs, then twenty, then a hundred are struck in perfect unison. Then there is silence. Nothing. Nirvana.

The hunger…

shakes Ari's whole body as she climbs away from me and crawls toward the man. He has finished the ceremony, prepared the sacrifice.

Ari sits before him, tying the strap of her halter-top around her upper arm. I have seen it before. Glint of needle.

The man now takes his fading, snaky manhood into his bony hands and squeezes the head. A jet of cream squirts into the air just as silver liquid fades into Ari's vein.

In the morning, Ari has gone. Our paths are no longer the same. In the end, Nirvana is only the illusion of a spartan room and a glazed, fallen goddess rocking on her knees, paying homage to the Priest of Smack.

vin ordinaire

꙳

GABRIELLE COYOTE

WOMEN HAVE BEEN COMPARED TO MANY THINGS IN
the history of love. Great ships that sail the ocean are named for
women. How many times has a woman's face been compared to a
rose or the stars? Helen had a face that launched a thousand ships.
Juliet would be as beautiful as a rose by any other name.

But to me, it is men that are like wine.

There was Tommy, my boyfriend from the university who
was a sunny California white wine. A sweet Chablis bought in
a big green jug to be taken down to the beach and picnicked on.
Everyone had a drink of him.

Or Andre: definitely Champagne, light and full of sparkle and
very fun at a party, but nothing you could drink every day or even
face first thing in the morning without quite a lot of orange juice.

I met Joerg in Germany, in the great wine town of Ruedesheim
on the river Rhine. That gentle river runs through German wine
country like a silk ribbon through the velvet, vine-covered hills.

Joerg was just like a bottle of the pale Riesling they produce there, light and sweet on the tongue, but with a bitter aftertaste.

We met by arrangement in a café on the river and sat watching the crowds of tourists go by, busloads of Japanese and Americans aplenty. I was there with my camera and laptop computer, writing articles for a premier wine magazine. Joerg, the son of a famous winemaking family, brought me back to the family estate for wine tasting and picture taking.

After a few days we could be found making love outside in the barns and stables. Joerg took me on the slopes of the sunny vineyard hills, dipping his clever and hungry tongue deep into my flesh while I sucked on him, bringing forth his own salty nectar. But he would not take me in his bedroom on the feather mattress. No stain of our sin touched the family linens and he kept his liaison with me a secret.

At first, the clandestine nature of our passion thrilled me. How lovely it was to sneak out to the garage and meet Joerg in the black and silver Rolls Royce! He slid his hand up my bare leg, pushing aside my skirt, his manicured fingers probing me until they found the soft wetness of my mound. One hand cupped my heavy breast under my silk shirt and his ardor excited me so much that I was delighted when he ripped the shirt from me, ivory buttons scattering around the interior of the car like snowflakes.

His own clothes cast off on the floor of the car, he looked like an alabaster statue with his pale, almost hairless skin and perfect musculature. He buried his head between my legs on those calf-leather seats, until I was so wet that my legs trembled and I pleaded with him. He flipped me over and entered me from behind, piercing me with his long, thick cock. Grabbing my hips, he thrust and ground his way into me until we were both groaning and screaming. Just as I was on the edge, a little sports car drove into the large garage and Joerg put his hand on my mouth. He pumped me harder than ever and fingered my clit too, forcing a wracking orgasm from deep within me. I climaxed just as a tall, beautiful blonde woman stepped out of the sports car and walked a foot from where Joerg was fucking me in the Rolls. She had long hair tied up in a knot and a perfect white face.

As she passed us, Joerg bent over me, and bit the back of my neck, thrusting one last time deep inside me, climaxing so violently that the car shook and he cried out in spite of himself. I could smell her expensive perfume as she sailed past us. The blonde turned on the doorstep and listened for a second while Joerg and I lay panting and sweating, his cock still deep inside me. We lay quietly, however, and the stately woman left.

"Who was that?" I asked as he withdrew and gathered his clothes.

"That was my fiancée, Marta," he said with a chuckle in his voice.

"Your fiancée?" My heart sank into my stomach. She couldn't have been more different from me. I am American, rather short, not statuesque as she was. I have a small waist, heavy breasts and rather round hips and thighs. My brown hair flows down my back in frizzy waves that could never have been tamed into the tight blonde coif that Marta wore.

"Yes. It made me so hard that she was there! I almost wish she had seen us. That would have put some color and heat in her face. I was not expecting her until next week." He eyed me rather coldly. How could I have not noticed that hard, unforgiving line of his jaw and the submerged glint of cruelty and selfishness in his eyes?

"Can we do that again, Emily?" Joerg asked me, pointing to his cock, which had grown hard once more. "Perhaps she will come back and fetch her luggage...."

I declined this gallant offer and removed myself from the area of the Rhine. The Riesling left a bitter taste in my mouth.

My review: "A seductive wine on the first taste, but the high acid content prickles the tip of the tongue. Pale and a little colorless, this wine is quite mineral-like on the back of the tongue, with an oily texture. Lusciousness is trying to unfold on the finish but this wine never quite gets there. It was probably opened about three to five years too early, although there is no telling that even maturation will help it. Disappointing."

I thought of Richard. He was a nice tawny port, just like his beloved Cockburnes. Rich, sweet and buttery, but a little cloying on the tongue. Port goes so well with chocolate! And sometimes he was the best thing after a heavy meal. But too much of him went to my head and I always felt horrible the next day, as one does when overindulging.

Richard owned a wine shop in a swanky section of London

that specialized in port. I wandered into his shop one day, looking for a rare, vintage port as a gift for a friend. Richard and I hooked up in a pairing as natural as port and pears. We would eat in a nice restaurant and talk about heady and important things and then stroll along the Thames back to his flat. Richard had an endearing way of pushing my glasses back up on my nose. When I get excited about something they tend to slip down and I end up peering over the top of them.

"Darling Emily, you have no idea how sexy you are when your glasses fall down your nose. I adore your sexy librarian look, all that pent-up sexual energy smoldering just under your intelligent and proper exterior," Richard used to say.

Sex was always the same with him, he really enjoyed his routine. He very much enjoyed watching me take off my clothes and I would sometimes catch him peeping at me in the bathroom as I disrobed for my shower, the door opened a crack, and his hand on his shaft. He said once that the mere sight of a woman taking off her coat could send him into orbit.

With Richard, I would make a big deal of the disrobing while he lay there panting and then I would join him in bed. He liked to be on top, Richard did, but he was a sweet and attentive lover. He would always make me come first with his clever hands and his quick mouth before he would settle on top of me and thrust his short but very thick cock into me.

He was very set in his ways, but as I got to know him he revealed a kinky side that was rather unexpected. One night after we had had more than our usual amount of the tawny port, he very politely asked me if he could tie to me to the bedposts. It sounded delightful and exciting and I consented.

He gently wrapped my wrists in silk cords and tied them onto the bedposts. Then my ankles, each one, until I was spread-eagled on the bed, legs far apart, and my pussy, with its dark, thick bush was wide open. It was a different Richard that appeared then, a wild man. He growled and bit my breasts and nipples. He shoved his face down into my crotch, biting and teasing my lips with his tongue while his fingers probed the depths of me. He made me come three times with his mouth and fingers before he mounted me and fucked me good and hard, coming, for a change, within minutes of entering me.

After that night Richard added the bondage into the pattern. I would strip while he watched, and then he would tie me up and fuck me hard and fast. It was nice for a little while but he was not interested in any variation of the theme. I soon realized that port was too rich for my blood to have on a daily basis and we parted ways.

My review: "This port is blessed with a copper-red tawny hue. Fragrant, spiced aromas follow through on a nutty, silky-smooth palate with a lingering praline finish that is a bit cloying. Sweet and hedonistic up front, it lacks mellowness and depth and doesn't hold up over the long haul."

I was on vacation in Provence when I met Guy. He was a Canadian by birth, but had come back to France to live and work at the family's winery. They made a simple table wine, a rich, subtle yet very unpretentious *vin ordinaire*, that supreme beverage so beloved by the French. It was a happy little wine, deep and earthy tasting, rich and thick in the mouth, with fine length and intensity. Supple, though well-structured, which is exactly how Guy himself turned out to be.

I shall never forget the day he brought me down to the family cellars where the huge casks of wine stood in their wooden barrels. This was the family store of wine and would never be bottled.

"Most of our wine never does get bottled," he explained. I liked his brown hair flopping down over his forehead and the deep brown eyes that matched the color of his hair exactly. He had fair skin to go with the dark hair and he blushed easily, two spots of color appearing on his cheeks as I looked him over and smiled. He was as honest and unpretentious as the wine his family made.

"We sell it in small casks to the other families and restaurants around here. I think there are only a few hundred cases that go out in bottles each year and never to the shops. They are all bought already by people that have been buying here for years."

Guy filled a chunky ceramic jug from one of the caskets and we sat around an ancient wooden table, in the dark cellar, sipping the wine out of small ceramic cups. To me it tasted like mother's milk and I told him so.

I took his hand in mine and dipped one of his strong, straight fingers into my wine cup. Then I lifted his finger to my mouth and sucked the wine off it, flicking my tongue over the tip and then, sliding my mouth down, sucking hard. Guy gasped and looked at me wide-eyed. Deep inside his eyes, a flame kindled and warmed me.

We kissed for the first time across that table, the taste of that *vin ordinaire* still on our lips. It tasted even better from inside his mouth. The table was in the way and he pulled me across it until I was sitting in his lap. His hand cupped my breast inside my shirt. We went very slowly, gazing into each other's eyes as we explored. I liked his style. He was in no hurry and took plenty of time to appreciate every aspect of me, drinking deeply from my lips and tasting his way down my neck to my breasts.

My hands played on his chest. He wore a pendant on a leather thong around his neck. It was a silver silhouette of the god Pan playing a flute, grapevines in his hair. A nice reference to the pleasures of wine, I thought and I smiled as my finger traced it.

He lifted me onto the long table so that I was lying on my back, shirt open, breasts tumbling out of my sheer silk bra. Guy looked me over like a hungry wolf about to devour a lamb and slid my trousers and panties off my hips. His eyes lingered over my exposed bush and I could feel the pink and wet lips of my pussy unfolding, opening under his gaze like a flower turned toward the sun.

He traced his finger around the rim, lingering on my clitoris, and then bent down to taste it. His tongue licked my lips, circled around my clit and then dove deep into me. He drank me like I was a bottle of the rarest wine. My toes curled, my back arched, and I felt a hot, tight coiling in my pelvis. He settled into sucking on my clit, lovely long, slurpy sucks, and when two fingers stole into me, I came around his finger like I was falling off a cliff.

He lifted his face from me and, looking me deep in the eyes, said: "A deep, saturated red color. The perfume is exotic and amazingly intense jasmine, oriental spice, and black fruit aromas fill the air. Mind-bogglingly intense flavors, honeyed and opulent on the tongue. Otherworldly in its power and persistence. This is approachable now, yet will certainly become richer and more honeyed with age. Hmmmm… The best I have ever had." He licked my juice from his chin and grinned at me.

I stared at him dumbfounded. I had met my match.

Then he unzipped his jeans and let them fall to the floor. His cock sprang free and I reveled in it. It was long and straight, very thick at the base with a graceful curve upward and a nice purple head. I fell in love with it on first sight.

Guy groaned as I fondled it with my soft hands. I bent over and licked the top of it, tasting him. He was rich and musky-scented and I loved the salty taste as a small drop of fluid eased out of him. I licked him all over, my fingers exploring his sack. I wanted to see how much of him I could get into my mouth, and he groaned again as I took him almost all the way in.

Then he withdrew and, parting my legs as I sat there on the table, guided his cock to my pussy and slowly thrust his way in. I grabbed his ass as he stood between my legs and pulled him in as deep as I could. I could feel my pussy lips stretch around the base of him and shivers ran up my back as he slowly pulled all the way out. I cried out as he left me, wanting more, and he thrust back in. The feeling of his silky head entering me thrilled me to the core and I felt another orgasm building in me. I wanted it hard and fast now.

Guy read my mind, for he slammed into me as hard and fast as he could until I was biting his shoulder and he was growling into my hair. I came again, from somewhere very deep inside me. I felt him tighten everywhere as he climaxed.

We held each other, panting and trembling on the table, and I knew that I had found my man. And so it proved to be. Guy was richly textured and complex enough to satisfy me every day. He was real, down to earth and immensely satisfying. I settled down happily in Provence and was easily incorporated into the family fold.

My review: "This is the perfect *vin ordinaire*. Long spiced finish. Rich, extravagantly textured mouthfeel. Extraordinarily aromatic and complex. Ripe and full on the palate marked by sweetness but balanced by vibrant acids. Intense finish. Amazingly complete and already drinking beautifully, this one has the structure to age magnificently. A truly glorious find."

Heartburn

༄

DIANE LEBOW

ONE AUTUMN IN A RESTAURANT BESIDE THE HARBOR in off-season St. Tropez, I sat eating mussels from a large silver bucket. Two tables away a handsomely dignified man similarly was sucking the soft bodies from their shells into his mouth. We observed each other licking butter and garlic from our fingers. Blond, silver-streaked hair hung oddly, somehow too evenly, across his forehead. He and the waiter joked back and forth; apparently he was a regular patron. When he smiled, there was just something lurking underneath: the hint of a sneer, perhaps?

Beside my dinner plate was Colette's *La Naissance du Jour* (*Break of Day*), my dinner companion. I had just attended an international conference on her here in St. Tropez where this particular book was written and set. Colette intended this work to be her farewell to romantic love but her intention only lasted for a few weeks, or about thirty pages into the book, when she begins a passionate affair with a young man. I was trying to solve Colette's riddle myself: the balancing act between freedom and romantic love, peace of mind and the insistent sexual urges of a middle-aged woman. In fact, my six-month sabbatical from teaching in Paris was giving me freedom to wander and think about these questions — and perhaps test out my theories.

At the end of my meal, the waiter approached me. "Monsieur wishes to offer you a cognac." I nodded. A large crystal goblet of warmed amber liquid was placed before me. When I raised my glass in acknowledgement to the man sitting at the neighboring table, his blue eyes seemed to spark like a struck flint. His glance shifted almost imperceptibly to my hands, which cupped the snifter. Then he looked back at my eyes with the slightest hint of amusement. My face heated as I realized that my hands cradled the glass as I might a man's delicacies.

"Madame, would it be too presumptuous on my part if I were to ask to join you at your table?"

Our conversation flowed along easily, aided by the comfortable setting, lovely meal, cognac, and something more. *La séduction,* as the French would say, not referring simply to a direct and perhaps crude sensual drive. No, something quite different. *La séduction,* a central lubricant of life: the tantalizing impossibility of ever quite comprehending the otherness of the man, of the woman: the mysterious and joyful interplay of male and female. The effort to mesh, to join, to enter each other, to fuse, seems also a metaphor for the destined final futility of getting inside the other's skin. Enter as we will through as many of the body's apertures as possible, still we remain — solidly alone.

I learned my companion had lived in St. Tropez much of his life, was a senior pilot with UTA, the French commercial airline, and had two yachts. Sailing was one of his passions and he would be hosting the judges for the Festival of the Tall Masts, an international gathering of antique sailing vessels from around the world that would begin within a few days. "Perhaps you would like to watch the competition from my yacht. All the judges will be sailing with me."

I found myself staring at his thumb. There are many ways of sizing up the measure of a man. For me, the thumb never fails. I had to remind myself to exhale. His thumb was broad, moderately long, but its breadth and overwhelming sturdiness and girth was — breathtaking.

"It is still quite early. If you have no pressing plans, I could show you around the harbor. We could stroll over to my yacht."

Fifteen minutes later I found myself on Jacques's yacht, listening to him rattle off the technical details: it was an Espace 1000 and so on. I really wasn't interested, although its name intrigued me: *La Hurlette.* I wasn't certain but I thought it translated as "The Howler." The soft dark navy-blue velvet of the cushioned cabin and the lapping Mediterranean outside eased the tightness in my shoulders. The slight night breeze off the water caused a chill to tide over my skin, contrasting to the warmth that was flowing down my spine, down to my thighs, increasing the tingling and throbbing between my legs. With a sweep of his hand, Jacques offered me a seat on one of the couches. He sat across the cabin from me. He spoke in a serious, calm tone, so that I expected more details about the upcoming sailing competition, more tales of his piloting days, his complaints about air-traffic politics and unions, perhaps something about his condo by the sea.

Instead he looked firmly and directly at me: "I would like to kiss you all over your entire body, lick between your toes, behind your ears—no, not yet there. First I will tease you, massage your thighs with my hands. Do you like a bit of strong pressure? I think you do. Finally my tongue will visit your sex, will delicately—oh, so delicately taste its way between your legs. No, I don't want you to open up too soon, not too soon. My tongue, my lips will find your soft folds, your 'chat,' your delicacies. You will help me to know what is best and better for you with your moanings, your cries, soft at first and then… Well, we shall see, won't we?"

I found it increasingly difficult to sit upright on the yacht's soft cushions, opposite him. His face and body were a bit larger and bulkier than would normally interest me. But already he had moved inside me even from that distance with only his voice, and I was wondering how his cock would look, smell, taste. I wanted to see the first drops of his lubricant seep out. Always that bit of pungent fluid seemed like magic to me when it appeared. First the penis was dry, almost like a lab study. Then almost between the blinks of an eye, it became enlarged, engorged, ruddy. Then the magical little drops. Some men didn't produce any of this lubricant. But it seemed to me the best ones did. I was anxious, impatient to know if he would. How would he respond to my tongue, my touch? Still we were both fully clothed and watching each other from a distance.

"Shall I undress you now? Are you ready for me to kiss you everywhere? I mean really everywhere. In places you perhaps have not been caressed before. Will you be ready for that?"

He moved closer to me, helped me to my feet — felt my nipples, which were already very hard and erect, through my thin summer blouse. He unbuttoned the top buttons. Then he slowly leaned over and took first one nipple then the other between his lips. Alternately he licked, sucked. Suddenly he bit hard for a small second. My legs parted. He slid one thigh up between my own legs — firmly, deliciously. I wanted only to open up and have him pleasure me. I wanted to taste him. Quickly now he pulled off my clothes; somehow while my eyes were closed for a moment he became naked. He was a tall man, athletically built. The slightest hint of thickening girth bespoke years of sensual pleasure at the table. The firmness of his torso and thighs affirmed sensuality of a different nature: his was a well-used, well-toned body.

Then we were in the king-sized bed in the master cabin with its navy-blue sheets. The lapping water and the soft breeze of the *Midi* tickled my heated body. The cool sheets further aroused my warm swollen genitals when I first sat on the bed. I wanted to look to see if my wetness had left circles on the navy sheets. But he slipped his hands over my mound, and with his tongue and fingers opened my lips, found my clitoris and began circling it. He alternated circling with sucking. Then he slipped his body around and let my lips find his engorged cock. It was what the French call *grosse*. The intended meaning always seemed to me to be "thick" rather than large. Somehow the word *grosse* excited me itself. To pronounce it correctly one's mouth has to move in three small syllables. The impetus of the word has to begin deep in your throat. Just saying "grow" makes me feel like I am preparing my throat to open up, to absorb one of the thickest cocks imaginable. So his was. Not too long. Length is not what women want. It is the breadth that parts our nether mouths, as Chaucer would say. Normally I am not able to reach orgasm in the traditional missionary pose: missionary so inappropriate. It is unlikely any missionaries enjoyed an experience like this one. When this thick *grosse* cock began its penetration I knew that coming with this man inside me would be effortless, spectacular.

As he entered me, I entered him. Our waves moved in and out of each other. I floated into the zone that is at once no thought and pure focus, that is beyond thought and focus. As I was on the edge of coming, he pulled out of me, lifted me backward so that my head was just hanging off the edge of the bed. Now he dived into me with his flickering tongue, his swollen wet lips, penetrating and pressing open both my vagina and anus—while at the same time, sucking and caressing my clitoris and labia.

"*Non, non,* not yet," he intoned.

He then turned me over. I climbed up on a mound of velvet cushions, green and blue and orange. His fully engorged penis thrust deeply and profoundly up into me, into my G-spot. H-spot. Who knows? I was feeling sensations I'd never enjoyed before. He stroked me with his words, which flowed over me continually. "*Elle est grosse, ma bite. N'est-ce pas? Tu es mouillée, totalement mouillée. Tu vas jouir, oui?*"

The French words for wet and for orgasm are onomatopoetic. "Wet," *mouillée,* requires a pursing of the lips and then a release like a water slide: *yaaay.* "I'm coming," *je jouis,* a different type of contraction, not unlike the full pelvic and body wave and contraction. "Je," "joo," plus "Oui." Like a gigantic affirmation: "OUI."

During the next week or so, I stayed at Jacques's house, sailing whenever I chose with him and the officials of the competition during the day. However, as absorbed and dedicated a lover as he was, in everyday matters in public he was like a ship in dry dock, dry, abrupt, even rude. During the Festival of the Tall Masts, especially when the judges were present, he almost ignored me. "No suntan lotion on my yacht. Shoes off before you get on deck." Of course he was equally abrupt with everyone. Although from time to time, when the elderly aristocratic French judges were on deck, we would sometimes stop below where he would slip his fingers and cock into me or lick me until I was writhing and moaning once again.

At his house, when we were not making love, he seemed to forget I was there. Every morning at 6 a.m. nautical reports burst out of his clock radio. He rushed out, leaving me on my own without a word about if and when we would meet again.

One night saddened by his coldness, I checked back into my

hotel. I lay there and talked into my tape recorder. My woman's body and soul had been penetrated fully by this man. Yet he never offered romantic love. Here was total freedom and passion and pleasure. I drove up to Colette's house. For a while I sat outside her yellow home and looked down at the bay. On the porch, a young woman was engrossed in her writing. Wandering the old gardens, which are open to visitors, I felt my calm and peacefulness return.

Each day now the restaurants were closing for the winter. The nights were chill; leaves were blowing in yellow and orange clouds on the *pétanque* ground in the square in front of my hotel. One night I went for dinner at the restaurant where I had met Jacques. The waiter told me this was their last night of the season.

The following morning I packed and put my bags in the trunk of my Renault. I opened the sunroof to better enjoy the autumn sun and blue sky. Checking my map, I picked out the route that would take me along the *calanche* to Antibes and later Menton. For a moment I looked in the rearview mirror, back at the reflection of the landscape where I had been. Then I put the car into gear and enjoyed negotiating the curves overlooking the luscious Mediterranean. I punched the record button on my tape recorder that I often used to entertain myself while traveling and began to tell the story of my time that autumn.

Some months later, on a plane back to the States, I sneaked a glance at the magazine article the elderly couple beside me was reading together. "Are You Afraid of Heartburn?" was the lead article in a retirement journal.

"No," I thought, "not anymore."

watching mammals

><

ROGER HART

THE PARKING LOT WAS CRAMPED, CARS, VANS AND SPORTS utility vehicles crowded together so tightly that Carl had to move the Accord back and forth several times before he had it squeezed into the parking space. "They don't give you enough room," he said. He worried about someone parking too close, opening a door and nicking the white paint. It also worried him that the Outer Banks had a reputation. Lori and Rick Andersen, two of the teachers from school, had lived in Duck for a year. "Skin and sex," they'd said laughing. Carl didn't like coming to that kind of place or that Lori and Rick were going to be here, too. This was the second marriage for each of them. He and Sylvia were different.

Sylvia smiled, patting his knee. "I can't wait to get to the beach," she said. She'd been looking forward to spring vacation for three months, telling him they'd have a good time and hinting that they might want to move here in a few years when he retired. "There's something about the South," she said.

Yes, he thought, *bugs, snakes, fireworks, pavement so hot it can blister your feet.* Carl had spent several months at Fort Jackson, South Carolina, and Fort Gordon, Georgia, in the late sixties. He'd been called a damn Yankee by drill sergeants — *You from Ohio, boy? Only steers and queers from Ohio* — and almost got bitten by a copperhead. He'd watched cockroaches the size of pocketknives march across the barracks floor, and eaten enough grits and red dirt to last a lifetime.

But Ohio winters are long, dark and cold. Gloves, boots, hats, heavy coats. People bend like tree limbs under the weight of a heavy snow. Legs and arms go chalky white. Teachers and students who can get away in the spring migrate south where the sun gets the juices flowing and tans the skin. Carl thought a quiet place inland might be better. He'd heard good things about Hickory, North Carolina, but Sylvia wanted to see dolphins.

She'd spent the winter reading about them and watching PBS tapes. Courtney, their only child, had sent her mother articles and pictures that she'd found in the university library. Sylvia had taped one of the pictures — a dusky dolphin leaping out of the water — on the refrigerator. It seemed to Carl that every time she opened the door, she'd say, "Look how sleek they are." On Saturday mornings while Carl drank coffee and stared out at the leafless pear trees in their backyard, she'd tell him when and how dolphins mated, the speed they could swim, the way they communicated.

"Think we'll see one?" she asked.

Carl looked across the parking lot, beyond the pink and white azalea bushes and the Beach Club restaurant to the thin slice of ocean visible between two houses on stilts. It bothered him that some of the teachers at school might think he and Sylvia had planned to vacation with the Andersens. Their coming to the same place was a coincidence. He looked around the parking lot one more time and didn't see their car, which made him feel a little better. Perhaps they'd changed their mind. "Maybe," he said.

Sylvia handed him the key and asked if he would check out the room while she walked across the street to the ocean. It would have been easier to wait until she saw the ocean, then go up to the room together. He'd read that you could get blood clots from sitting too long, and he didn't like making extra trips, not after driving eight hundred miles. He waited for a second, hoping Sylvia would change her mind, but she was already halfway across the parking lot and heading toward the water.

He climbed the steps to the Sun Suites and shuffled along the open corridor. The railing was low and looked flimsy. It would have been easy to fall over and splatter like a fat southern bug. A quick knife-like pain shot up his leg, maybe a clot.

He pushed the key into the lock, turned the knob and opened the door.

The room was dark but he saw her immediately: there on the unmade bed, talking on the phone was a nearly nude woman. A girl, really. Maybe twenty. She was wearing lime-green bikini panties and the phone cord fell across her bare breasts.

Carl pushed his glasses up his nose and stared. He was surprised, shocked, and a little frightened. There was an odd odor in the room, and it was so strange—a nearly nude woman on the bed—that drugs seemed to be the only explanation. He felt a flash of anger and wondered if it was too late to turn in their key and get the deposit back. He looked at the girl again. She didn't look crazy or glassy-eyed and her skin was, as nearly as he could tell, free of needle marks. She was talking with someone, but he couldn't concentrate on what she was saying because of all that bare skin.

She didn't scream. She didn't even act surprised. He took another small step into the room, then stopped. She continued talking on the phone, although now that he'd moved closer, she looked a little alarmed; or not alarmed so much as maybe embarrassed, perhaps suddenly aware of her near nudity. But still, she didn't scream or drop the phone or hide behind a blanket. Later, he would think of how she should have kept her hand on the bed, how touching herself, spreading her fingers, her red fingernails over those small but perfect breasts, made her look even more sensuous.

Bare legs. No tan lines. The bottoms of her feet pink and soft. He'd never seen so much pretty skin. She was young, almost as young as the seniors he lectured in his office: the smokers, those who cut class and the girls with the obscenely short skirts.

He wanted to walk across the room, sit on the edge of the bed and ask what she was doing in his room.

"Someone's here," she said into the phone.

Carl held up his key. He wasn't a troublemaker. He was

waiting for her to stop talking, so he could explain there had been some mistake and she would have to find her own room. He wanted to make it clear that this was her fault or maybe the fault of the registration center.

He glanced at the key.

Nothing made sense, the number on the key, how he had opened the door, why she wouldn't stop talking on the phone to scream or tell him to get out. Hadn't Sylvia said 217? "Sorry," he said.

The girl leaned back against the headboard and pressed the phone to her ear. He hesitated, expecting her to say something. He looked at her legs, her knees pulled up in an effort to hide her breasts. Her feet were small; tissue paper was stuffed between her toes. Her nails were bright red and wet: the odor in the room was nail polish.

He nodded, hesitated, backed out, carefully closed the door behind him, then hurried along the corridor, found 214, tried the key and quickly went inside. He wondered if he had done anything wrong, if he could get in trouble. What if she reported him? And why had she stared at him that way? Did she think he was going to touch her? He tried to remember her face, her expression, but he could only recall smooth legs, bare breasts and the lime-green underwear. After a couple of minutes, he checked the peephole and then, not seeing anyone, left the room and walked to the far end of the building, so he wouldn't have to pass her room.

• • •

"The bugs," Sylvia said, scratching her ankles while trying to pull a suitcase out of the trunk.

"There was a woman," he said, "a naked woman." He listened for police sirens.

"What?" she asked.

"A girl."

Sylvia scratched at her ankle. "Is the room okay? And the television? Is it big enough for you to see the basketball games?"

He didn't remember seeing a television. "Fine," he said, thinking surely there had been one. He picked up the larger suitcase. "She was wearing underwear, bikini bottoms, green ones. No bra though. Nothing else."

Sylvia reached for the other bag, stopped again to scratch. "What are you talking about?" she asked.

"You gave me the wrong room number," he said. "A naked woman on the bed." He checked the parking lot to make sure no one could hear. "Almost naked anyway," he whispered. He slapped at something biting his neck.

Sylvia slammed the trunk and looked one more time in the direction of the ocean. "Let's hurry," she said.

In the room Carl changed his shirt, hoping it might make him more difficult to recognize. "She was doing her nails," he said.

Sylvia pulled back the curtains on the windows. "You can glimpse a corner of the ocean from here." She pressed her head against the glass, and then said, "What? What? I'm not following you."

Carl pointed down the hall. "I walked into the wrong room." The room smelled of insect repellent and saltwater.

Sylvia pulled a pair of sandals out of a bag. "Bet she was embarrassed." She dug through several other bags until she found a can of insect repellent, then sprayed her legs. "Let's go."

Carl was no longer hungry and a walk on the beach sounded good, although he worried about being seen. "I don't think so," he said.

"What? You don't want to go to the beach?"

"No, I mean yes. I mean I don't think she was embarrassed."

• • •

The beach was littered with jellyfish. Two young boys were walking along popping them with a piece of driftwood. Carl didn't think it was a good idea. "Boys," he said just as the older one raised his arm to whack another jellyfish. He'd been a teacher for ten years, a principal for twenty. Telling kids to behave had become a habit. He should have said something to the girl, told her to be more careful about locking her door. Such pretty skin. He tried to think about something else but couldn't. Nothing like this had ever happened to him.

The boys shrugged and ran off down the beach.

Half the teachers in his school were divorced, many had affairs. And this past fall Charlene Nelson, a junior forward on the basketball team, went to his assistant's office and put her foot on the chair and told him to feel the bruise on her thigh. She had beautiful legs and a skirt so short he should have cited her for violating 3G of the dress code. She grabbed his hand and said, "Here, feel it?"

When he told Carl he had laughed but he never said whether or not he had felt her leg, squeezed the muscles as if looking for the bruise, and Carl was afraid to ask.

Nothing like that had ever happened to Carl. He thought temptation found those who were susceptible to it. That was why he had always been spared.

Sylvia stared out at the waves. "They like to play close to shore," she said. "They're very friendly."

He was glad the Andersens had not yet arrived. He wondered what they would say if they heard he'd walked into the wrong room and seen a nude woman. They'd tease, that's for sure, but he didn't want anyone thinking it was his fault. "I don't know about them being friendly," he said. "Maybe the ones at Sea World."

"If I see one, I'm going to jump in and swim with it," she said.

They walked closer to the water and let the waves break over their feet.

"Too cold," he said, although a few teenagers and college-age kids in black wetsuits were splashing on surfboards thirty yards from shore.

. . .

That night, while he sat in front of the television waiting for the North Carolina-Charleston basketball game to begin, he watched Sylvia's reflection in the wall mirror. She was pulling a pink nightgown over her head. She'd mentioned while packing that she bought something for the trip and thought they might have some fun while they were away. Carl figured it was part of the plan to get him to like the South.

"Too many distractions at home," she said from the bedroom as if reading his thoughts.

Carl wasn't sure what the distractions were now that Courtney was off at school. He thought about the girl in 217, who at that very moment might be wearing nothing but the briefest of pajamas, maybe nothing at all.

Sylvia walked into the room and stepped in front of the television. Flickering images showed through the gown. "What do you think?" she asked. The gown stopped at her knees. Carl thought Sylvia had good legs even if she was fifty-three, but he couldn't concentrate on them now.

"Nice," he said. "Very nice." Carl stared at the hazy image of a man's face between her legs.

"It'll look better when I get a tan." She brushed the bottom edge of the nightgown with her hand.

He wondered how it would have been to press his fingertips against the girl's hip, feel her muscles and skin move beneath her thin cotton panties. He imagined sitting on the edge of her bed, his face inches from her breasts. He dropped the newspaper on his lap, made an apologetic face. "I'm tired," he said.

As Sylvia stretched her hands toward the ceiling her gown slid up her thighs. "It was a long drive," she said. She paused in front of the television. "Maybe in the morning."

"In the morning," Carl said.

• • •

But at dawn he quickly dressed and stepped outside. A few cumulus clouds drifted toward the ocean. Lori and Rick's car was in the parking lot next to theirs. He walked down the corridor and paused in front of 217. The curtains were drawn and it was quiet inside, no shower going, no sound from the television. He wondered if she'd left the door unlocked again. A mockingbird sang from a palmetto tree.

Most men looked for opportunities to see an almost nude girl, but he wasn't like most men. Perhaps the long, cold Ohio winter had made him more than unusually sensitive to the sight of exposed skin. Back home people were still wearing jackets and not even the senior girls had begun showing up in shorts skirts. Seeing her had caught him off guard, that's all, so much beautiful skin. He stood at the railing hoping she might come to the door or step outside, but when she did not, he returned to the room.

Sylvia was on the phone. "Here's your father," she said, passing him the phone.

Carl asked Courtney if she was OK and if she was studying. When he hung up he felt mildly depressed. Sylvia was ready for the beach. "You coming?" she asked.

• • •

The water was calm and Sylvia stopped from time to time to scan the surface and tell Carl about dolphins. "Females initiate courtship," she said.

Carl wondered if Sylvia was hinting at his promise of the previous night. He wasn't a robot, though. He'd been tired. He'd done most of the driving. Still, he was glad they hadn't done anything. He had been experiencing strong desires, which almost felt new to him, and he wanted to hold onto them a little longer. When a cool breeze began blowing off the ocean, they returned to the Sun Suites and sat at the edge of the pool where it was warmer.

Sylvia read her book on marine mammals. Carl held the latest issue of *Sports Illustrated* and tried to read an article on the golf tournament at Augusta, but each time the gate to the pool clicked open, he looked up and studied the newcomers. The last girl to enter had long legs and walked in that funny way girls do when barefoot on hot pavement. Carl watched as she dipped her toes in the pool, then tossed her towel on a chair. Her face was hidden by a large hat and dark sunglasses, but she wore a black bikini and he could tell she was the one. She sat on a chair and rubbed lotion over her stomach, legs, and arms until her oiled skin reflected the sunlight like a mirror.

Sylvia began telling Carl a story about dolphins saving a couple, how the dolphins jumped and sliced in front of their sailboat.

"That's her," he whispered.

Sylvia looked over the top of her sunglasses, and he immediately regretted saying anything. "Who?"

"The girl," Carl whispered, holding the magazine close to hide his face.

Sylvia glanced around the pool. "What?"

He sighed, leaned over the edge of his chair. "The girl, the woman on the bed."

Sylvia looked around the pool, then frowned as if he weren't making sense.

"You know," he said.

"Oh, yes. How embarrassing." She shook her head, studied the girl for a second. "She's no older than Courtney."

Carl wondered why she would say such a stupid thing.

Courtney was nineteen, this girl was twenty-one or -two. And what did one thing have to do with another? He watched the girl over the top of his magazine. She flexed her toes.

He tapped Sylvia on the arm. "I have to run up to the room," he said.

• • •

He found the binoculars in Sylvia's bag, popped off the lens caps, and peeked through a small gap between the curtains and the edge of the window. The binoculars brought the girl up so close he could see the tiny, almost invisible, pale green veins that ran along the tops of her feet. Slowly, he moved the binoculars up her legs, her thighs, her hips. So many forbidden hills and valleys. He wanted to run his hand over her legs, press his fingers and palms against her thighs and breasts. Wanting to touch her made him feel guilty but then he reminded himself that when he had been in her room, he had kept his distance. She opened her eyes and looked around as if she sensed she was being watched, and he backed away from the window.

When he looked again, she was rubbing more lotion on her stomach and shoulders, her fingers splayed, moving slowly over her skin. She leaned back, moved her legs slightly apart: *her thighs warm, almost hot.* Perhaps she would return to her room in the next couple of minutes for something to drink or more suntan oil. He could see it all happening:

At the very moment she passes he steps out of his room and walks with her along the corridor.

She smiles. Would you mind doing me a big favor? This is embarrassing, but I can't reach the middle of my back. Would you...?

He closes the door to her room, backs her toward the bed, takes the lotion and begins rubbing it on her shoulders.

I don't need lotion there, she says.

You need lotion everywhere. He slips the bikini strap off her shoulders.

She cocks one eyebrow. Everywhere?

He eases her back on the unmade bed and rubs the lotion on her feet, between her painted toes, her calves, her knees.

You're not rubbing it in, she says.

Later, he answers, and he squirts more lotion into the palm of his hand, enough lotion to do three or four bodies and he spreads it on her thighs, pushing her legs slightly apart as his hands go up and down the insides of her legs which are still hot from the sun. He reaches down and puts his thumbs on the inside of her bikini bottoms and slides them down. Don't want to get lotion on these do we?

She shakes her head as the bikini bottoms drop to the floor. And then he's kneeling between her legs, pushing her legs apart and then untying the straps to her bikini top. It falls aside and he sees her bare breasts again, just like the previous night only now he's going to touch them. He squirts lotion directly from the bottle onto her breasts, making little circles around the nipples, then bigger and bigger ones while she watches.

He smears the lotion across and around her breasts, both hands at once. Her face is flushed, and she reaches out and touches him, wraps her fingers around his penis. He's about to push inside her when she sits up and rolls him onto his back, then straddles his hips. She lowers herself a fraction of an inch, just enough so that he has begun to slip inside her, then she stops, suspends herself above him. He has both hands on her breasts and he wants to compliment her on them, tell her how beautiful they are, how firm, and he wants to plunge deep inside her but she's grinning and he can't say anything because he knows any second she's going to lower herself completely on him although he doesn't think he can stand it much longer....

As his own hand moved faster, there was a knock on the door.

At first he thought it was the girl, and he sat there holding himself, not sure what to do, but a man's voice said, "Hey, Carl. Come on out and play." Rick Andersen. Carl hid behind the curtain and waited until he left. *Damn,* he thought, *Rick's been here for ten minutes and he's already a nuisance.*

When Carl returned to the pool, someone had taken his chair, and he looked at Sylvia, wondering where he could sit. "You're beginning to turn pink," he said. The girl across the pool had rolled onto her stomach, her toes curled over the end of the lounge chair.

Sylvia pressed a thumb against her thigh. "You were gone a long time," she said.

He didn't like standing there where everyone could stare at him. A few college-age kids splashed in the pool, everyone else was stretched out on a chair or a blanket. Music he didn't recognize blared from a poolside CD player. He felt out of place and conspicuous.

"I saw the Andersens," she said.

Carl sat on the hard concrete next to her chair, pulled his knees up to his chest, and wished he had a better tan, more muscles.

• • •

That evening Sylvia and Carl met the Andersens down by the pool and went for a walk on the beach. Sylvia's arms were pink but she said they didn't hurt. She didn't think she would peel. Lori and Rick were red too. Rick was wearing a white t-shirt to show off the muscles in his arms and Lori was in a yellow sundress that the wind blew dangerously high on her bare legs. Carl was pleased he'd had the good sense not to get burned.

"They're out there," Sylvia said, staring over the water with the binoculars.

Rick had been saying that women who are menstruating shouldn't go in the ocean. "Sharks," he said.

A gust of wind caught Lori's dress. Carl saw yellow panties.

"Maybe the dolphins are asleep," he said. It was a stupid thing to say, but seeing Lori like that had caught him off guard.

"Only one-half their brain sleeps at a time," Sylvia said. She closed one eye and let her right arm drop to demonstrate.

Carl wasn't sure. How could you sleep with half your brain? And why wasn't Rick upset about his wife's dress flapping in the breeze? A gust of wind hit them and Carl quickly glanced sideways at Lori, then looked out at the water.

"Sharks can smell blood a mile away," Rick said. He stared at a group of young women sunning on bright blue beach towels.

"Rick!" Lori said. "Keep your eyes in your head."

Everyone laughed but Carl. He didn't think a married man should act like that.

"It reminds me of Pearl Harbor," Rick said. "All those ships lined up just…"

Sylvia and Lori laughed again but Carl pretended not to hear. He hoped Sylvia wouldn't mention the girl. Sylvia would exaggerate as she often did with the little episodes and events of their lives. *She was nude, not a stitch of clothes, and she asked Carl to sit next to her on the bed!*

Lori pointed at a small ship, barely visible, crawling across the horizon and they all stopped and speculated where it might be going. Rick said it was probably a navy ship out of Norfolk.

The warm sand felt good on Carl's bare feet but he worried about the jellyfish. More had washed ashore during the night, little blobs of blue with almost invisible tentacles that stretched for a foot or more from the body. A small wave slapped over his feet and ankles. Lori stopped to pick up a shell.

"Oh, oh. Look," Sylvia said, and then, "Never mind, it's just a pelican sitting on the water. It looked like a fin."

"Dolphins have been known to kill their young," Rick said. "They could be dangerous. I'd never go swimming with them."

"I don't believe that," Sylvia said. "They wouldn't hurt anyone. I've never heard of them hurting anyone."

Lori handed Rick the broken shell and he threw it into the ocean. "They're promiscuous too." Rick taught biology, and supposedly knew those things. Before he and Lori were married Carl heard a rumor about him sleeping with a former student. Carl didn't tolerate things like that at his school, but he never had proof.

"They use their beaks like clubs and then rip with their teeth." Sylvia stopped. "They wouldn't do that to humans."

"And they mate belly to belly." Rick said smiling, and wrapped his arm around Lori's waist. "Can you imagine—" Lori punched him in the arm before he could finish and the two of them giggled at what Carl figured was a private joke.

The clouds were building behind them, blocking the sun. Carl felt chilled. "Ready?" he asked, looking back in the direction of the Sun Suites.

"A little farther," they said.

• • •

That night Carl couldn't fall asleep. He spooned Sylvia, imagining she was the girl down the hall. Soon, his hard penis pressed against the groove in Sylvia's buttocks. He pressed harder, then pulled away, pushed down his boxer shorts. His penis sprang free. *The girl has her back to him but she knows what he has done. Yes, she says, then slides her own panties down. Go ahead.*

He wanted to pull Sylvia's pajama bottoms down to her knees but was afraid she would wake up and begin to ask questions. Carefully, he guided the head of his penis into the valley of her backside.

Go ahead, yes. She reaches back, lubricant magically appearing in the palm of her hand, and she grabs the tip of his penis. Her hand, so warm, so soft, her fingers rubbing the silky liquid up and down his shaft. Then she begins to press back against him.

Carl presses forward, pushing deeper into that valley. He can't remember ever being so aroused, so hard. He pulls back, then pushes again, slowly slipping inside her. She rocks her hips, and as he sinks deeper and deeper into her, she grabs his hand and clamps it to her breast and she's saying, Yes, Yes, Yes, and Carl feels the spasms coming from a long way off, from down in his knees and then his thighs and she says, Yes, again and he can't stop....

"Ouch! My sunburn," Sylvia said.

Carl released his grip on Sylvia's arm and rolled away. He waited for her to ask what he'd been doing or for her to comment about the wet spot on the back of her pajama bottoms. "Sorry," he said. "I forgot." He hesitated. "I was dreaming." He stared at the ceiling, at the parallelogram of light from the partially opened curtains. Most of the time after an orgasm he immediately lost interest in sex and fell asleep, but this time something was wrong. He felt guilty and fragmented, unsatisfied. He wanted the girl more than ever. Within a couple of minutes Sylvia was back asleep and breathing deeply. Carefully, so as not to disturb her, he slid out of bed, walked across the room, pulled on his shorts and a t-shirt, then slipped out the door and tiptoed down the corridor in his bare feet. It was after midnight and the rain had stopped.

Nearly a dozen people were standing in the parking lot talking, but the girl's room was in the shadow of the stairwell and made him almost invisible to anyone watching from below. Carl stood by her door and listened. A dim light, perhaps from the bathroom or from the television, came through the heavy curtains. She was probably in bed, her tanned legs warm on the cool sheets. *Oops! I keep getting the wrong room,* he'd say.

She'd hold her hand, those bright red fingernails against her breasts: *What makes you think it's the wrong room?*

A woman in the parking lot laughed. It sounded like Lori. Couples leaned against the cars, the tips of their cigarettes tracing red arcs as they flipped them into the sand. Carl rested his fingers lightly on the knob and squinted through the peephole. At first, he saw nothing, but then the distorted images began to sort themselves out. The room appeared upside-down and a light shined in one corner. He wanted her to whisper, tell him to come in. God, how he wanted to run his hands over her skin, to hold his body against hers, to explore all her hills and valleys. She was a college girl who wore black bikinis and lime-green panties and lounged on her bed half naked. She wouldn't say, "No," or "Watch my sunburn!" Carl figured she would like doing things he and Sylvia had never even tried.

He thought about some of those things, things they never discussed, and he felt his erection return. He leaned against the doorframe. Yes, he and the girl would even do it standing up, her hands high over her head while she looked him in the eye and grinned. *Come on in,* she'd say, and he would.

Slowly, he tried to turn the knob.

"Yes?" a soft voice called from inside. "Yes?"

Carl hesitated, then hurried back down the corridor to his room and closed the door. He imagined she had been thinking about him, the man who walked in and caught her on the bed. Perhaps she had been in bed waiting for him to return. She'd been thinking about the two of them together on the beach, riding one another, the surf slapping the sand and the waves going up and down, up and down, and the two of them rocking back and forth.

Carl kicked off his shorts, tossed his shirt on the floor and stepped into the shower. He ran the tips of his fingers up and down the length of his penis the way the girl would, playfully but firmly. He turned on the water and soaped his hands. He thought of her down in her room, naked on the bed, touching herself, and although they weren't together, in a way they were. His hands were slippery with soap and as they moved faster and faster he thought of all that pretty skin and what it might be like to be buried inside it as she arched her back and groaned and this time when the spasms came there was only the sound of the shower and the girl saying *yes, yes.*

• • •

He looked for her the next day at the pool and when he and Sylvia walked by the tennis courts. He looked for her when they waited for a table at the Brown Pelican with Rick and Lori and while eating barbecue at the Bad Wolf Café. He looked for her on the golf course, on the beach, in the parking lot, at the Bike Barn, at the Wright Brothers Memorial and at Surfside Treasures. He wondered if she'd gone home, and he worried that he might not recognize her fully dressed. Perhaps she'd been the girl with the deep voice he had heard talking about shrimp in the booth behind theirs at Awful Arthur's.

There were no dolphins either. "I know they're there," Sylvia said. It was their last morning and they were standing on the beach. Her sunburn had blistered and long, ghostly white strips of skin were peeling from her arms and legs.

Rick debated whether or not he should go for a swim. "After all," he said, "we're here and it'd be a shame to go home without getting wet. Want to go, Carl?" he asked.

Carl shook his head, stopped and grabbed a beach ball rolling along the sand. An old couple in sweatshirts and sweatpants walked by with a bucket full of shells. He looked up and down the beach for a black bikini. "Our last day," Sylvia said.

"Yes," he said.

A string of pelicans sailed over and Sylvia screamed. "There!"

At first Carl thought she was pointing at the birds and then he saw two dark fins moving parallel to the beach not more than thirty yards away. Sylvia jumped up and down, squeezed his hand, then grabbed the binoculars out of her bag.

Twice, they circled and came back. The fins disappeared beneath the surface, and Sylvia stepped closer to the water. She leaned forward with anticipation, waiting for them to reappear. Up and down the beach, people were pointing. And then Carl saw her not more than ten feet away. She was wearing the big hat, dark sunglasses and a white sweatshirt that said *GATORS*. He glanced down at her feet, her pretty small ankles, her painted toenails.

Sylvia nudged him with the binoculars. "Look," she said.

Before he could think about what he was doing, he kicked off his shoes and ran toward the ocean, high-stepping as far out into the waves as he could. When he could run no farther, he began to swim.

Someone shouted on the beach. Maybe it was Sylvia or Lori or the girl. He thought he heard his name. He was not a great swimmer but the waves were small and the current seemed to be helping him move away from shore. Within a few minutes he was in deep water. When he looked around he was surprised to see he was alone. No one else, not even the surfers had jumped in. He had the feeling that the dolphins were somewhere below, watching him. Perhaps they would surface close enough to touch. He swam a few strokes farther out into the ocean. When he stopped and looked back, the people on the beach were small and they were all waving.

He was sure the dolphins were friendly but his legs, dangling beneath him, felt vulnerable, almost as if they were no longer attached to him, and he tried to pull them up so that he was in a little ball. People on the beach continued to wave and yell. He felt like a hero and he waved back. A woman's voice, maybe the girl's, shouted something he couldn't understand. At first he thought she was cheering, then she shouted again. This time louder. "SHARKS!"

Bakewell, Revisited

჻

Mitzi Szereto

DERBYSHIRE. So many years since I was among the rolling green hills and sheep-dotted valleys, the stone walls lining the roads and crisscrossing the pastures. So many years since I walked the village streets of Bakewell. Ate a Bakewell Pudding. Licked the last jammy traces from my buttery fingers. Nostalgia is a powerful tool. It makes people return to their pasts.

To Bakewell. A place where you might expect to see Colin Firth decked out as Mr. Darcy alighting from a horse-drawn carriage. Where in the nineteenth century a cook at the Rutland Arms misunderstood instructions while making a strawberry jam tart, inventing the confection that put Bakewell on the map. The one that lured me back here on this first day of spring.

The last remnants of snow like cake icing in the shadows. A crisp cold day. A perfect Derbyshire day. The daffodils are enthusiastically in bloom thanks to global warming, despite the sudden cold snap that whipped through the region last week. England will soon have the same climate as the Mediterranean. Or so everyone keeps saying. Of course I'll be dead by then and won't need to worry about how much SPF is in the sun cream I bought at Boots.

Before heading down into the village, I take a drive along the winding road above Chatsworth House. A spectacular edifice. Surreal to think that people actually live there. Far below me the visitors' car park is already jammed full of shiny metal rectangles. Easter break. I offer a regal wave from my car window at the Duke and Duchess of Devonshire, who are nowhere to be seen. The sheep grazing on the hill seem to appreciate my greeting, making me wonder whether they might be the same sheep I saw there in my youth. Doubtful, considering all the culling that went on in the countryside.

I leave my vintage Mini Cooper in a pay-and-display lot in the center of Bakewell. It's too early to get a pint even by bibulous British standards, so I take a stroll along the bank of the River Wye, thinking about the past and those who inhabited it. A few pensioners loiter at the water's edge, tossing hunks of bread to the mallards and the swans, which stretch their elegant white necks to receive them. The rejected bits and pieces float sluggishly along the river's surface until finally sinking. Raucous laughter comes from the ducks and I turn to see who cracked the joke. Hell, maybe the joke's on me for being here. Even with the chill in the air the ice cream van is already ensconced at the edge of the park, waiting for the punters to line up. The tourists. The locals. The children just off school. *Award Winning Ice Cream* it says on the side. Award winning. How can there possibly be that many awards for ice cream in a small country that's always cold?

Bored watching bread being masticated by rubbery bills, I return to the village proper, passing by the shops with their local handicrafts and their racks of postcards outside on the sidewalk. Fifteen pence — a real bargain. I know exactly where I'm going; my taste buds have been telling me all week. The old parish church stands guard on the hill before me, its bell tolling the noon hour. I've been up there countless times. Not to worship, mind you, but to daydream in the watery light among generations of leaning headstones. Daydream of things that were never to be, as I ate the Marmite sandwiches my mum had made me although I was old enough to do it myself. I was old enough to do a lot of things by then, given the chance. But the one thing I most wanted to do I never did. Fear of rejection, I suppose. Of being laughed at.

I liked to walk up to the church via the steep roads lined with terraced cottages, each competing for attention with their hanging baskets and window boxes exploding with red and orange and purple. Sometimes *she* came with me. Sometimes. Then I'd bring along a Bakewell Pudding with the Marmite sandwiches, which we shared. She would lick her fingers afterward and once, as a lark, she even licked mine. Our special feast left her lips gleaming with butter and speckled with bits of eggy pastry flake. I wanted to lean forward and clean them away with my tongue. Only I didn't dare.

Monday. A dull day by village standards, but not in Bakewell. It's market day. I could buy a heifer if I wanted to, or a bunch of leeks. Neither tempts me. I'm more interested in my reveries of what might have been had I been more daring. Fantasy and drink go well together, so I nip into the first pub I see, the pub of my youth and the youth of so many generations who came before. Although the crowds haven't yet arrived to fill it with their clamor and their stink of cigarettes, I take a table over in the corner by the window, wanting to be left alone with my thoughts of the past. My thoughts of her.

Time passes quickly when you've got a warm pint in your grip. I order a second to draw things out. I don't want to leave, since I've only just got here. Not that there's that much to see, but I did drive all this way for my Holy Grail. Besides, my pay-and-display sticker is valid for another two hours. After I exhaust every memory I have as well as some that are more illusion than memory—of parted thighs and tiny gasps with my name imprinted on them—I am left with the conclusion that nothing much has changed in Bakewell, except me. But then, I'm not a part of Bakewell anymore.

With the approach of lunchtime, the pub gets busier. I glance up from the muddy depths of my stout and notice a woman standing at the bar while the publican pulls a pint for another customer. Her fingers drum the aged wood—the only indication that she might be impatient for the man to get on with it and serve her. She's dressed in typical country fare: brown corduroy jeans, beige Fair Isle sweater, earth-caked hiking boots. Probably one of those hale and hearty types on a walking excursion, although I see no evidence of the requisite rucksack and walking sticks. She shrugs her heavy brown coat from her shoulders and whips off her plaid scarf, which — surprise, surprise — has brown woven into it.

Wild waves of chestnut hair. Creamy skin. A rosy blush on the cheek turned toward me. I stop breathing.

It can't be. It can't.

But it is.

Drink in hand, she turns around, apparently searching for a suitable place to drop her over-garments and partake of her half-pint of what looks to be cider. A ray of sun from the window by my head catches on the contents of her glass, turning it to liquid gold. She spies me at my lone table and her eyes widen. "Um, aren't you — "

"Yes."

Without waiting for an invite, she settles into the chair adjacent to mine. The chair with the wooden seat made shiny by generations of pub-crawling bottoms is now being made shiny by hers. The thought causes a fluttering that begins in my abdomen and spreads lower and lower until I have to cross my legs within the confined space to quash it.

"You all right? It's been so long..." Mundane words, but nevertheless exciting. Her accent still has the north in it — that curious Derbyshire-Yorkshire crosshatching with the dropped *thes*, and the *sommat*s in place of the *somethings*. But then, she probably never left here.

I nod. I don't need to be reminded of how long it has been. The evidence shows in my face. My eyes. Not hers though. She's still beautiful. Still young. Even after two decades I can taste my desire for her. It's as strong as it was when we picnicked among the dead of Bakewell. I watch her lips move as she offers me small talk. I feel a dampening as they form the vowels and consonants that make up speech. A trickling in my armpits and groin, followed by a stirring. A pulsing. A staccato beating. "Do you still live here in Derbyshire?" I manage to ask.

"Never left," she says with a smack of her lips, which have the delicate tincture of Belgian strawberries. "Why leave heaven?"

Heaven. Yes, it might be to some. It never was to me though. Not as long as my desire for her remained frozen on my fingers and tongue. Frozen in my genitals.

She shakes her head and sighs. "Market day."

"Eh?"

"Suppose I shouldn't complain. Did fairly well in morning, considering."

"Considering?"

"Competition. Gets worse every year."

A two-foot expanse of weathered pine separates us. I want to kick the table away. To grab her up in my arms and have her right there on the gritty pub floor. To do all those things I've wanted to do since I was old enough to think them. Instead my right hand begins to close up the gap between us under the table, a thief in the night as it seeks out a corduroy-clad knee. Contact is made. A slight widening of eyes. An intake of breath. She dips her lips back into her cider, taking a long draw from the glass. I am imagining that she's taking a long draw from me.

The warmth of her knee scalds my fingers. My heart. "I heard you got married," I say, not wanting to talk about the market, but about her. About what she's been doing with her life since I last saw her.

"I did."

"And?"

"And nothing."

"What happened?"

"He paid more mind to footie than he did me."

I can't help but laugh. "Blokes!"

We grin at one another conspiratorially and her knee presses closer, killing me. Does she know?

"What's in bag?" she asks with one of those mischievous twinkles I remember from years past. She was very skilled at those mischievous twinkles, even when she was still running about in pigtails. Problem was, I never knew if they meant anything.

"Actually, it's a Bakewell Pudding."

She smiles with what I take to be a remembered fondness. After all, she liked them as much as I did. Maybe more. Her teeth are so white and perfect. She could have been a toothpaste model. A shining exponent among a nation of dingy gray. "Reliving your past?"

"Yes. I mean, no. There really isn't anything from the past I want to relive."

The smile turns to a frown. I can tell that my offhanded remark puzzles her.

The strong stout I'm drinking makes me reckless and my

fingertips trickle light as summer raindrops up her thigh. Does she notice? Yes, she notices. "Bad memories then?"

"No, not bad. Just not particularly memorable. Or not as memorable as I would have liked them to be."

"That's sad."

I want to tell her that my memories are all of her and how much I wanted her. Of all those times I dreamed of her silky skin beneath my fingertips, playing it like the strings of a harp. A melodious cascade of notes that reach a crescendo as I pluck the string of her womanhood. As I think this, my hand moves higher, toward the warmth held safely between her corduroy-encased thighs. Toward the humid place that haunted so many of my youthful nights and the nights leading to my middle years. She doesn't flinch from my touch. Surely she can feel it beneath those cast-iron jeans of hers?

"You mentioned the market. What exactly do you do?" I say, hoping to divert her attention from my meandering fingers. Just a little while longer let me touch you. Just a while longer. Let me feel the wetness through the corduroy. I know there's wetness. There must be.

"I run me nan's farm."

"*Farm?* Somehow I never envisioned you in the role of lady farmer."

"She died five years ago. No one else but me. It's not a bad life, really."

I find it. That sweet core of moisture. That hint of female desire. I press my fingertips to it, as if they can pass through the fabric and into her. I smell the butter from the Bakewell Pudding. It has soaked through the bag, forming a dark spot on the white paper. It probably matches the dark spot soaking the crotch of her jeans if only I could steal a peek beneath the table to see it. I would like to taste her with the rich butter of a Bakewell Pudding. Taste her with fingers glistening with it, glistening with her. A heady pudding, indeed.

"Any problems with foot and mouth?" I ask inanely.

"No. Keep mostly hens. For eggs. Free range. Also grow organic veg. I don't go in for this killing of animals for profit." Her words are coming quicker, as do her breaths.

"That's very admirable." I press my fingers harder into her. Her mouth opens like a pink flower bursting into bloom in time-lapsed photography. "So I take it you're a vegetarian?"

She nods. Her left eye has begun to twitch. As I stare at it, she reaches up and rubs at the corner with her knuckles.

They say you taste like what you eat. I've never tasted a vegetarian before. I would like to. "Do you eat any animal products at all? Like butter, for instance?"

"I'm not vegan, if that's what you mean."

Good. Then she won't mind my buttery fingers dipping inside her. But not without first rubbing her outside. Rubbing that slippery little node of flesh—that sentient string on a harp—that I know is getting stiffer with need for my touch, maybe for my tongue. "I hope you don't mind my asking, but can you actually make a living from a farm like this?"

"I get by."

Is that a gasp I hear? A slight catch in the voice? Her cheeks, already rosy with the brisk Derbyshire air, are now even rosier.

"Well, I envy you."

"Envy me? Why?"

"Because it's an honest way to live. True to the land. It beats climbing all over each other to see who can grab the most dosh."

"Suppose that's one way of looking at it."

My fingers begin to move in a circular motion in the place where I imagine her clitoris to be. I must have estimated correctly, because she catches her lower lip between her teeth, biting the strawberry color out of it. "Are you enjoying it?"

"What?" she says breathlessly.

"The farming life."

"Yes, yes. I enjoy it."

Now that I'm in the correct location, my fingers move faster, push harder. The legs of my chair scrape the floor as I urge myself sideways, closer to her. So close there's hardly any space separating us. Her booted right foot has hitched itself up onto the brace of her chair, which causes her legs to part. She is opening herself to me. I look down at her lap and see that she has undone the zip on her jeans. When did she manage to do that? She takes another sip of cider. Should I? Should I do it?

The locals have gone over to the darts board with their pints, thankfully moving farther away from our table. Not that their presences would have made much difference at this point. I am too far gone, as is she. I abruptly remove my hand from between her thighs and she deflates. "Would you like some Bakewell Pudding?" I dip my blessed right hand inside the butter-soaked bag to tear off a piece.

"N-no. No thank you."

"Are you sure? There's more than enough here for both of us."

"Thanks. No."

"Remember how we used to share it? That and my mum's Marmite sandwiches?"

She doesn't answer.

I eat what I have taken, enjoying the flavor of my youth. The slippery butter coats my fingers, but I don't lick them clean. Instead I plunge them down the unzipped front of her jeans. Down to the rich oleaginous pudding that awaits me there. She cries out from the shock and parts her legs even more, her head lolling backward into space, chestnut hair billowing behind her. Her clitoris is stiff and greedy, as I knew it would be. I purposely neglect it, running circles around it, torturing it, before taking that heart-stopping plunge. Her own butter drips onto my fingers, and I am able to easily fit three inside her.

I worry about that lower lip of hers. It has been absent of blood for too long from the biting of her teeth. Her perfect white teeth. "It's funny, but I'd forgotten how truly lovely it is here," I say.

"Where?"

"Bakewell. I shouldn't have stayed away for so long."

"Why did you then?"

"I guess I didn't think I had anything to come back to." My fingers slide back out of her melting butter and hone in where they are most needed. She mewls as I stroke her. As I fondle the upstanding bit of flesh that so identifies her as a woman—the woman I have long dreamed of having. Touching. Tasting. Why did I wait so many years to return to Bakewell? So many wasted years!

Her hips begin to gyrate on the seat of her chair as my strokes turn into more concentrated circular motions, which I intersperse with teasing little tweaks between thumb and forefinger. She likes those; I can tell by the quivering of her eyelids. I know what a woman likes. Of course I do. I lean in close, smelling the wild waves of her hair and smelling the wild waves of her desire. She is a hot flame beneath my fingertips. The sound of darts hitting their target reaches my ears, as do the moans being manufactured beside me. She's close. I can feel it. I speed up and that's it: I push her over. She cries out her pleasure, which gets lost beneath the dart players' excited shouts. Someone has scored a bull's-eye.

As she suffers her last shudders, I raise my fingers to my lips to lick off the buttery remnants of my Bakewell Pudding.

I've come home. At last.

Butterfly

༄

LISABET SARAI

AFTER NINE MONTHS LAYING PIPE IN THE SAUDI ARABIAN desert, the dusty concrete towns of northeast Thailand seemed to me like paradise. Although accommodations were simple, the food was fantastic, and the local people shy but friendly. Our engineering crew was working on a dam near Khon Kaen. Irrigation and hydropower would help enrich the farmers who eked out a living from that salty soil.

Videos and beer were the only entertainment in Maha Sarakan, the little town where we were staying. The beer was good, true, amazingly refreshing after the heat and dust, but my crewmates wanted something spicier. So on our first free weekend, after three weeks on the site, we piled into the minivan and headed south to Bangkok.

When I had arrived the previous month, the airport was all I had seen of that loose and lascivious metropolis the Thais call the City of Angels. My first real trip there was a shock after the tranquil boredom of the northeast. Chaotic traffic, constant noise, mile after mile of grimy cement apartment blocks interrupted occasionally by skyscrapers and the graceful eaves of Buddhist temples.

One of my mates, Charlie, knew the city well. He checked us into a comfortable, ridiculously cheap hotel in the middle of the tourist district. Bewildered and dazzled, I followed him along sidewalks crammed with vendors hawking watches, T-shirts and toys, trying to avoid tripping on the broken pavement.

Beggars with shriveled limbs extended their bowls in silent entreaty. Blond, ragged-haired tourists in shorts and sandals; slender Thai women in tight jeans and silk blouses; monks draped in saffron; policemen standing stiffly at corners, their revolvers prominently displayed: it seemed that the whole of Bangkok was here on this one street. Meanwhile, an endless line of vehicles crawled by us: tint-windowed Mercedeses, sooty trucks, and rickety buses with people hanging out the doors. The air was heavy with diesel fumes, frying garlic, and jasmine. We dined at a quiet restaurant on a side lane, where the young waitress giggled every time we spoke to her. Then Charlie took me off to see what he called "the real Bangkok" — the go-go bars and sex clubs.

I can't say that I was completely enthusiastic. Yes, I admit that I come from the Bible Belt, but it wasn't that. I've been to strip clubs in the States a few times, and I simply found them depressing. Everybody looking guilty as they try to have a good time. Drunks acting crude, dancers acting coy, everywhere the desperate smell of dirty money and sexual frustration.

I've been with hookers, too. I didn't enjoy that much either. It relieved my physical needs, but it left me feeling empty, sour and old.

My job makes it hard to have a real relationship, though. I never know where my next project will be, but I can bet that it won't be in America's heartland. So I read a lot, and seek my own five-fingered companionship. I didn't think I needed what Bangkok had to offer.

We sauntered into the "entertainment plaza." Three stories of indoor bars and clubs surrounded a central court, which was crowded with open-air bars and stalls selling skewers of grilled chicken, fresh fruit, and fried locusts. As we walked along the second-level balcony, bikini-clad girls tried to lure us inside their establishments.

"Come inside," they crooned. "One beer fifty *baht*. No cover charge." Briefly, the women would hold back the dark cloth draping the door, offering a tantalizing glimpse of flickering lights and bare flesh. "Take a look, no charge, come inside."

The more energetic of these young marketeers would grab us by the hand, and laughing the whole while, try to pull us in. It was all good-natured, though. We'd extricate ourselves from her strong fingers and thank her. "Not now," we'd say. "Maybe later."

"Why not now?" she'd say, stamping her foot in mock anger. "Don't you like me?"

Charlie stopped in front of a doorway surmounted by a blinking neon butterfly. "I came here last month," he said with a grin. "The girls are hotter than average." As if to prove his point, an exquisite creature wearing a fringed bra and a practically nonexistent skirt came out to greet us.

"Welcome to Butterfly Bar. Come inside, please." We followed her through the curtains and found ourselves in a space much deeper than it was wide, lit like some disco nightmare. Everywhere, clashing multicolored lights flashed, vibrated, spun on the ceiling. Rock music pounded in our ears. Our guide settled us on a plush upholstered bench that ran along one wall. In a moment, two frosted mugs of Singha beer sat invitingly before us, and we could turn our attention to the entertainment.

The bar that ran along the opposite wall was also the stage. Half a dozen women wearing next to nothing danced there, churning and writhing to the music. Every single one was drop-dead gorgeous.

One wore a bikini bottom made of chain mail, and thigh-high, spike-heeled vinyl boots. Her long hair fell over one eye, Lauren Bacall style, as she squatted on the bar and circled her hips suggestively.

Another beauty had short, curly hair that looked bleached, and a faraway look. She cupped her perfect breasts absently as she swayed to the beat, sequins flashing from the heart-shaped patch that covered her sex.

Two other dancers were doing a playful lesbian pantomime, grinding their pelvises together and struggling not to laugh. They all seemed so young, despite their salacious behavior.

Other women, wearing brief kimonos, circulated among the

patrons, serving drinks, cuddling, or simply chatting. It wasn't long before we had an entourage of three of these little imps. "You want massage?" asked one, kneading my shoulders with clever hands. "What is your name?" asked another. "My name Ao."

"They want you to buy them drinks," Charlie told me. "Whenever a customer buys them a drink, they get five *baht*."

"Is that all they want?" I was overwhelmed by the feminine flood surging around me.

"Well, of course they want tips. And if you like one of them enough, you can pay to take her out of the bar."

"They're prostitutes?" I suddenly felt slightly queasy. The atmosphere was so different from a Stateside joint, lighthearted and innocent; I didn't want to think about how it might be tainted.

"Well—it's up to them. The bar pays them to dance and to push drinks. If they want to make a private arrangement, it's their prerogative. When they decide to leave for the evening, they simply compensate the bar for lost drink income."

"Hmm." As I pondered this, the music changed, becoming slower and more sensual. Meanwhile, the leftmost dancer stepped down from the bar, and the remaining women moved left to new positions. A figure appeared at the right end of the bar.

Something about her caught my attention. With casual elegance, she shed her kimono and draped it over a barstool. Then she turned toward the shrine in the corner near the ceiling. Touching her fingertips together, she brought them to her forehead and bowed, her reverent gesture totally at odds with the environment.

I felt a strange ache in my chest as I watched her mount the steps to the bar, smooth and sure on her stiletto heels. She was taller than many of the girls, slender and willowy. Her long hair rippled around her as she moved, perfectly attuned to the melody and rhythm.

She was a natural dancer. Her fluid gestures held me transfixed. She grasped one of the poles leading from the bar to the ceiling and arched backward until her hair brushed the floor. Waves flowed through her, sweet undulations that began in her pelvis and shimmered up her spine. By comparison, the other girls seemed clumsy and coarse. She was not trying to entice, it seemed; she was lost in the music. Yet there was something supremely sexy about her performance. I found myself hardening as I gazed at her, turned on for the first time since entering this den of flesh.

As if she felt my gaze, she released the pole, turned and looked in my direction. Her red-painted lips curved in a smile of invitation. Her eyes locked to mine, she unhooked her bikini top and let it slide off her shoulders, revealing sweet, small, firm-looking breasts, capped with almond-hued nipples that surely were erect. She brushed her palms over them, closing her eyes as if savoring the sensation. My penis throbbed uncomfortably in my jeans.

The song changed to something more upbeat. She shook her hips, did the same bumps and grinds as the other dancers, but the effect was totally different. She was listening to some inner voice. Every now and again her eyes would meet mine, and that luscious smile would light her face. I found myself holding my breath, willing her to turn again in my direction.

Finally, her set ended. She slipped away into the crowd before I could call to her. I felt a sense of loss totally out of proportion to the situation. Then, suddenly, she was beside me. I discovered that I was blushing.

"Hello," she said, her smile even more intoxicating close up. "You like me? You like my dancing?"

"I certainly do."

"You buy me drink?"

"Of course." She waved over another bargirl. "Mekong Coke," she ordered. "And you, mister, you want one more beer?"

"Sure, why not?" I looked over at Charlie, hoping for some guidance. He had one girl in his lap, and another whispering in his ear. All three of them were giggling. Charlie caught my slightly desperate glance and shrugged.

"Go for it," he said. "We are. Come on, girls!" He stuffed three five-hundred-*baht* bills in the bamboo tube holding our bill, then headed for the door, one girl on each arm. "Have a great time, Pat," he called over his shoulder. "I'll see you on Monday." Damn him, leaving me alone like that.

I was almost trembling when our drinks arrived. My companion seated herself beside me, her bare thigh pressed against mine, and raised her drink. "*Chok dee*," she said, clicking our glasses. "Good luck to you."

I was tongue-tied with nervousness. Fortunately my lovely friend managed the conversation.

"What your name?" she asked.

"Patrick. Pat."

"Hello, Pat. My name Lek. Means small." For the first time, she giggled in that girlish way I associated with the other women. "It's a joke, because I'm so big."

"You're not big," I said. "At least, not next to me." In fact, she seemed diminutive and fragile beside my six-foot-two, two-hundred-eighty-pound frame.

She took my hand, and a little shiver ran up my spine. Her skin was smooth and cool. "You have a wife, Pat?" she asked.

I shook my head. "Would I be here with you if I was married?" She doubled over with laughter, apparently finding this hilarious.

"Most men come here have wives. Never mind. You have girlfriend?"

I smiled into her shining eyes. "No, no girlfriend."

"OK, then, maybe Lek can be your girlfriend." Without warning she laid a gentle hand on the bulge in my pants. "You like me, I think."

I swallowed hard, not knowing what to say. "Yes, I like you."

"I like you, too. Maybe we go to your room? You pay the bar five hundred *baht*, then we can go."

I felt a chill. All at once this had turned into a financial transaction. Still, I wanted her. "What about for you?" I asked. "How much do I have to pay you?"

"Never mind. Whatever you want, no problem." She pulled me to a standing position. "Come on, let's go. I like you a lot."

On the way back to the hotel, I wondered what I was getting into. Lek was nothing like the hookers I had known. Was she just pretending not to care about the money? She chattered away, apparently unaware of my concerns.

My room was cooler than the muggy night outside, but still humid. The whisper of the air-conditioning drowned out the traffic noise from the street. As soon as the door was closed and she had slipped off her shoes, Lek was kneeling in front of me working at my zipper.

I tried to make her rise. "No, you don't have to do that."

She looked disappointed. "You don't want my mouth on you?"

"Of course I do, but…"

"Then let me," she said softly. "I want to." With a hooker, I had to pay extra for a blow job. Lek acted as though I were doing her a favor. As soon as my fly was open, my penis popped out, full and solid as a sausage. She pursed her lips and mouthed the tip, leaving traces of lipstick on the bulb. Then she slithered her tongue down my length, circling the base with her thumb and forefinger while cupping my balls in her other palm. I groaned. It had been a long time since I'd known anyone's touch but my own.

"Your cock very nice, Pat," she murmured, in between mouthfuls. She took me deep into her throat and kept me there, sucking hard, nursing my cock like a baby at its mother's tit. I'd never felt anything like it.

Already I could feel the come boiling up in me. I began to thrust, jerking my hips, banging the tip of my cock against the back of her throat. She responded by sucking harder, till I felt that her hot vacuum would literally pull the come out of me.

I wanted to stop. I didn't want to come so soon. I wanted to be inside her, those graceful, muscular legs wrapped around me, when I came. But she wouldn't let me go, and finally, I didn't want her to. I twined my fingers in her hair and pulled her head into my crotch, fucking her face until I could bear it no more. The semen surged up my shaft, filling her mouth and overflowing.

She kept licking me gently as my dick shrank back to its normal size. Then she looked up at me and smiled, an angelic smile made sweetly perverse by the creamy remnants of my come on her lips.

"You like that?" she asked archly.

"What do you think?" I pulled her to me and embraced her, tasting my own bitter fluid on her ripe mouth. "That was amazing, Lek." After a while, I released her and looked down ruefully at my limp penis. "Unfortunately, I was hoping to use that to explore some other parts of your anatomy."

"Never mind," she said. "Long night. You lie down there and watch me. You'll be hard again pretty quick."

She was so charming that I couldn't contradict her. I reclined on the bed, while she did a little private striptease.

She wasn't wearing much, but she made every garment count. Moving to some music in her head, she strutted across the carpet, then turned her back to me. She untied her halter-top from around her neck. Then she turned and slowly lowered her hands, gradually revealing to me those luscious little breasts. Her skin was a dusky ivory that reminded me of the erotic figurines carved from elephant tusks that I had seen in Okinawa. Her nipples seemed large in proportion. I ran my tongue over my lips, thinking about having one in my mouth. My penis twitched, already coming back to life.

Next she unbuttoned her miniskirt, shimmied it down to her ankles, hooked it with one foot and flung it playfully onto the bed. Only her panties remained, a black thong that hid the merest sliver of the flesh between her thighs. Looking into my eyes, she undid the ties at each hip. With agonizing slowness, she drew the cloth forward, through her cleft. Then she held the garment out to me.

My hands trembled as I took it from her. It was warm and moist from her body. I held it to my nose, breathing deeply. Her musk was fainter and more delicate than the Western women that I had known, but still strong enough to bring me half-erect.

She posed for a moment, silent and desirable, her gold chain and Buddha amulet glinting between her breasts. Then she came and stood by the bedside, her thighs parted, her hairless mound close to my face. "Touch me," she said. As nervous as a virgin, I reached out my finger and slid it into her folds. She sighed as if in bliss and closed her eyes, twisting her nipples between thumb and forefinger.

Her flesh was slippery and unbelievably smooth. I thought of sun-warmed porcelain, or stones rounded and polished by the river's kiss. My fingers found her clit and massaged it gently. I was rewarded by her soft moans. My cock swelled to fullness as I imagined probing her more deeply.

Lek saw that I was ready. She climbed onto the bed. On all fours, she presented her ass to me. Her pale, swelling cheeks flowed like sculpture under my hands. I wanted her as I had never wanted any woman.

Fumbling in my pocket, I found a condom and slid it over my now-rampant penis. Then I slipped my fingers back into her cunt, spreading her juices.

Lek looked back at me over her shoulder. "No, not there," she said. "Take me the other way. In the other hole. Like a whore."

Her crudeness, so out of keeping with her earlier manner, shocked me and excited me. I spread her cheeks and placed my forefinger on the crinkled ring of muscle. "You mean here?"

"Yes. There. Like that. You want to, don't you?"

I did. I had never done such a thing, but oh, I had read and I had imagined. I was afraid, though, afraid of hurting her, afraid of the dirtiness of it, afraid of the unknown.

"Are you sure?"

"Do it. Please, now. Fuck me like a whore, Pat."

"You're not a whore, Lek..." I began, but I couldn't continue. My cock surged, hardening to pain. I didn't hesitate any longer. I smeared some of the lubrication from her pussy over my cock, until I was as slippery as she was. Then I pressed my knob against that tight whorl, that gateway to the forbidden, and pushed. To my surprise, I slid halfway in, halfway into the tightest, hottest space my cock had ever known.

I grabbed her hips and pulled her toward me, fully impaling her. She sobbed, in pain or delight. From the way she arched her back and pressed herself against my hardness, I thought it was the latter. I began to move inside her. Her muscles gripped me, rippling around my rod. Each time I thrust into her bowels, she moaned, urging me on.

The sensations and the thought of what I was doing fed on each other. I was buttfucking a beautiful woman. Reaming her. Screwing her brains out with my cock buried to the hilt in her ass. And she loved it, I could tell, from her mewling cries, from the way she writhed beneath me and thrashed her head about until her hair was tangled all over her back.

It lasted a long time. My cock seemed to swell with each stroke. Her passage got tighter and tighter. Finally, I could bear it no longer. With a yell, I rammed myself into her and let the orgasm take over. It tore through me, sweeping away all thought in its path.

When I came back to myself, she was stretched out beside me, stroking my hair. Sweet satisfaction shone in her eyes. "*Khorp khun kha,*" she whispered. "Thank you."

"Thank you, Lek." I gathered her in my arms and showered her with small kisses. I had never imagined such generosity in a woman.

We spent the weekend together. The next morning, breakfasting late in the hotel coffee shop, I was self-conscious. Then I looked around and realized that we were by no means the only Thai-foreign couple in the place

She was magnificent company, and a wonderful guide. She

showed me the bejeweled Grand Palace and the National Museum. In the Temple of the Emerald Buddha, she lit incense and knelt silently for a long time. I watched, amazed, remembering her reverence in the bar.

We wandered through the weekend market laughing and sweating in the sun, while she bargained for sarongs and cheap jewelry. We toured the canals on a rice barge, ate fiery curry and fried bananas.

And of course, we made love, a dozen times in a dozen different ways. Finally, I got the chance to sink myself into her cunt, while looking into her eyes. It was clear even to me, though, that she preferred entry via her back passage. I was more than happy to oblige.

On Monday morning, we held hands while waiting for the minivan. All at once, I remembered that I had not paid her. I had bought her gifts and given her money for treats, but nothing to recompense her for her time and her physical bounty.

I reached for my wallet. She put her hand on mine. "Never mind," she said.

"But I haven't given you anything. I have to pay..."

"No, no pay, Pat. I'm your girlfriend now. Just take care of me, OK?"

I shook off her hand and slipped five thousand *baht* from my billfold. Folding it, I stuck it into her palm. "You know I'm going to be gone for the next three weeks. This should help you take care of yourself. I'll see you when I come back, OK?"

"OK, Pat. I miss you."

"I'll miss you too, Lek." The van pulled up, and at the same time, Charlie and the other guys tumbled out of the hotel, looking tousled and somewhat the worse for wear. I kissed her lightly on the lips. "See you soon."

The next three weeks were the longest I had ever endured. The days crawled by in a haze of sunburned dust. The nights I spent fantasizing, remembering Lek's sweetness and her lust, thinking of new things we would do when I saw her again. I wished that I had a picture of her, but then I knew no photo could do her justice. No photo could capture her dancer's grace, her whimsical sense of humor, her gentleness, or her blazing carnality.

Finally, I couldn't bear it anymore. I had to hear her voice at least. I asked one of the Thai members of our team to find the telephone number for Butterfly Bar, and one evening around six, when I figured it would not be busy, I tried calling.

The phone rang and rang. Finally it was picked up. "*Kha?*" a woman's voice answered.

"Is Lek there?" I asked, miserably aware that I might not be understood. "I'd like to speak to Lek, please."

There was a silence, then the woman laughed. "Oh, Lek, yes, of course. One moment, please."

The line crackled with static as I waited. Dimly, I could hear the thumping beat of rock 'n' roll. I had no idea what I was going to say. I only knew that I needed Lek in some way that was totally new to me.

Finally, I heard a clicking, and then her softly accented English. "Hello? Lek speaking."

"Lek, it's me. Pat."

"Pat!" she almost squealed with excitement. I heard her say something in Thai to someone in the background. "Pat, I miss you!"

"I miss you too, Lek. That's why I'm calling. I just had to hear your voice."

"When you come back to Bangkok?"

"Not until the end of next week. Friday. I'll meet you at the bar, OK?"

"OK, Pat. See you then." There was a pause, filled with static. "Everything good with you?"

"I'm fine except that I wish you were here with me."

"Want me to come up-country to see you?"

I laughed at her enthusiasm. "No, no. I've got to work, and this place would be pretty dull for a gorgeous girl like you."

"If you there, not dull," she said firmly. "We make excitement together."

"You're certainly right on that score, young lady. But no, I'll see you in Bangkok. Maybe we can go down to Pattaya and hang out on the beach."

"Crazy *farang*," she laughed. "No Thai girl goes to the beach. Make us black."

"Well, whatever. Maybe we'll spend the whole weekend in my room."

"Mmm," she sighed. "I like that."

Another moment of staticky silence. Finally, she spoke, so softly I could hardly hear. "Pat? I love you."

"I love you, too, Lek," I heard myself say. I realized I meant it. "See you next week."

The last week seemed even longer than the previous two. Then, when Friday afternoon finally arrived and I was packing for the trip south, my boss dropped by. He needed me to stay until tomorrow, he said, to supervise the grading of the site. "Can't Charlie do it?" I asked, a bit testily.

"Charlie's sick. Got some stomach bug or something."

As soon as the boss left, I tried calling Lek's bar. This time the phone rang and rang, unanswered. I tried again, around eight o'clock, and again near midnight. No response. I prayed that Lek would not be worried, or angry with me for standing her up.

The grading went like clockwork. I was headed toward Bangkok by 2 p.m., driving one of the company jeeps. My spirits rose with each kilometer that brought me closer to her. I pulled in at the hotel around six, took a quick shower, and then immediately set out for the Butterfly.

The place was already jumping, full of men in white naval uniforms. Maybe that was why no one had picked up my call the previous night. I sat down with a beer and looked around for Lek. There was no sign of her.

"Hello, mister. Remember me?" I recognized the round face and pixie haircut from my last visit.

"Hello, Ao. Of course I remember." She looked delighted. "Would you like a drink?"

"Yes, thank you." As she was leaving, I grabbed her hand.

"One moment, Ao. Do you know where Lek is? The tall dancer with the long hair?"

She shook her head. "She not here tonight, I think."

A bolt of panic surged through me. Did she think I had abandoned her? Had she left the bar with some other man?

"You ask the mama-san," Ao said, pointing to a woman behind the bar. "Maybe she know about Lek."

I picked up my beer and sat down at the bar, inches from the spiked heels of one of the dancers. I gestured to the mama-san.

"Excuse me, but do you know where I can find Lek?"

The woman looked me over critically. She was a well-preserved forty, with short-cropped hair and glasses, wearing a fitted hot-pink suit.

"Lek buy herself out of the bar tonight. Today her birthday. She want to take the night off, celebrate with her friends."

"Do you have any idea where she might have gone to celebrate?"

"Why? Who are you? You her new boyfriend?"

I blushed, but then nodded. "Yes, I'm Pat."

The mama-san's suspicious manner changed abruptly to friendliness. "Oh, Pat. You call her last week?"

"Yes, that was me."

"Oh, Lek very much in love with you."

My heart did a little flip of gratitude. My dear girl was not angry with me.

"I love her, too."

The mama-san took my hand. "That is so good, mister Pat. She looking for someone to love her for such a long time. Ever since her operation."

Some vague uneasiness gripped me. "Her operation? What was wrong? Is she ill? Did she have an accident?"

The mama-san laughed. "Oh no, no accident. But last year, she have operation to make her a real lady. No more *katoey*, lady-man. She always want that, save her money for five years to have operation."

"Lady-man?"

"Yes, you know." The mama-san gestured toward one of the dancers, a long-legged, sultry-looking temptress. "Like Nong. Before, Lek a man but look like woman, dress like woman, want to be woman. Now, after operation, she really a woman. No more pretending."

My stomach lurched. I thought for a moment that I would vomit. Lek, sweet, delicate, feminine Lek, was a man! I was in love with a man. I had had sexual relations with a man. The flesh of my penis was crawling, as if loathsome creatures swarmed over it. I was filled with shame and disgust.

"No!" I yelled. I jerked upright, spilling my beer all over the bar. It made a little pool around the heels of the dancer looming over me. She watched me curiously, surprised and shocked by my outburst, wondering what the crazy *farang* would do next.

"Mister, never mind. Lek good girl. She love you. You lucky man."

"Lucky?" I roared. "She played me for a fool. She defiled me! She's a devil in angel's guise!" I stormed out of the bar. The girls cringed and shrank away from me as I passed.

Without knowing how I got there, I found myself in the shadowy cocktail lounge of my hotel, gulping down a double bourbon. I lay my head in my hands and sobbed. The Filipino band was warming up. I hoped that I would pass out before they started playing their set.

Suddenly there was warmth next to me, and a faint hint of jasmine. Cool, slender fingers touched my arm. I opened my eyes.

"You!" I hissed, jerking away from her hand. "Get away from me, you filthy whore!"

"Pat," she said softly. "Please forgive me. I want to tell you, last weekend, but no time. Always we were laughing, or making love."

A vision of her taut flanks straining back at me. A recollection of the dark scent of her butthole. "Get out of here. Don't touch me, you, you abomination!"

I could see tears gathering in her eyes, making them shine even more than usual. I felt a brief pang of guilt, and something else I could not name.

"Never mind, Pat. You love me. I know you do. Man, lady, lady-man, same-same. All human, all love. Please, Pat."

She looked tiny suddenly, frail, crushed like a wilted flower. My anger left me, but I still came close to retching when she took my hand. "Look into my eyes," she said softly. "Look at me, and tell you don't love me. Then I go."

I took one last look. Her raven hair shimmered in the multi-colored bar lights. Her ivory skin glowed golden, stretched firm across her high cheekbones. Wet traces of tears streaked her face, but her lips smiled that same luscious, sensuous, loving smile that I first saw across the room, three weeks, a thousand years ago.

I looked at her, and I wanted her. My cock stiffened even as my gut turned over and tried to expel its contents. I was more terrified than I had ever been in my life. I wrenched my hand away.

"Go away," I whispered. "Leave me alone. I don't love you."

She did not hesitate any longer. She turned on her heels

196

and walked to the door, an epiphany of grace. I bit my lip, and wondered what I had done to deserve this hell.

My work on the dam will be finished in another two months. Meanwhile, I don't bother to go to Bangkok on the weekends anymore. Charlie keeps bugging me to join the rest of the guys. He knows that something happened between Lek and me, though of course he doesn't know the whole story.

"Come on, Pat. Forget her. You've got to be a *phee-sua*, as the bargirls say, a butterfly flitting from flower to flower." I just shake my head and turn back to my Orson Scott Card novel.

After this gig is through, I think I might go back to the States. I'll settle down in Cedar Rapids to be near my folks and find some nice girl. Someone blonde, comfortable, totally unexotic.

Then I catch a glimpse of some nymph in the Maha Sarakan market, sarong hugging her hips, jet hair trailing down her supple back and I'm drowning in memories. My cock like granite, my throat burning with nausea, an ache knifing through my chest. Desire, disgust, unbearable longing.

In those moments, I wonder if I'll ever find a place to rest.

crossing borders: milan to paris through the simplon tunnel

✣

JOY JAMES

I WAS BLONDE THEN, AND YOUNG. Italy was ancient, and all the men seemed swarthy. I remember the way they would look at you. Or was it just me whom they looked at that way? Did they know? I worried, but was also pleased. Even alone in the morning in my third-class hotel in a particularly ugly section of Milan, performing the difficult chore of styling my much-too-fine, too-thin hair, I would look in the mirror and imagine the Mediterranean men's eyes caressing my Nordic body.

Now you can lead an even fuller life. Softer, fuller hair. No fuss.

Hair was the hardest, I had always thought. Now, however, dressed in the laciest bra and panties, I happily tossed my head upside-down, with my hands tightly grasping the wire brush and blow-dryer as if they were phallic tools. I made believe it was a public performance for Giovanni or Gianni or Giacomo or Giuseppe or whatever the name behind the anonymous, leering eyes I would encounter that day.

Enjoy the pleasurable sensation of your whole body turning satin-smooth. And the touch of clothes against your body feels better than you ever remembered.

Yes, even shaving and moisturizing was fun, as my body tingled in anticipation of the fixed male gaze. Rolling on each leg of some brand-new pantyhose, I smiled. They had been my very first purchase in Italy. The salesgirl hadn't spoken English; the extent of my Italian, *per favore* and *grazie*. In a foreign country, even the most quotidian activity becomes a test. And I had passed. The salesgirl had smiled and called me *Signorina*. I was no longer just a tourist; I was a fuckable female, just like her. *Signorina*. I liked that. It sounded so sensual…it made me feel so…

Fluttered. Ruffled. Rippled. Frilled. Flirty and feminine.

I had come to Milan hoping to catch a glimpse of the fashion shows. After all the endless, adolescent-like moments of flipping the glossy pages of *Vogue* and *Elle* and *Bazaar* adding up to idle years of dream weaving, I would discover the truth behind the pictures and words. Oh, the words. Oh, how I loved the sound of them, like a melodious foreign language. You didn't have to be fluent to be aware of layers, like petticoats, of meaning.

Flirty and feminine. Flaunt your feminine flair.

I'll never forget what I had on that very last morning in Milan. It wasn't Gucci or Ferragamo or Armani or Brioni or Prada or Versace or Dolce & Gabbana, but it might as well have been, because I wouldn't have been caught dead dressed like this back home in the heart, if there is one, of suburban America. Black leather boots, almost knee-high, with three-inch heels. A snug knit skirt, also black, maxi in length but with a side slit almost up to you-know-where, exposing my silky black pantyhosed thigh with even the tiniest step I took. A black, tight top, snapped at the crotch like a bodysuit, long-sleeved dolman style but low-cut with the fabric fluted between the breasts. And a wide, red belt in the style of a corset-like cinch. Yes, red, so I wouldn't be totally monochromatic. Plus lots and lots of jewelry, so that I jangled conspicuously when I walked.

The dark, narrow corridor leading to my morning coffee at the hotel's *trattoria* felt like a fashion show's catwalk as I sashayed along; and I, a nervous novice. As with any travel experience, there was fear of the unknown. Fear mixed with desire; there's exquisite excitement in that: what would happen next?

. . .

"Hey, honey, I love the way your ass wiggles. You want me to fuck you, don't you, baby?" Those words, or the Latin equivalent, were, I confess, what I secretly wanted to hear. Not that we would actually fuck — in fact, I would disdainfully ignore the speaker. To be desired, that was enough. To be validated as a real woman — what men jokingly, crudely refer to as a life-support system for a cunt — a sex object, no more, no less: that was my desire.

Oh, how I wanted it, needed it, so.

Sipping the dark-roasted coffee and picking at a pastry in the *trattoria*, I waited. A bell tower chimed. I waited for watchful male eyes to latch onto me. I loved the sound from the bell tower, its ritualized tolling punctuating the waiting. *Il dolce far nienta*, the Italians call it. It is so much more than "delightful idleness." It is knowing that to be a woman is to wait. Waiting for watchful male eyes. There's contentment, even wisdom, in that.

I heard the bell tower chime again. How had time passed so quickly? I didn't care. I was a woman, surrounded by attentive, appreciative male eyes. I didn't necessarily need to be fucked. To be seen and desired, and thought to be fuckable, that was enough. I strolled out of the *trattoria* and onto the street.

Italian men are such exquisite flirts — all talk and no action; they might leer, make lewd yet flattering comments, even pat my bottom, but they would never actually try to find out if I was for real: a cock tease or a genuine, fuckable cunt? It would remain a mere question of semantics, lost forever in translation.

One man, bolder than the rest, kept circling me as if I were prey. I liked his eyes. What did they see exactly, how did this vision of me make him feel? Did I make him hard? I wanted to know. I felt as though I had just entered a museum, about to view for the very first time masterpieces familiar from years of flipping through their reproduced images in coffee-table art books. I wanted to know what the real art was really like. Was I like the sensual subject of a Caravaggio portrait? I wanted to know.

But whenever I would turn to face him directly, his eyes would ricochet off my own and quickly drop downward, pretending to browse the magazine he had in his hand. Then, I, too, would look away, scanning the window displays, the sales tags I couldn't read. And the ritualized, visual dance would happen all over again:

he would stare; I would catch him; his eyes would dart away. I wanted to smile invitingly if only his gaze had lingered. Then as I turned away from the shop window, suddenly he moved closer and grabbed—yes, pinched!—my ass. That he wasn't disappointed to feel a padded girdle was at that moment all I desired.

"*Sind Sie Deutsche?*" The voice, unmistakably female, seemed to come from nowhere. Was it, like the pinch on my butt, meant for me, but properly to be ignored? I kept walking.

"English?" The voice spoke again. I turned and saw a woman, a gorgeous woman, expectantly smiling at me. The man who had pinched me was nowhere in sight. Her smile demanded an answer.

"American, actually," I said.

"Oh, you fooled me," she said and laughed. It felt like a compliment. Her own English was impeccable, in that university-schooled, indeterminate-nationality, Continental way. Definitely not an American, but just as definitely a real woman, a gloriously glamorous woman, the kind of woman I wanted to become, a model for me to grow into being. She could have passed for a real model had she been younger. Maybe now a fashion writer? I wondered. I couldn't take my eyes off her clothes, the way they hung so effortlessly on her body.

"And I believe you fooled your admirer as well," she said.

I must have blushed, for she quickly added:

"Oh, dear, don't worry. Don't be embarrassed. Men are so stupid. They would never know."

"But how…" I stammered. "How did you know? How can you tell?"

"Oh, I can just tell." She smiled and grabbed my arm. "Let's go have coffee."

• • •

One of the wonders of the world, I thought: the wisdom of women. She could tell, she just knew; words were unnecessary. What she knew, I needed to know. To learn, after all—that's perhaps the primary purpose of travel, isn't it? As with a foreign language, total immersion is the best way to learn. And the very first thing I learned was this: just as only visitors can truly appreciate what natives take for granted, I was awestruck by the easy camaraderie and shared intimacy of natural women. As my new friend nodded and smiled and touched my arm, I found myself confiding everything. How I had brought two suitcases to Europe: one so big, it was almost like a steamer trunk, brimming with all my feminine finery surreptitiously collected over the years; the other, very small, like an attaché case, containing a pinstriped suit, starched white shirt, tie, socks, and boxer shorts, for my return trip back to reality.... How I had a letter from my therapist in case my male passport was called into question at a border crossing.... How that same therapist had prescribed estrogen-replacement patches for me to test on my trip, and I was already beginning to feel a not-unpleasant tenderness and tingling in my nipples....

"Can I touch?" She laughed. "I'd like to feel them grow."

"It would be a long wait." I laughed, too. "Apparently it takes months and months for any measurable breast development to occur. So the good news is it's not irrevocable. I can change my mind. This time in Europe really is just a test, to see if I'm comfortable transitioning and really want to go all the way." I giggled. "With all the sex-change surgery and stuff. Now that *is* irrevocable!"

"You're so brave," she said, "but you can't be expected to do it all by yourself!" She squeezed my hand. "Every girl needs a mentor, doesn't she?" As I squeezed her hand back, she smiled and said: "I'll help."

That's when I decided to call her Gigi—GG, for genetic girl. She thought that was funny.

"Well, the very first thing," she announced, "we just have to do something about your hands." Suddenly self-conscious, I moved my hands away from the coffee cup into my lap. She laughed. "Don't worry, sweetie. Nothing a good set of sculpted nails, complete with a French manicure, can't fix." She paused. "I know a salon right down the street."

As we walked through what seemed a maze of watchful male gazes, she asked me about the men in my life. I confessed, alas, there were none. Moreover, I was a virgin.

"We'll have to do something about that, too," Gigi laughed. I tried to explain that until I sorted out my own gender identity, I wasn't at all sure I really wanted to have sex with anyone, man or woman.

"Rubbish," she said. "It's fucking that creates gender."

"So I may not need a sex-change operation after all?" I laughed. "Just find a man to fuck me, and I'll automatically be a cunt?"

"That's a lot less expensive, isn't it?" She laughed again as we entered the salon.

. . .

Gigi's Italian seemed fluent and flawless as she and the manicurist talked nonstop, all the while gesturing toward me. I had no idea what they were saying. All I knew was that my nails were being miraculously transformed. They seemed to belong to someone else, no longer a part of my own body. While they were drying, Gigi finally said something in English, addr essed to me: "If you don't mind, I'm going to have the salon's proprietor give you a brow wax and a little touch-up on your makeup. It's her specialty. You'll love it."

"Whatever you say, Gigi." I laughed. "You're the boss." I was excited but also apprehensive; I had never had a brow wax before.

The room where the waxing was to be done was like a doctor's office. I stretched out on the crisp, white sheet of what could have been an examining table and submitted myself to the procedure. It was over quickly and the pain seemed somehow pleasurable. Gigi was standing there, right next to me, like a well-intentioned nurse, figuratively holding my hand.

"Whoops!" she said. "She took a bit too much off, so she's going to pencil in a nice artificial arch." Before I could reply, I heard what sounded like a dentist's drill tracing lines above my eyes. Then Gigi asked me to close my eyes, and I felt the same sensation on my lids and then just beneath my eyes. I started to ask what was happening, but Gigi put her finger to her lips and said: "Don't move your mouth. She's about to work her magic on your lips right now. Maybe she'll inject some collagen, too. You don't mind, do you?" I didn't say anything; I didn't mind. I knew collagen would wear off within a few weeks; back home, no one would notice.

. . .

Late that evening, back at my hotel room, it seemed to take forever to unscrew the caps for my cleansing and moisturizing lotions. I hadn't yet become used to my talon-like nails, I told myself. But actually I was nervous. I wasn't yet ready to know, really know. But I couldn't not know any longer.

And, yes, just as I had feared or hoped—are the two verbs ultimately the same?—my eyeliner, cupid-shaped lip line, and pencil-thin, arched brow would not wash off. I scrubbed and scrubbed. Yes, these feminine facial markers were now embedded in my body. The person I saw in the mirror looked like a girl even when naked! And yes…no…I didn't want to believe it…or did I? Gigi had instructed that permanent makeup be applied at the salon!

No wonder she had insisted on paying the salon's bill. We had then spent all day together, shopping, trying on clothes, visiting an art gallery, flirting with men. About the makeup, Gigi didn't tell, and I never asked. I was afraid to ask. I preferred to know but not know, to know only innocence and ignorance. Uncertainty became me. And I didn't know this: how I would, or should, react if I knew for sure? Especially, how would I react in front of Gigi? Would I dissolve in tears? Would I get angry? Would I disappoint her?

Now, staring into the hotel mirror, totally alone yet never more socialized, I used the new extensions of my body, my sculpted nails, to trace the feminine imprints on my face. At first, I was horrified at the exaggerated cupid's bow of my lips and the fuck-me highlights around my eyes. But then I had to admit it: my face looked good, and that made me feel good, so good the feeling was foreign.

And so it was that I, an innocent abroad, first tasted the ambivalent nature of desire. It wasn't as if I had been chained to the table while the permanent makeup was being tattooed on my skin. But neither had I actively consented. To be forcibly transformed into an object of desire—was that what deep down I desired? To will away my will—was that what I really wanted? Was it as simple and crazy as that? And lacking the will and the wisdom, I needed Gigi, my Pygmalion—or was she Dr. Frankenstein?

• • •

That night I dreamed of desperately seeking a plastic surgeon to remove somehow the permanent makeup before I returned to the United States. It was a nightmare. I didn't know what to wear to the first consultation. He didn't speak English. He laughed at me and said he didn't "do" queers.

When I awoke, I looked in the mirror to see if my new face hadn't been a dream, too. It was real, all too real, so real that I didn't know what to do. So I called Gigi. She had told me she was going to Paris that day, and had left her phone number in case I wanted to join her.

"I absolutely love your makeup," was the greeting she gave me when we met at the *Stazione Centrale* that early afternoon. I felt my cheeks blush, and we never spoke of it again.

"Here, let me help you with your luggage," she said and reached for the small bag that held my men's clothes. Something told me I would never see it again.

Our tickets were first class. Gigi insisted that she pay.

"It will be a beautiful trip," she said. "The views of the Piedmont and then as we climb through the Alps are really quite stunning." She smiled. "You'll truly feel like a new woman by the time we get to France." She paused, and her face suddenly seemed to radiate a sense of joy. "And then Paris! Ah, Paris. I always love showing first-time visitors around."

"I'm so excited!" That's all I could say.

After settling into our cozy, quite private, compartment, Gigi surprised me with some clothes she had brought along for me to try on: a black leather micro-mini, fishnet hose, strappy high heels, and a low-cut, peasant blouse.

"Gorgeous! You look fantastic," she announced after I had donned my new look. "Very fuckable." She laughed and gave me a hug. "Yes, a bit tarty, I admit, but where we're going, you'll be overdressed!"

I didn't ask what she meant exactly, but I did learn a little about Gigi as we shared a bottle of the best Chianti I've ever had and she teased and sprayed my hair. She considered herself a successful businesswoman. That's why she was going to Paris—on business. She owned a number of franchises throughout Europe.

"Euphemistically, let's call them modeling agencies." She smiled and took my finely French-manicured hand in hers. "And I'm always looking for new talent."

I laughed nervously, then finally got up the nerve to ask: "Are you offering me a job, Gigi?"

"I like to think of it as more fun than a mere job," she said. "Certainly, you'll be handsomely rewarded. In more ways than money." Gigi then stood up from our seat, said she had to run a little errand, opened the compartment door, and blew me a kiss.

I gazed out the window. Only two hours out of Milan, the train was now climbing the Alpine heights. There were craggy peaks and snow everywhere. The view took my breath away. Or was it what Gigi had just said? I contemplated her meaning. It was like the permanent makeup. I knew but I didn't know. There was excitement in the uncertainty: what would happen next? Embarking toward a destination I couldn't even imagine, on a trip of possibly no return, was I being railroaded? The American slang came to mind, like a Freudian slip. I had to smile.

• • •

"You look happy," Gigi greeted me as she slid open the compartment door. With her was an older man; though distinguished looking, he was certainly not handsome. He had a huge grin on his face, but still appeared nervous. "This kind gentleman here very much wants to meet you," Gigi continued. "I've told him all about you."

Then she closed the door, drew the shades, took my hand, squeezed it, and placed something in my palm. I looked down, and, yes, it was a condom.

"All my girls use protection," Gigi said.

Then I saw that the man was unzipping his trousers.

"Don't worry," Gigi said. "I'll stay here with you since it's your very first time. I'll help you along every step of the way." She paused. "And he knows that already. I think it's an added turn-on. A real woman coach and her sissy boy student." She giggled, then touched my shoulder to gently push me to my knees.

As I sank to the floor, I glanced out the train window. The sun and snow had disappeared, for we had just entered what I would later learn was called Simplon, the tunnel carved through the Alps. On the other side would be Switzerland — or was it France? — and my new self, I realized, forever altered, on this transgressive, transformational train ride. Transfiguring even.

The snug micro-mini exposed my panties when I kneeled, and the man reached down to feel what was between my legs, as if to ensure that I was as Gigi had advertised, a girl with something extra. This seemed to excite him, for immediately his own cock popped out of his pants, hard and huge. He took it in his hand and moved it, like a makeup powder brush, around my face.

"Now put the condom on the very tip of his penis," I heard Gigi say, "and then roll it down his shaft with your lips." She was sipping wine, sitting so close to me we almost touched, but her voice seemed far away. I tried to do as she said, but it was a technique that surely required practice. I cheated a bit and used one of my hands.

"Make believe it's a giant lollipop," Gigi said. "Go ahead, use your tongue all over his cock. And when you lick his balls, grasp his cock with your hand. Hold it nice and tight and move your hand up and down." I did as I was told, vigorously. "That's a good girl," Gigi said.

"Now comes the fun part," she told me. "You get to suck. You get to do what you've always wanted. You get to feel it and taste it. You get to be your true self, at last. And you don't have to worry about whether it's something you should actually be doing, about whether it's wrong, or some silly notion like that. You're doing it simply because I'm telling you to do it."

I nodded my head and then slid the cock between my lips into my mouth.

"Yes, suck! Go ahead and suck, suck him dry. Let yourself go, sweetie. Don't be bashful. Abandon yourself. Don't be ashamed. Relax in the contented knowledge that you're just a hole for cock that forever needs to be filled. Ah, luxuriate in the sensation."

I pushed my head down the shaft as far as I could without gagging, then I pulled it back to the very tip, then down the shaft yet again and back, again and again. The rhythm came naturally — like the rocking of the train — this most basic of techniques I would later learn was called the "bob and slide." The sucking was instinctive, as I played with and puckered my lips to add variety to each head stroke. All the while I heard Gigi's words in the background:

"Gaze up at him and smile with your eyes while you're sucking…. Use your hands to let him see you play with your own tits…. Let him know you're getting turned on, too. I know that you are, aren't you, sweetie?"

With my lips tight around his cock, I nodded my head up and down, yes, yes, yes. Gigi kept talking: "There's a surgeon in Antwerp I've heard about. He specializes in facial feminization. We'll need to have a brow and forehead reduction, some cheek implants, and of course your Adam's apple removed. And breast implants. We can't wait for the hormones to kick in. Also buttock implants would be helpful, don't you agree?"

My eyes glanced toward Gigi, as my nose nuzzled the man's pubic hair. I no longer felt the gagging reflex; I was able to swallow him whole, all the way, deep down my throat.

"Yes, I know that surgically feminizing your body will make you blissfully happy, just like a mouthful of cock. Then you'll be just the perfect little she-male, and you can get all the cock you crave. There's a great market, real demand, you know, for very special girls like you, and I need at least one she-male in my stable of escorts. Aren't you honored and glad that I picked you?"

Gigi's words washed over me, adding to the eroticism of the moment with her promise of many moments just like it to come, filling me, a would-be woman, with cock after cock after cock, forever into the future, sucking and being fucked, desire unending, desire for me, for the hole that I had become. I no longer had to travel anywhere; my body was now a destination. Gigi's seductive words, like the ones I had heard and read all my life, were what dreams were built of.

Now you can lead an even fuller life. Flirty and feminine. Flaunt your feminine flair with the body you deserve, the body you were meant to be. Only a sensual, sexy body can express the real inner you.

Suddenly, there was a rush of whiteness everywhere. We were emerging from the tunnel. Snow and sun, cold and hot whiteness, everywhere — and white hot semen. Yes, he came just at that moment, pulling off the rubber so he could shoot all over me, on my now permanently made-up face and down my soon-to-be increased cleavage. I closed my eyes and licked my lips. We were in the mountains but I tasted seawater. And I imagined the eyes of the Italian men on the street back in Milan, and the eyes of strangers yet to come, ogling me, wanting me, filling me with their desire. Yes, that's what I wanted, all I wanted; that was enough. To be forever an incomplete woman, who could never get enough; that was now more than enough.

The vodník

ॐ

G. MERLIN BECK

According to Czech legend, Prague's pubs are haunted by a water sprite called the Vodník. He wears an overcoat, and can be distinguished by the pool of water that collects under his seat. The Vodník lures young women to his home under the Charles Bridge and thence to an unspeakable fate.

GEORGE WAS LOST IN PRAGUE. He'd spent half an hour wandering the curved, cobblestone streets and had only managed to reach the old clock tower. He studied his map, trying to ignore the crowds of tourists gathered around. Especially that one, the young man standing a few feet away, the slender one with the honey-colored hair and the sweet, coy smile. The one that might let George follow him back to his hotel room, where he would close the door and push George onto the bed. And then seize George's wrists in one big hand while tearing at their clothes with the other, letting George's hard cock spring free, to be enveloped in a warm, hungry mouth.

George shook his head and forced himself to concentrate. There wasn't much time. His parents would be back from the office at midnight, which meant he had four hours to find a certain street: a street that held one of Prague's few gay bathhouses. He searched the map laboriously, his hands shaking, his teeth chattering with anxiety. What if he couldn't find the street? What if he weren't brave enough to go into the bathhouse when he did? He knew that Prague was a safe place, and that bathhouses were safer still. But none of that was very comforting. It was his first time, and he was scared. Once again, he considered just giving up and going back to the hotel. But then he thought about the men, the beautiful Czech men. Tiny little waists, flat stomachs, tight asses. Kisses tasting of good Czech beer. George's cock stood up straight and hard. He heard someone panting nearby. And then he realized that it was his own labored breathing. Embarrassed, he turned and started to walk away.

"Excuse me!"

George started. He had almost collided with a small, dark-haired woman in a long black overcoat.

"You speak English?" she said, with a heavy accent.

"Yes, I do." He smiled, figuring she was a lost tourist who needed help.

"Do you want sex?"

George stared for a moment, unable to speak.

"With you?" he finally said, incredulous. The woman nodded and licked her lips.

"Uhh, no thank you," he said, backing away.

"But it is very good," she said.

"No, really. No thank you."

"You will like it. Good price. Come. I not hurt you, little boy." She grabbed his wrist and pulled. George panicked and tore himself out of her grasp. He ran into the nearest alleyway, ankles buckling on the cobblestones. Several streets later he stopped to catch his breath and look around. He was on a narrow road that twisted between curve-walled buildings. He huddled beneath a dim streetlamp and consulted his map. It was frustrating; street names in Prague were a jumble of consonants. He stuffed the map into his pocket and decided to ask directions. There was a pub across the street, decorated with the omnipresent *Pilsner Urquell* sign. George hesitated. What if nobody spoke English? And besides, he had never been in a Czech pub. His parents had only taken him to expensive tourist restaurants.

There were footsteps at the end of the street. A short, shadowy figure walked toward him. George squinted. The person seemed to be wearing a long, dark overcoat. *Well,* George thought, *that decides that.* He walked quickly into the pub, anxious to avoid another encounter with the dark-haired woman.

A cloud of cigarette smoke and Czech words greeted him. George stood there, uncertain what to do. A haggard, sad-looking waitress walked by. George opened his mouth, hoping to ask her for directions. Without looking up, she pointed at an empty chair at one end of a long table and walked away.

Might as well, George thought. At eighteen, he was old enough to drink in the Czech Republic. And besides, he was still shaky; a beer might help him relax. Feeling a thrill of naughtiness, he sat down at the table. A group of Czech men sat at the other end. They looked at him curiously. He was small-boned, with long black hair and his mother's delicate, girlish Chinese features: a rarity in a Czech pub. The men muttered among themselves. One of them shrugged.

"Uh, hi," George said. They immediately turned away from him and went back to their conversation. *Drat,* he thought. *They were really cute.* He sighed. The waitress walked up to him.

"*Prosím?*" she asked.

"Huh? Oh, could I have a beer? And maybe some directions, please, if you have a second?"

She frowned at him, not understanding. He pointed at one of the Pilsner signs and smiled. She put a coaster down in front of him and wandered off, looking exasperated. George felt embarrassed. For a moment, he was tempted to just get up and leave. But he forced himself to stay in his chair. He looked around. The pub was strange. Its walls were decorated with obscene cartoons: ugly, badly drawn men with big cocks; fat women with pendulous breasts and red, leering mouths. It made him slightly ill. He turned away, and bumped into a young man sitting alone at the next table.

"Excuse me!" he said. "Uh, *prosím!*" He smiled. The young

man smiled back. He had dark curly hair, penetrating blue eyes, and sharp, chiseled features. George could feel his heart beating.

"You American?" the young man said.

"Yes," George said, relieved to find someone who spoke English. "Just visiting. With my parents. They work for an American company."

George's new friend looked at him quizzically.

"You are man, yes?" His tone was one of curiosity, without any hint of derision.

"Yes!" George felt his face tighten with irritation. He hated being mistaken for a woman, but between his smooth face, slender body and shy manner it did happen. A lot.

"I'm sorry. No offense, please." The young man smiled, and put a friendly hand on George's arm. "You like Prague?"

"Oh, yes, very much. But it's hard to find your way around."

"Ah. Maybe you would like me to help you? I could give you directions. Where do you go?"

The young man slid his chair over to George's table. George told him the name of the street he was looking for: Martinská. The man raised one eyebrow and then grinned at George.

"And what you want to do there?"

A blush crept across George's cheeks. "Nothing. Just…some shopping." He looked away from the man's steady, friendly gaze.

"This late, most shops are closed in that street. Except one."

George glowed red. Fortunately, at that moment, the waitress brought him his beer. She set another down in front of his new friend. George stared. The beer was huge, far bigger than American beers. *Oh well,* he thought. He picked up his glass. His friend did the same.

"Cheers!" he said, clicking glasses. They drank. George was surprised. The beer was good, smooth and rich. He put down the glass.

"So," his friend said. "It seems to me you still blush. A bit."

George looked down. "OK, OK. So I'll admit it. I…"

"Sorry, just teasing. By the way, I am Petr." He reached out his hand. George shook it, thrilling at his gentle strength and at the warmth of his flesh. Petr held on two heartbeats longer than necessary, then let go.

"I'm George. Good to meet you."

They chatted and drank their beers. George tried to relax, but impatience tickled at the back of his mind. When he set down his empty glass, Petr's was still half full. The waitress saw the empty and walked over. George glanced up at her and then at the clock. Petr gave him an amused smile and handed the waitress some money. He stood up, motioning to George, who fumbled with his wallet.

"Please," Petr said. "I pay all. My gift. Come. Let's go. I take you there."

They walked out into the still-warm night. Petr strode confidently over the cobblestones; George scurried to keep up with him. As they walked, Petr told him about some of the buildings, what they were, how they came to be. They walked up to an iron gate that was set deep inside a thick stone wall. Petr stopped.

"Come here. I show you something else."

Petr walked toward the gate. George raised his eyebrows in surprise, but followed. Petr stood in front of the gate for a second and then turned to face George, taking one small step toward him.

"What did you want to show me?" he asked, sure that Petr could hear his heart thudding in his chest. Thin streams of darkness seemed to seep out of the stone and metal: ancient ghosts, pressing in on him. Petr reached one tentative hand toward George's head and stroked his thick black hair.

"I want to show you that Prague is very friendly city." Petr's hand trailed down to George's chin and tilted his head back. George was shaking now, barely able to stand. Their lips met. George returned the kiss, tentatively. Petr's arms circled around George's slender frame, pulling their bodies close together. Their tongues touched, and suddenly George was desperate. He clutched Petr, showering him with hard, slightly inept kisses. Petr turned him and pressed him against the cool gate. Their hands slid up and down each other's bodies. Petr's hand found George's cock and squeezed the hard flesh through the fabric. George moaned out loud. Petr pressed a hand over his mouth.

"Shh! People hear," he whispered. Petr knelt down in front of George and nuzzled against his cock. George bit his lip, trying to keep from crying out. Petr reached up to unbuckle George's pants. He slid the fabric down, inch by inch. The head of George's cock peeked out, red and hot in the night air. Petr reached out his tongue, and licked hungrily. George clenched his teeth, trying to be quiet. And then Petr yanked hard, pulling George's pants down to his knees. In one smooth motion he swallowed George's cock.

George's mouth gaped open. His cock had only been in a man's mouth once before, and that had been an amateurish, hurried affair. This was different. The sensation was stunning, almost overwhelming. He wanted to scream out loud at the intensity of the pleasure; he forgot about everything else in the desperate need for more. Petr pulled his head back and then swallowed again. George put his hand to his mouth and bit hard to keep himself from crying aloud and alerting passersby. Petr growled deep in his throat, a growl that George could feel vibrating in his body. Petr's lips slid down George's cock and touched the soft, black pubic hair. George felt the approaching orgasm burning in his groin. He fought it, trying to will it away, praying that he would be able to dwell in this heaven just a little bit longer.

They both heard the footsteps. Petr stood up quickly. He pulled George back into the darkest corner of the gate, and then helped him pull his trousers back up. Petr wiped his lips with his shirtsleeve. It was all George could do to keep from whimpering in frustration. The footsteps stopped. George could see Petr frowning in the darkness. They waited, breathing silently, but they heard nothing more. After a moment, Petr beckoned to George.

"Come. We go." They walked away from the gate. Petr pointed at the opposite building, as if he were explaining it to George. As nonchalantly as they could, they both looked down the street, in the direction that the footsteps had come. A short figure stood there, shrouded in darkness. It watched them, hands stuffed in the pockets of its overcoat.

Petr led George away. They turned a corner. The footsteps started again. Petr turned more corners, slipping into alleyways, between buildings. He circled a few blocks. But no matter where they went, the footsteps seemed to follow them.

"There is pub," he said in a whisper, pointing to a building with a worn *Pivnice* sign. "Let us go to there, wait for our friend to leave."

"Who is it?" George whispered back. Petr looked worried, which made George uncomfortable.

"Don't know. Probably ugly old troll who want you, too." He smiled at George. George looked down and grinned, blushing furiously.

They walked into the new pub. It was long and narrow with a low ceiling. Like the last pub, it was crowded and smoky, but it was free of obscene artwork. As soon as they had ordered their beers, Petr stood up.

"Excuse me. I be back." He headed toward the restroom with a smile and a quick squeeze of George's shoulder.

The waitress brought the beers. George's head was buzzing from the first one, and from the excitement that still raced through his body. He decided not to wait for Petr; he picked up his glass and drank, taking big gulps. The beer took the edge off of George's frustration, and turned it into a warm glow of pleasure. Things were definitely looking up. This was turning into the kind of adventure he had always dreamed of. He stared around the pub and waited for Petr to return.

"*Prosím? Jak se máte!*"

George jumped. Petr's seat was occupied by a short man in a long dark overcoat. He was the strangest person George had ever seen. The hair that flowed out from under his cap was gray, but had an odd, almost greenish cast to it. His beard was black and silver. And he seemed to be soaked to the bone. Hair, beard, clothing were all dewy and glistening. Water dripped from his body, gathering into a puddle under his seat.

But the most alarming thing about the man was his eyes. They were huge, and they fixed George with a look that made him glad that there were other people around. George sat there, mouth open, trying to keep his psyche from being pulled out of his skull and into those eyes. Finally, he managed to stammer out a response.

"I, I'm sorry, I don't understand. You speak English? Um, how do you say it? *Mluvíte anglicky?*"

The little man's lips slowly curled into a wide, toothy grin.

"*Ano,*" he said, with a very heavy accent. "Yes. For you it is lucky. I speak your English."

The grin faded, and the man licked his lips. He leaned toward George, seizing his arm in a powerful grasp. George tried to lean back, but the man pulled him closer.

"I watch you. You and your friend. I heard you in pub. I know where is Martinská. But I think now you come with me. I take you. Your friend, he make you happy. I make you more happy. I am new friend."

The grip tightened further, making George wince. Panic fogged his brain. He looked around for help. Just then, he saw Petr return from the restroom. The little man let go of George.

"Petr!" George said frantically. "Um, sorry, but it looks like this fellow took your seat. Want to sit here?" George gestured to the empty chair beside him. But instead of sitting down, Petr stopped and stared at the little man, eyes wide. The man slowly rose. He was shorter than Petr, but bulkier. He took one step toward Petr and said something in Czech. George couldn't understand a word, but the threatening tone was unmistakable. Petr shook his head, and took a step backward. The little man growled. And then he slowly reached up one hand toward Petr.

To George's amazement, Petr turned and walked away, hurrying for the door.

"Hey, wait!" George said. The little man laughed, and then seized George's arm. With the other hand the man fished in his pocket, pulled out some coins and threw them on the table. He pulled George's arm, making him scramble to his feet.

"Let me go!" George panicked and tried to wrench free. He looked around, hoping someone would come to his rescue. The other patrons, who had watched the whole scene, simply looked back down at their beers as George stumbled between the dark wood tables.

The man dragged George out the door and propelled him down the street. His steps squished wetly on the cobblestones. George looked around, hoping that Petr was waiting outside to rescue him. But the street was empty. George gave one last glance back at the pub as he was pulled around the corner. He saw that the little man had left a trail of water behind him. George frowned and then concentrated on keeping up. The man chuckled and mumbled to himself in Czech.

George's fear quickly ebbed as he trotted beside the little man. The fellow was weird and pushy, but he didn't really seem hostile or malicious; if anything, he seemed to be delighted. And he said he would take George where he wanted to go. George told himself that this was another adventure, like the one with Petr. Petr, who had left him to fend for himself. Suddenly angry, George decided that he would go with this troll, but he was not going to be dragged like a sheep. He twisted his arm suddenly.

"Hey, look, let me go, will you? I'll follow you," George said.

The little man shrugged without looking up and let George go. George breathed a sigh of relief. If the man was dangerous, he certainly wasn't acting that way. George started falling behind; the man motioned to him to keep up. George ran. Moments later, the Charles Bridge loomed ahead of them. The man quickly stomped to the middle of the bridge, passing the ghost-encrusted statues of dead kings and saints. Beggars crouched on hands and knees under each statute, their heads buried in their hands, their hats in front of them. Prague's castle glowed in the distance, casting light on the low clouds.

"Hey, hold on!" George said. "This isn't where I'm going. I know for a fact that Martinská is on this side of the river." He pointed back the way they had come and reached for his map. The man laughed, his mouth opening wide. He fixed George with his gaze, and George froze.

"You are worried, yes? Do not be so. Almost, we are there."

"Now wait a minute!" George began. But the man grabbed his wrist and with one motion hurled him over the edge of the bridge, into the Vltava River.

George hit the surface hard. He floated facedown, stunned. Then something grabbed his wrist and pulled him down into the cold water. Panic cleared George's head. The little man was dragging him under! George struggled and thrashed, desperate to get back to the surface. But it was no use. The man was too strong. George clenched his teeth, trying to hold his breath. A dim glow caught his eye; the little man was dragging them toward it. George soon realized that it was a small hole in an outcropping of rock. And then his body began screaming for air. Just as he was dragged into the hole George's lungs heaved and then expelled the stale air that they held. He felt a pang of bloodless regret that it would end this way, in this dark river. And then he relaxed, preparing to die.

Fingers twined through his hair and pulled his face out of the water. George breathed hard, his gasps echoing. Slowly, shakily, he stood up.

They appeared to be in a dimly lit, underground cavern. The little man grabbed George's wrist and pulled. George stumbled after him, still panting, too disoriented to do anything but obey. His eyes grew accustomed to the dark as they walked. He saw that they were walking past columns, squeezing under crumbling archways made from large blocks of stone. They skirted around a heap of rubble. On the other side stood a stone wall, into which was cut a large window. The little man pointed at the window. George stared. The man grabbed him by the waist and lifted him up, depositing him into the darkness on the other side of the window.

"Do not move!" the man said. He followed, landing on the ground with a thump.

George finally found his voice. "Wh…Where are we?" he said, teeth chattering from the cold.

"Under!" the man said, pointing up. "Long ago, many floods from Vltava. They bury old Prague, build new Prague higher!"

"You live here? Why?"

The little man grinned. "I am Vodník. Vodník lives under bridge. Finds pretty girls. Bring them to Vltava. Do this to them!"

The Vodník pushed George hard. George toppled and fell. He landed in a pool of cold water. The Vodník splashed in beside him. George found himself held by powerful arms. At first he was afraid, and struggled. But the Vodník was warm; his body was a furnace, radiating heat. George slowly relaxed, and nestled in close, hungry for the warmth that the muscular body provided.

"You are good girl, do not fight Vodník." The man's voice was a husky whisper. George felt a flash of anger at the familiar mistake. But then, in the dim light, he saw the Vodník's eyes glowing with that look he had seen in the pub. George's cock rose in response to the desire that burned in the man's face. A bristly beard touched George's chin, and warm lips met his. George pulled back with a little whimper, but this only excited the Vodník further. He pressed his lips against George's. Their tongues met and George relented. He kissed back, tentatively at first and then harder. They stumbled backward, their harsh breathing echoing off the silent black walls.

George tripped, and suddenly they were underwater again, still kissing. George was too lost in his growing arousal to care. But in a moment his lungs began heaving, demanding to breathe. He struggled; the Vodník held him under the water. There was a moment of panic, and then George was free. He stood up, gasping.

The Vodník reached for him. Grinning, he tore at George's shirt, exposing his smooth, hairless chest. George looked down. In the dim light he could see fingertips reaching toward his nipples.

He felt the Vodník's other hand grasp his hair. And then suddenly he was underwater again. The Vodník held George's head under while he explored his chest. George gazed up at the man's dark outline, feeling helpless in the face of his strength. Strong fingertips fastened on a nipple, tweaking and pulling it, sending sharp, hot flashes of pleasure to George's groin. The pleasure and the fear combined into a sickly sweet, potent mixture. But then it was swamped by the sudden need for air. George struggled. After a long while, the Vodník let him up.

"Stop that!" George said, breathing hard. "You're going to drown me!"

There was a menacing pause. "You not tell Vodník what to do!" the man said, with a growl. He pulled George toward him, kissing him furiously, pinching his nipples, hurting him. George's cock jumped in response, hardening under the wet fabric. George clasped the little man to him.

George took a deep breath, preparing at any minute to be pulled under again. But instead the Vodník let him go. The man stripped, pulling off his clothes and letting them fall to the bottom of the pool. George could see that the Vodník was beautiful, with the raw muscular body of a manual laborer. The Vodník grasped George's belt. He pulled, tearing leather and cloth, making George's head spin with fear and need. George pulled off his pants, whimpering, and let them float to the bottom of the pool. Growling again, now with passion, the man reached down between George's legs. The strong fingers clasped George's cock, and George gave a loud moan of pleasure.

The Vodník froze. He looked down, his dark features creased in a frown of surprise and dismay. Seconds ticked by.

"You! You are...man!" the Vodník said.

Guilt quickly infected George's lust, turning it queasy.

"I...yes."

"But you did not say!"

The Vodník did not wait for an answer. He let go of George, shaking his head, and then turned away.

"I never had a chance." George said to the retreating back. "I'm sorry! But couldn't we..."

"No! Vodník only bring here girls. Only girls. Pretty girls."

The Vodník's voice trailed off as he drifted away into the

darkness. George could barely see the man's outline. He panicked. What if the Vodník left him down here? He'd never be able to find his way back. He would die in this buried city! He moved quickly toward the Vodník, desperate for the warmth, desperate to keep the man near. George found him, and circled his arms around the hard torso. But the Vodník was stiff and unyielding. George wasn't sure what to do. And then he remembered something. That night on a high school camping trip, tucked into a tent with his very straight best friend. They had talked long into the night, about life, about sex. The talk had aroused them both, for different reasons. And when the talk had run out, George had simply snuggled close and let his hands drift down to his friend's cock. It had worked, even though it had ultimately cost them their friendship.

So George let his hand gradually crawl down the Vodník's chest, then to his stomach and then to his cock. It was semi-erect. *Good,* George thought. He grasped the cock gently and stroked. He could feel the Vodník's flesh harden. The man breathed harder. George smiled in the dark. He took a few deep breaths and then slipped under the water. His mouth found the Vodník's cock, and closed around it. He sucked hard, letting the cock bump the back of his throat. His head thrashed back and forth. The Vodník's hips bucked; his strong hands closed around the sides of George's head. He kept George there, until the familiar need for air asserted itself. George held out as long as he could and then his body struggled of its own accord. The Vodník pulled George out of the water.

"You are very strange boy," the Vodník said, panting. But then he pushed George's head back under, forcing his cock into George's mouth, deep into his throat. Soon George's lungs were heaving again, and he was pulled back up to the air. The darkness seemed to pulse; the cold was gone. George breathed quickly. The Vodník grasped his head again, preparing to shove him under.

"No!" George said. "Wait."

The Vodník's fingers tightened in George's hair; his face twisted in anger at George's impertinence. But George lifted his legs, wrapping them around the Vodník's body. The Vodník's eyes widened with surprise. George bucked his hips until he could feel the head of the man's cock sliding between his ass cheeks. The Vodník gasped aloud. George reached under him, and guided the cock so that it touched his asshole. And then George pressed downward. The thick cock stretched him, sending sparks of pleasurable pain shooting up through his body. George moved his hips, up and down, relishing the agony, until the Vodník's entire shaft was swallowed up.

There was a moment of silence. George felt like the cock inside of him was pushing against his own, sliding into it, filling it. He reached for the edge of the pool and shoved. They were both in the water now, rolling over and over. George's hips bucked. The Vodník slowly overcame his surprise and began to thrust back. He held George tightly, fucking him. And then George needed to breathe. This time, the feeling of panic was gone, replaced entirely by lust. The Vodník held George down, until he thrashed. And then they broke to the surface, gasping.

As they panted, George dared to reach forward and kiss the Vodník again. The man's lips relaxed and their tongues met. And then the Vodník grasped George's hair and pulled his head back. George couldn't keep his ass from squirming around the big cock inside of it. He moaned aloud.

"What you want, my little…girl," the Vodník said. "What you want?"

George took the Vodník's hand, and guided it down to his swollen cock. Teeth flashed in the darkness. The Vodník's mouth found his again, and they went under, sinking down to the bottom of the pool. The Vodník's cock pounded deep into George's body. The man's hand pulled up and down George's shaft. The sensations met deep in the pit of George's stomach. And then they were joined by the third sensation, the stabbing, desperate need for air. The Vodník's hips bucked wildly. George saw a red fog drift before his eyes; there was a loud humming in his ears. And then there was a little flare of white light near his groin. It grew, and ignited the red fog. George's mind felt like it was exploding, burning. Orgasm tore through him. He pumped come into the cold water. He could feel the Vodník's cock grow huge as the man came, thrusting, scraping George's body against the bottom of the pool.

And then, as quickly as the fire had ignited, it went out. George was enveloped by the subterranean blackness.

• • •

"George? George!" The voice pulled him out of the blackness, and toward a blurry yellow light. Slowly, the light came into focus. It was a single, dim bulb, hanging from the ceiling. George looked around. He was lying, naked and wet, in a small room. A man sat next to him, naked save for the towel around his waist. It was Petr. George sat up.

"You are OK?" Petr said, putting a hand on George's shoulder. "How do you get here?"

"Where am I?" George finally managed to say.

"In bathhouse. Like you wanted. But how…"

George stood up and coughed. There was still water in his lungs. His ass burned, and the burning licked at his groin, making his cock harden. He lurched to the door and looked out as Petr watched him, concerned. At the end of a dimly lit corridor a group of men was milling around, each wearing a towel around his waist. They were staring at a ventilation grate that had been pushed open, exposing a black hole in the wall. Another man, wearing jeans and a t-shirt, was shining a light into the hole. As George watched, the man put the grate back on and screwed it down. The man gave a curious glance at the trail of water leading away from the grate and then walked away. The men dispersed.

George turned back to Petr.

"You left me. In that pub."

Petr glanced down at the ground. "I am very sorry. But that man, he…"

"I *said* you left me. And I think now you're going to make it up to me."

Petr looked up at George, into his eyes. And when he saw what was there he could not look away. He sat, very still, as George reached for him and twined his dripping fingers through his dark, curly hair.

About the Authors

G. MERLIN BECK lives in San Francisco and works in Silicon Valley, helping to make the world safe for the machines that will one day enslave humanity. While we wait to be conquered, Merlin entertains us with tales that are meant to weaken our moral fiber and sap our will to resist. Merlin's work appears in the anthology *Roughed Up: More Tales of Gay Men, Sex and Power* and in the upcoming anthology *Love Under Foot: An Erotic Celebration of Feet*.

MARGUERITE COLSON is an Australian high school teacher in Queensland who enjoys breaking boundaries and experimenting with genres. She has been published at www.literotica.com, www.sliptongue.com and www.slowtrains.com.

GABRIELLE COYOTE is a freelance writer from Boston, Massachusetts, and has been writing in one guise or another for ten years. She has done everything from tech writing and features for magazines to erotic novels in various stages of completion. Her erotica has been published in a variety of venues, including www.mindcaviar.com and www.sexilicious.com. She also has a busy sideline writing erotic content for adult websites and crafting custom pieces. Read all her erotica at her website *Gabrielle's Erotic Letters* (www.gabrielleletters.com).

LESLEY GLAISTER is the author of nine novels, as well as numerous short stories and radio dramas. She is the winner of a

Somerset Maugham Award, a Betty Trask Award, and has been shortlisted for several major prizes including the *Guardian* fiction prize. Her most recent novel is *Now You See Me* (longlisted for the Orange Prize), and her next will be called *As Far As You Can Go*. She teaches novel writing on a Master's Degree at Sheffield Hallam University and is a fellow of the Royal Society of Literature.

GRISELDA GORDON was born in Scotland in 1961 and grew up in Edinburgh. She began writing five years ago, but only recently with publication in mind. She's the recipient of the Canongate Prize for New Writing, with the winning story appearing in an anthology published by Canongate, entitled *Writing Wrongs*. She has another story appearing in *New Writing Scotland 20* (2002). This is her first attempt at erotica. Having read Arabic at Oxford, she is currently completing an M.Phil. in Creative Writing at Glasgow University. She lives in rural Ayrshire with her husband and three young children.

MYRIAM GURBA is a graduate of UC Berkeley and works as a teacher in Long Beach, California. Her fiction has appeared in *Tough Girls*, *Pillow Talk III*, *Best American Erotica 2003*, and *Best Fetish Erotica*. She regularly contributes to *On Our Backs*. She lives in Los Angeles.

MELANIE HANNAM is an award-winning journalist and travel writer whose work has appeared in newspapers and magazines worldwide, including *Independent and Specialist Travel*, *The Times*, *Trailfinder Magazine* and *The Hull Daily Mail*. She lives in the North of England and is currently working on a screenplay, *A Girl's Book of the Wild West*.

ROGER HART'S fiction and essays have been published in numerous magazines, and included in various anthologies. His short story collection, *Erratics*, winner of the George Garrett Prize, was published by the Texas Review Press. He is the recipient of an Ohio Artist Fellowship and holds an M.A. from Antioch University. He and his wife, the poet Gwen Hart, are presently living in Minnesota, where he is working on a novel and a new collection of stories.

DEBRA HYDE'S erotic fiction has most recently appeared in *Erotic Travel Tales, Ripe Fruit: Erotica for Well-Seasoned Lovers, Body Check: Erotic Lesbian Sports Stories, Herotica 7,* and *The Best of the Best Meat Erotica.* She is a regular contributor to *Scarlet Letters* (www.scarletletters.com) and maintains *Pursed Lips,* a sex-in-the-arts web log (www.pursedlips.com). While she loves her home in the Land of Steady Habits (Connecticut), she always welcomes an excuse to vacation elsewhere. Especially if everybody involved gets naked.

MAXIM JAKUBOWSKI is still toiling for a living wage in the galleys of erotica. Since his appearance in the first volume of *Erotic Travel Tales,* he has published a novel about sexual jealousy, *Kiss Me Sadly,* a handful of erotic, crime and SF anthologies, and dozens of columns for the *Guardian* and amazon.co.uk, as well as various short stories, and visited countless hotel rooms on a diversity of continents in the interest of culture and lust. He is about to embark on a survey of modern erotic fiction for the Pocket Essential imprint and is pondering the substance, mood and style of his next novel. He lives in London where he collects too many books, CDs and DVDs when not seeing movies.

JOY JAMES is a freelance writer based in suburban Washington, DC. Her essays and fiction have appeared in such erotica websites as www.cleansheets.com, www.mindcaviar.com, and www.peacockblue.com, and in print in *Best Fetish Erotica.* She has also been a newspaper reporter, magazine editor, and advertising copywriter as well as, ever so briefly, working for an escort service.

ARABELLA LAINTON grew up in Sydney, Australia. She did a degree in Anthropology at the University of Sydney in 1994. In 1999 she won the Australian Women's Forum erotic fiction competition. She is currently living in London where she is writing a novel.

MICHÈLE LARUE, a Sorbonne-educated journalist, has used her six languages freelancing around the world. As a director, she's made two documentaries in Cuba, and another on the European S/M scene. Les Editions Blanche (Paris) has published her erotic short stories since 1994, including "Rapture at Cartagena" (in

Passion de femmes). Editore Mundadori (Milano) picked up two of her stories for their collection of erotica *Spicy*. And another, "Lilly's Loulou," was included in the first volume of *Erotic Travel Tales*. In France, she has also published BDSM novels under the name Gala Fur: *Les Soirées de Gala* (now available in English as an e-book at Renaissance E Books), and *Séances*. She lives in Paris.

DIANE LEBOW, when not at home in her Victorian cottage in San Francisco, lives and loves her way around the globe, looking for the best of all possible worlds—and how people satisfy their needs for love and community. She spends her time with—among others— Afghan women, the Hopi, Amazon people, Tuvans, Mongolians, Corsicans, and Parisians. She has scuba dived with sharks in the Red Sea, trained champion Morgan horses, pioneered college women's studies programs, and served as a union president. She has a Ph.D. from the University of California in the History of Consciousness and publishes in Travelers' Tales anthologies, Salon.com, *B for Savvy Brides,* and numerous national newspapers and magazines.

CATHERINE LUNDOFF lives in Minneapolis with her terrific girlfriend and less terrific cats. She's a computer geek by day and writer by night. Her writings have appeared in such anthologies as *Shameless, Below the Belt, Zaftig, Scarlet Letters, Best Lesbian Erotica 1999* and *Best Lesbian Erotica 2001, Electric* and *Electric 2: Best Lesbian Erotic Stories.*

MARY ANNE MOHANRAJ (www.mamohanraj.com) is the author of *Torn Shapes of Desire,* editor of *Aqua Erotica* and *Wet,* and consulting editor for *Herotica 7*. She is also the author of two choose-your-own-adventure erotic novels, *Kathryn in the City* and *The Classics Professor,* forthcoming in 2003 (Penguin/Putnam). She has been published in a multitude of anthologies and magazines, including *Erotic Travel Tales, Herotica 6, Best American Erotica 1999,* and *Best Women's Erotica 2000* and *2001*. Mohanraj founded the erotic webzine, *Clean Sheets* (www.cleansheets.com) and serves as editor-in-chief for the Hugo-nominated speculative fiction webzine *Strange Horizons* (www.strangehorizons.com). She also moderates the Eros Workshop and is a '97 graduate of Clarion West. Mohanraj has received degrees in Writing and English from

Mills College and the University of Chicago, and is currently a doctoral student in Fiction and Literature at the University of Utah. She has received the Scowcroft Prize for Fiction, a Neff fellowship in English, and currently holds a Steffenson-Canon fellowship in the Humanities. Mohanraj serves on the 2002 Tiptree Award jury, and lives in Chicago.

LISABET SARAI (www.lisabetsarai.com) has been writing fiction, nonfiction, and poetry ever since she learned how to hold a pencil. She is the author of three novels, *Raw Silk* (Black Lace, 1999) *Incognito* (Blue Moon, 2002) and *Ruby's Rules* (Blue Moon, 2003), and the coeditor, with S. F. Mayfair (who appeared in the first *Erotic Travel Tales*), of the forthcoming anthology *Sacred Exchange* (Blue Moon), a set of stories that explore spiritual or transcendent aspects of BDSM relationships. Lisabet has traveled widely, especially in Asia, but currently lives with her husband and two extremely spoiled cats in a renovated eighteenth-century mill in New England.

JACQUELINE SILK is thirty-three years old and has recently moved to a small village in North Wales. Previous to this she lived in Cambridge, Manchester and North London. Although she has only recently started to write erotica, she has been published in Black Lace's erotic short story collection, *Wicked Words 6*. She has also had a short story published in *Mslexia*. In the last year, she completed an M.A. in novel writing at the University of Manchester and is currently looking for a publisher for her first novel.

ALISON TYLER is the author of erotic novels including *Learning to Love It, Strictly Confidential, Sweet Thing*, and *Sticky Fingers* (all published by Black Lace), and the coauthor of the best-selling anthology *Bondage on a Budget* (Pretty Things Press). Her short stories have appeared in anthologies including *Erotic Travel Tales, Best Women's Erotica 2002 and 2003, Guilty Pleasures, Sweet Life, Best S/M Erotica, Sex Toy Tales, Noirotica 3*, and *Wicked Words 4, 5*, and *6*. She is the editor of the erotic short story collection *Naughty Stories from A to Z* (Pretty Things Press) and *Best Bondage Erotica* (Cleis). Ms. Tyler lives in Northern California.

GERARD WOZEK is the author of *Dervish*, which won the Gival Press 2000 Poetry Book Award. His poetry and erotic fiction have appeared in various journals and anthologies including *Erotic Travel Tales, Queer Dog, The Road Within, Best Gay Erotica 1998, Rebel Yell 2,* and *The Harrington Fiction Quarterly*. Last year, his short film *Elemental Reels* won top honors at the Edgewise Poetry Video Festival in Vancouver, BC. The video can be viewed online at Planet Out's *Popcorn Q* cinema (www.planetout.com). He is an associate professor of English at Robert Morris College in Chicago.

About the Editor

MITZI SZERETO is editor of the first *Erotic Travel Tales* as well as author of *Erotic Fairy Tales: A Romp Through the Classics,* and the e-book novella *highway* (Renaissance E Books). Her writing appears in various books and publications including *The Mammoth Book of Best New Erotica 2002, Wicked Words 4, Joyful Desires: A Compendium of Twentieth Century Erotica, The Erotic Review, Moist, Writers' Forum,* and *Proof.* She's also known as M. S. Valentine, author of the erotic novels *The Martinet* (Chimera Books Ltd.), *The Captivity of Celia* (April 2003, Blue Moon), *Elysian Days and Nights, The Governess,* and *The Possession of Celia* (all from Blue Moon, 2003-2004). She's the pioneer of the erotic writing workshop in the UK and Europe, which she conducts for arts organizations and literary festivals. A regular fixture on the interview circuit, she's appeared on BBC radio and in the Bravo television documentary series *3001: A Sex Oddity.* Her work as an anthology editor has earned her the American Society of Authors and Writers' Meritorious Achievement Award. Her current literary projects include a pair of anthologies, a novel, and a screenplay for television. An itinerant spirit, she has lived in Miami, upstate New York, Los Angeles, Seattle, and the San Francisco area. She resides in Yorkshire, England (not far from Bakewell), where she's working toward an M.A..